WITHDRAWN
NDSU

GALAHAD

GALAHAD

ENOUGH OF HIS LIFE TO EXPLAIN HIS REPUTATION

By

JOHN ERSKINE, 1879-

The story of the legendary immortals King Arthur,
Lancelot, Galahad, Guinevere and the Elaines. It
opens when Arthur, Guinevere and Lancelot are young,
four years after Arthur's wedding. Twice in his
life a woman asked Lancelot for his love, both
women were named Elaine. These two incidents begin
and end the story spanning twenty years. Galahad
is Lancelot's son by the first Elaine, but
Guinevere remains the abiding love of Lancelot's
life.

INDIANAPOLIS
THE BOBBS-MERRILL COMPANY
PUBLISHERS

To

JOSEPH ANTHONY

CONTENTS

GALAHAD

PART ONE
ELAINE

GALAHAD

ELAINE

I

Twice in his life a woman asked Lancelot for his love. Two very different women, both named Elaine. But as all the world knows, Lancelot cared for no woman except Guinevere.

To take the second incident first. In his middle age he came to the house of Sir Bernard of Astolat, who had a daughter. She was called Elaine the White, from her appearance and because she knew nothing of the world. This is the Elaine we usually hear of. The old books say she loved Lancelot incurably and died of it. Their words at parting are recorded.

"I would have you for my husband."

"I thank you," said Lancelot, "but I shall never be married man."

"Then, fair knight, will you be my paramour?"

"God forbid!" said he. "Your family would not like it."

"Then alas," said she, "I must die of love."

"Don't," said he. "I might have been married before this, if I had applied myself to it. It's too late now. But since you feel about it as you say, I will do what I can. When you marry—oh yes, you will—I promise a part of my lands to you and your heirs, and as long as I live I will be your true knight."

"No," she said, "—not unless you will marry me, or at least be my paramour."

"Fair damsel," said Lancelot, "from these two things I must be excused."

When he said he might have married before, he was not thinking of Guinevere. He was remembering his youth. There had been another Elaine, King Pelles' daughter. She too had offered herself, heart and body, and though at first he had said no, in the end he tired of saying it. Galahad was their son.

Galahad's mother came of a distinguished family. King Pelles was keeper of the Holy Grail, and a near relative of Joseph of Arimathea. But this is thought to be legend.

Many fables attached themselves to King Pelles, some of them hardly befitting a man of saintly lineage. It is said, for example, that he determined to marry his daughter to none but the best knight in the world, and her standards for a husband were equally severe. But how could he tell who was the best? There happened to be a lady near by, a beautiful but dolorous lady, shut up in a tower. An enchantress had kept her there five years, immersed in scalding water, and she was never to get out till the best knight in the world should come and take her by the hand. King Pelles was sorry for the lady, yet she would serve as a barometer of chivalry. When handsome Sir Gawaine arrived at the tower, the king paid close attention. The lady was still in distress when Gawaine rode away. But when Lancelot came, the doors unlocked themselves and unbolted, and when he took the lady by the hand, she immediately stepped out of her discomfort. Though at the moment she was, they say, naked as a needle, the five years' parboiling had had no ill effect, and she seemed to Sir Lancelot the handsomest lady he had ever met, next after Queen Guinevere. His opinion seems irrelevant. But the whole episode is fictitious.

It is said also that King Pelles selected Lancelot another way, by his success with the dragon in the tomb. There was a tomb, and on it in letters of gold these words: "Here shall come a leopard of king's blood, and he shall slay this serpent. And this leopard shall engender a lion, the which lion shall surpass all other knights." The king determined to have this leopard in the family, and the lion too, of course. Lancelot killed the dragon. Then the king asked his name, but he knew already, from Lancelot's way of killing dragons. But there is no more warrant for the dragon than for the scalded lady.

Finally, it is said that King Pelles and his daughter went to some trouble to insure the truth of these prophecies. Since Lancelot was loyal to Guinevere, they had the family necromancer put enchantments on him, so that Elaine seemed the woman he loved, and he spent the night in her arms. In the morning the charm was gone. His impulse was to kill the girl who had tricked him, but she got down on her knees and pleaded the desperate state of her affections. She was very beautiful, and anyway it was too late to help it. This comes nearer the fact, but there was no necromancer, and King Pelles was not involved.

It is well to mention these legends because they are known, and if we did not warn the reader he might be looking for them in this book. But we shall tell the story as it happened in our world, to people like ourselves or only a little better—the story, that is, as it was before poets lifted it out of its origin and used it as a language for remote and mystical things. In its humble form it had its own meaning. We say nothing here of the Grail, nor of Joseph of Arimathea, nor of the Round Table, nor of Excalibur; we confine our report to the first causes, as it were, of these famous dreams.

The story begins when Arthur, Guinevere and Lancelot were young. Four years after Arthur's wedding, to fix the date. The plot is composed of three women and one coincidence. When the White Elaine offered her love and Lancelot declined it, he was an experienced man and on his guard.

II

"You will admit I have loved you faithfully," said Sir Bromel.

"I admit it," said Elaine. "You keep coming to my father's castle, you swear your heart is broken, you hold out the possibility of its mending if I marry you. You think I ought to reply with my thanks and my person. That's a queer idea—that a man can earn a woman by saying over and over how much he'd like to have her. Sir Bromel, I shan't pretend to be grateful. I'll not thank you for offering what you know I don't want."

"You are hardly civil," he said, "and if I weren't a fool I should leave you now. But I love you, that's all there is to it, and in love no one gives up before he has to."

"I shall never love you," said Elaine. "Do give up now, and find some other girl! You are still young, but time passes, and if you dream of a home and a family, you ought to be getting on with it faster. You've wasted three years."

"Don't you want a home and a family, too?" said Sir Bromel. "I should think any woman would."

"Bromel, you're a nice boy, but every word you add reassures me that I shan't lose my heart to you. You miss the point. No, I don't want a home, and at the moment I have no ambition to provide any man with a family. You think me old enough to feel the call of

17

sex and the maternal instinct. I'm happy with my father
here, and having children, I understand, is a disagreeable
experience."

"I wish you wouldn't talk so," said Bromel. "It's
coarse and vulgar, and I see no wit in it. Where do
you get such ideas? You will soil your mind."

"What I said about sex and children?"

"Yes."

"Why, I got that from you! You're always hinting.
Of course my mind is soiled. If I loved you I'd want to
marry, and we'd have the children, but you've made me
so self-conscious, I doubt if I shall ever fall in love."

Sir Bromel went to the tower window and gazed down
into the courtyard. His back was turned to her. An
over-fed spaniel woke up from beside her chair and
walked across to see what Sir Bromel was looking at.
Elaine sat watching their two backs. Then she looked
at her hands and examined one of her fingers.

"If you hadn't pestered me, we could have been good
friends."

At the sound of her voice the spaniel returned to her
side and went to sleep again. Sir Bromel did not move
from the window. She took up her embroidery frame.

"Your father's men are busy," said Sir Bromel.
"There's quite a stir."

"Yes, he told the steward to have the place in good
order. Sir Lancelot is coming."

Sir Bromel turned around.

"Oh, he is, is he? When?"

"I don't know, but father expects him soon."

"Well, of course I can't rival Sir Lancelot."

Elaine laughed at him.

"I shouldn't be jealous if I were you. I have never seen Sir Lancelot, and he's father's guest, not mine. Besides, he's Guinevere's lover."

"I don't believe that story," said Bromel, "and if I did, I wouldn't repeat it. The queen is a noble woman, and the king is a fine man."

"No one doubts it."

"Lancelot is the soul of courtesy," he continued. "That man never did a mean thing in his life."

"I'm sure he never did."

"Then don't say such things."

"I shall probably not mention the subject to you again. It seems to make you forget you are a guest in my father's house, with no authority over me."

"You are right. I spoke out of my manners," said Bromel, "but no one should slander the queen and Arthur and Lancelot. I'm too fond of you to enjoy your growing habit of reckless talk. I must protest, for your own sake!"

The spaniel woke up again and looked at him.

"Bromel, if you came this afternoon to persuade me, you choose strange arguments. I can see exactly the sort of home you think I ought to long for—you presiding over me and the children, telling us what thoughts to have. But since I'm not your wife, I'll use my freedom to say again in your presence that Lancelot and Guinevere are lovers, and they are the best people in the world, and so is Arthur."

"You don't think it is wrong of the queen to love Lancelot?"

"Not having seen Lancelot, as I told you, I assume Guinevere made no mistake."

"I had better go," said Bromel. "We are not likely to agree, and we may lose our tempers."

"Perhaps you are right," said Elaine. "When you come again, Bromel, remember the subject is closed."

"The subject is hardly opened as yet," said Bromel. "I intend to marry you."

"Look out for that bad turn in the stairway as you go down," said Elaine. "The stone is worn and slippery."

The spaniel came to the top of the stairs and stood beside her.

III

KING PELLES was a proud man, but before Lancelot he knew his place. The castle was in exceptional order when the great knight rode in. He was on an errand from Arthur. They took his horse away, helped him out of his armor, and led him to a corner of the hall where he and his host could talk at ease. When Arthur sent messages by Lancelot, there was little to discuss, but Pelles made the conference last out till nightfall, and the servants brought candles, and prepared the room for the evening meal.

"My daughter, who presides at my table," said King Pelles, "will be here presently. If you don't mind, we will wait for her."

"Your daughter?" said Lancelot. "You are fortunate. And old enough to preside over your house!"

"She presides at the table," said Pelles. "She is only twenty—in some matters young, in others too old. I wish I knew what to do with her. Her mother died four years ago. Elaine thinks too much."

"Elaine? A beautiful name."

"It does well enough," said the king.

"And she thinks too much?"

"She won't marry. I have offered to let her choose the husband, but she says the whole matrimonial program, regarded with the eye of reason, is unattractive."

"A nunnery, perhaps?" said Lancelot.

"I've suggested that, too, but she says she hasn't the temperament for the religious life, and I doubt if she has. I'm very fond of her, but she's a difficult child."

"In a home so well appointed," said Lancelot, "she would have little to occupy her. Perhaps she is forced to think, for want of something better to do."

"Oh, I don't know," said Pelles. "There's a good deal going on here, and I share as much of it with her as she will let me. We hunt in season, and I take her to most of the tournaments. She was at the one last year, where the man got killed."

"There will be jousting at Lonazep in a few days," said Lancelot. "When I leave you I'm to join Arthur on the way there. I hope your daughter will attend."

"She won't," said Pelles. "I invited her to go, but she said the sport was out of date. That's the mind she has. Even in murder, she said, one should keep up with the fashion."

"She calls it murder?"

At that moment Elaine came in.

"Daughter, we are honored to have Sir Lancelot at our table."

"We are indeed," she said, and smiled up at the tall warrior with the deep eyes and the scarred face. When they had taken their places he looked across at her. She was not so tall as Guinevere, and her hair was not so brown. She had cut it short, and she was slender as a boy, but the mischief in her blue eyes seemed to Lancelot anything but boyish.

"Do you know," she said, "I hadn't the slightest idea you were so young. It's your fame, of course. I thought you must be at least fifty."

"Lady—" began Sir Lancelot.

"My name's Elaine. It saves time." She smiled at him again.

"Your manners, daughter!" said King Pelles. "What were you about to say, Sir Lancelot?"

"I should like the fame, but the lady, I fear—"

"It's Elaine," she said.

"—I fear Elaine is too generous."

"But you aren't fifty, are you?"

"Just half of that."

"Old enough for a man."

"Sir Lancelot, I'm covered with confusion!" said King Pelles. "My daughter is—"

"She is charming," said Lancelot. "She is everything your daughter should be."

"Good—!" said Pelles.

"You don't always have to ride around, do you?" said Elaine. "They let you stay at the Court sometimes?"

"Wherever Arthur sends us, but at Camelot, of course, much of the time. I'm on my way to meet the king now—we are riding to Lonazep, to the tournament. I was just saying to your father, I hope you will be among the ladies there."

"Nothing I'd like better. Shall we go, father?"

"Why, when I asked you, you wouldn't!"

"Oh, was this the one? I thought it was another. Yes indeed! Which ladies did you say would be there, Sir Lancelot?"

"All the ladies of the Court."

"They are very beautiful, I suppose."

"One of them," said Lancelot, "one who is sure to be there, is often said to be the greatest beauty in the world."

"I've heard that Guinevere is lovely," said Elaine.

"The queen will not see the tournament," said Lancelot. "She is recovering from a severe illness. I referred to Iseult."

"Iseult? Sir Tristram's Iseult? She doesn't belong to the Court."

"She is visiting the country," said Lancelot, "and Tristram will enter the tournament."

"They are famous lovers!" said Elaine. "I never hoped to see them. But then I had no hope of seeing you, Sir Lancelot."

King Pelles spoke sharply to the servants. "Sir Lancelot will have some more meat. Perhaps better done this time, Sir Lancelot?"

"No more meat, thank you."

"They are, aren't they?" said Elaine.

"Who are? And are they what?" said King Pelles.

"I meant to ask Sir Lancelot if Tristram and Iseult are not wonderful lovers."

"How would Sir Lancelot know? And if he knew, you shouldn't ask him. I think Sir Lancelot will have some more wine, daughter."

"Will you?" said Elaine.

"No more wine, thank you."

"You know them personally, of course," said Elaine.

"I know them," said Lancelot. "They seem to interest you."

"Immensely! They are the happiest people in the world."

"They certainly are remarkable," said Lancelot, "but I never before heard them praised in those terms."

"Oh, yes. They really are living. If I thought I could—"

"Daughter!" said King Pelles.

"Did you speak, father?"

"You forget yourself. You forget our guest."

"Sir Lancelot? Why, I was talking to him!"

"You were. Your talk was neither appropriate nor entertaining."

"I protest," said Sir Lancelot. "Everything your daughter has said interests me."

"Then I'll go on. With your permission, father. I was about to say that if I could love a man as Iseult does Tristram, I'd think myself happy. I'm afraid of stagnating."

Lancelot stared as though he had not noticed her before. King Pelles looked at Sir Lancelot, then at the servants. One of them thought he wanted something, and hurried over to him.

"Don't you think so?" said Elaine.

"No, daughter, I don't think so at all."

"I wonder if Sir Lancelot will tell us what he thinks," said Elaine.

"Ah, yes," said her father. The servant retired with dignity.

"Stagnation would be serious of course—I've a friend who warns me against it," said Lancelot. "But you are safe from that danger, I should say. And there are other ways of leading a full life. They are not completely happy."

"What's wrong with them? They haven't grown tired of each other, have they?"

"So far as I know, they have not," said Lancelot. "But think how much they miss."

"I'm very stupid. I can't see they miss anything."

"Why, they probably feel they were made for each other, and it looks as though they were. But then, what was King Mark made for? She's his wife, after all. Besides, they never can have children."

"Do they want them?"

"I can't imagine being in love and not wanting them," said Lancelot.

"You can't imagine it of any great lovers?" asked Elaine.

"Of none whatever."

It was her turn to stare at him—so hard that he looked away, and appealed to her father.

"Isn't that so, King Pelles?"

The king roused himself.

"To be sure—of course it is. Shall we have the minstrel in to sing for us, Sir Lancelot? Or shall we move over into that window and entertain ourselves? The conversation in this house is not profound, but then the minstrel isn't very good, either. Out here we miss the privileges of the Court."

"The conversation is profound enough for me," said Lancelot. "My habits are of the most active kind. Ordinarily I'm not what you'd call a thinking man."

Elaine kept her eyes on him. Her father made a slight bow in her direction, less a tribute than a signal not to delay them. She walked to the window, a deep bay with tall leaded panes, and perched herself on the cushioned ledge. She must have known by experience that her feet could not touch the floor, for she promptly drew them up and sat on them. Lancelot took the seat opposite. Pelles placed a chair for himself precisely between them.

"The prospect from this window is very fine," said the king.

"I'm sure," said Lancelot.

"It's best when you can see it," said Elaine.

"Of course—in the daytime," said her father. "And we shall have the moon shortly."

"Moonlight is vague," said Elaine.

They gazed through the open window, into the darkness.

"If you're devoted to the active life," said Elaine, "you must envy them for having to do what they did."

"Who's this now?" said Pelles.

"Tristram and Iseult, father. Didn't they drink some magic? Rather pleasant to do what you're compelled to, and can't argue about, and aren't responsible for. Especially when you'd like to do it, anyway."

"That story isn't true," said Lancelot. "Tristram told me it wasn't."

"I wish you'd tell me something about Guinevere," said Elaine.

Lancelot started from his window-seat.

"Since I'm not to see her at the tournament."

Lancelot settled back again. "Is there anything to tell about the queen, beyond what everybody knows?"

"Is there something everybody knows?" said Elaine.

"They know she's the queen," said Lancelot. "If they've looked at her, they know she is beautiful."

"More so than Iseult?"

"It's a different kind. Guinevere lifts you up."

"I suppose that's why Arthur is such a great king," said Elaine. "Or did he get most of his best work done before he married her?"

"Daughter, I can't permit this to go on," said her father. "Your talk this evening has displeased me, as I have intimated. Now I must forbid any flippant discussion of King Arthur. At no time would it be proper to speak of him as you are doing, and least of all before Sir Lancelot, who is his best friend."

"But, father," said Elaine, "I had to ask these questions of some one who knows. If you had let me go to Court and see the world, I should have had the answers long ago. Of course Guinevere has a gift for inspiring men. I wish I had. But Arthur was at the peak of his glory when he married. I want to know what Guinevere could do for so supreme a man. It isn't disloyal to ask that, is it, Sir Lancelot?"

"He was a great man when Guinevere married him," said Lancelot. "He ought to be still better, I should say, for having had her love."

"Ought to be, but is he?" said Elaine. "And do you imply that he hasn't her love now?"

"Some men don't seem to need so much inspiration as others," said Lancelot. "That's what I mean. Even if he had never met Guinevere, Arthur would have been remarkable."

"I've heard he's rather uninteresting," said Elaine.

"He interests me," said Lancelot.

Elaine said nothing more. The moon was well up now, and King Pelles called attention to it. Lancelot thought it a very fine moon.

"I hope we may keep you for some time," said the king.

"I must ride early to-morrow morning. I ought to have gone on to-night, but your hospitality was too pleasant to leave."

"I'll see you at breakfast," said the king. "Any hour you prefer."

"I shall, too, Sir Lancelot," said Elaine.

"It's not necessary, daughter."

"No," said Elaine, "not because it's necessary."

IV

Lancelot was up first, before the household were ready to serve his breakfast. Elaine was up before her father. She came down with the stout spaniel at her heels, and found Lancelot walking back and forth in the garden just outside the window.

"I hope you slept well," she said.

"Very. And you?"

"I haven't slept the whole night."

"What on earth have you been doing?"

"I've been thinking."

"Thinking!" said Lancelot. "Your father told me you overdid it, but he didn't say you did it at night. What were you thinking about?"

"You, Sir Lancelot. I came to two conclusions about you. I got up early to tell you one of them."

"Why not both?"

"After the first, perhaps you won't listen to the second."

"What's the first?"

"I love you, Sir Lancelot."

"You mean—"

"Just that. Since you may not come here again, I thought I'd better tell you. If you don't love me, I'm no worse off, and anyway I'd like you to know. . . . I suppose you really don't?"

"To be frank," said Lancelot, "I don't."

"Not marriage," said Elaine. "That would be too much, of course. But just your love, for a little while?"

"I can't."

"Never?"

"Never."

"Well, I shan't give up thinking about you. You don't mind, do you?"

"You know, I'm sorry about this!" said Lancelot.

"You needn't be. It might happen to anybody."

She leaned over and petted the spaniel at her feet. Lancelot looked down at her hair in the sunlight.

"It's hardly decent of me to mention it," he said, "but you've roused my curiosity. There was another conclusion?"

She straightened up and laughed. "Yes; I'm sorry you are in love with Guinevere."

"Who says I am?"

"It makes it hard for me to solve my problem—you can see that."

"What problem, Elaine?"

"Why, of winning your love—or of winning you! I suppose I can't have everything."

King Pelles came out of the door so fast that he slipped and had to recover his balance.

"I'm shocked to be late, Sir Lancelot. I gave orders to have your breakfast ready half an hour ago, but they didn't wake me in time. It's on the table now—don't lose a minute. When was it you have to meet Arthur?"

V

LANCELOT and Arthur rode toward the tournament, along one edge of a plain, with the forest shading them. Across the plain another path led toward Lonazep, and behind the path another forest began. In the sunlight they could see two armed men, with a woman riding between them.

"Those people are bound for the tournament," said Arthur.

"They certainly are," said Lancelot.

"I don't recognize the armor," said the king, "and it's too far to see who the lady is. She has black hair."

"She has," said Lancelot. "It's Iseult. One of the knights must be Tristram, and since the other looks quite as powerful, my guess is he's Palomides the Saracen, Iseult's other lover."

"You don't mean she has two at once!" said Arthur. "If I had known that about them—"

"Oh, no," said Lancelot. "Tristram is her lover, but Palomides worships her, and I dare say he's the nobler man, if there's a distinction, for he has no reward—never will have."

"She couldn't encourage a Saracen, of course," said Arthur.

"There's something in that," said Lancelot. "I doubt if Tristram tries hard to convert him to the true faith. But if changing his religion would win Iseult, Palomides would confess to the first priest he met. Christian or not, he's a wonderful knight."

"I've heard Iseult is extremely beautiful," said Arthur.

"She is, but your wife is far lovelier."

They rode half a mile or so without conversation.

"You've seen her, then?" said Arthur.

"I've seen them both," said Lancelot.

"I've seen Guinevere myself," said Arthur. "What does Iseult look like?"

"Her hair is black, as you noticed, and her skin is white. She has remarkable blue eyes. Long, dark lashes. They seem misty and swimming."

Another two hundred yards in silence.

"I've a mind to cross that next field," said Arthur, "and welcome the two knights to our tournament."

"I wouldn't, if I were you," said Lancelot. "If you greet them now, you'll have to ride the rest of the way with them, and the others coming to the jousts will be offended that you honored two contestants with your personal escort, two strangers and one a Saracen."

"Quite right, as usual, Lancelot. It will be better not to disclose who we are. I'm in the mood to join them incognito, with our visors down, pay our compliments to the lady and her two lovers, and then ride ahead."

"If you ride up to those two men with your visor down, especially if you address the lady without first disclosing yourself to Tristram, you will have the tournament beginning on the spot. Tristram or Palomides will knock you out of your saddle."

"Will he?" said Arthur. "I'll take care of that."

He put his horse across the field, and drove in the spurs.

"For God's sake, Arthur!" cried Lancelot, hurrying after him. "Think what you are doing! Even if you could handle those men, you'd be insulting Iseult. If you won't consider her, at least give a thought to Guinevere. She'll get no honor out of this. What you'll get out of it, the devil knows! A broken neck, perhaps."

"I'll be back in a moment," said Arthur. "My intentions are good, and no one will misunderstand them."

"I've followed you when you were sane," said Lancelot. "I must stay by you now."

They got across the field and rode hard after Iseult and her men. Tristram and Palomides heard them coming, and stopped. When they saw that Arthur and Lancelot had their visors down, they covered their own faces and waited for an attack. Arthur puzzled them by slowing up his horse. He rode by at a walk, peering out through his helmet at Iseult, and Lancelot came at his heels, looking hard at the two lances. Arthur entirely forgot to salute the knights.

"Good morning, fair lady," he said.

"Good morning," said Iseult.

He was quite a distance away before Tristram called after him.

"See here, whoever you are, the insult to the lady is an insult to me. I'd rather not strike you in the back. Turn round!"

Whether he heard or not, he rode calmly on. Lancelot took a firm grip with his knees and got his lance ready.

"You're a poor judge of courtesy!" called Sir Palomides. "I don't wish to strike you in the back, either, but if you don't turn, that's where it will be!"

Arthur came to himself in time to hear the hoof-beats, and turned round just soon enough for Palomides to lift him clear of the saddle and drop him on the grass. In his anger Palomides had spurred so savagely that his horse wouldn't stop. When he got back he saw Tristram climbing into his saddle, and Lancelot talking to him, not at all in a hostile manner. Arthur was mounted again, but looked rather dazed. At sight of Palomides, Lancelot got him out of the way.

"Where are they going, Tristram? Why did you let him off so easily?"

"Well, in the first place," said Tristram, "if you hadn't been riding across country you would have noticed that the tall knight did to me what you did to his friend. I was in no position to detain them. Besides, the tall one explained there was no discourtesy meant. His friend, your adversary, is of high degree. They will probably hang you at Lonazep for lifting your hand against the Lord's anointed. You being a pagan."

"What do you mean?"

"The knight who unseated me was Lancelot. I knew it the moment his spear touched me. The apology he made, too, was like him. You can guess who the other was."

"Who?"

"Arthur, of course. They are inseparable."

"It couldn't be!" said Palomides. "Arthur would not be speaking to ladies on the road in that insulting familiarity."

"It was Arthur," said Tristram.

"Why didn't he address himself to you or me?"

"He liked Iseult's looks better."

Lancelot and Arthur rode in silence for several miles. "I shall have to see them again," said Arthur at last.

"Who's that?"

"Tristram and Iseult."

"You're hard to satisfy," said Lancelot. "I thought you had seen enough of them for a lifetime."

"No," said Arthur, "I must straighten out the misunderstanding. I'll make an occasion to call upon them after the tournament."

"I beg of you not to! No good will come of it."

"But certainly no harm. What I did was foolish—the least I can do now is to explain myself. I'll see them for a few moments alone."

"Worse and worse," said Lancelot. "I shall have to go with you."

"I say again," said Arthur, "I will see them alone."

"And I say again, with more reason," replied Lancelot, "I'll have to go along to see that you get out alive."

VI

IF ARTHUR had not looked at Iseult, Galahad would not have been born. Or if Bromel had not come once more to plead with Elaine. Or if Bors, Lancelot's cousin, had not happened to ride by King Pelles' castle.

Bromel, of course, was hardly welcome, but he had to be let in.

"Haven't you changed your mind at all?" he began.

"Oh, yes," said Elaine. "I'm much wiser—improved to an extraordinary degree. I'd rather not joke about it. I'm sorry for you—I know how you feel."

"You begin to understand!" he said. "I shall have your promise some day. I can wait."

"I said I knew how you felt, but I don't feel that way toward you. I don't love you, Bromel. Let's be friends—I can be a kinder friend than I was."

"If you don't love me, what's the point of saying you've changed?"

"You said some sides of my nature were asleep. Well, they've all waked up. I don't think contemptuously of love now, not even of marriage. I'd like to have children."

"What has happened to you?"

"I told you. I'm wiser."

"Haven't you anything else to tell me?"

"Nothing."

Bromel began to walk up and down the room. He

stopped finally at the tower window. For some time he stood looking out.

"When I was here before," he said, "your father was getting the place ready for Lancelot. He came, I suppose?"

"He did."

"He must be quite a person," said Bromel. "I spoke foolishly about him then, but I envy you that chance to see him."

"I envy myself," said Elaine. "I'd be glad to see him again. He was here only one night."

"Would you mind telling me what he's like?" said Bromel. "I confess to curiosity."

"Tall—dark—deep eyes—a number of scars on his face. He's only twenty-five, you know, and—well, he's quite a person."

"I don't believe those stories about him," said Bromel.

"You'd better; they're true," said Elaine. "He's Guinevere's lover."

"Then I'm sorry," said Bromel.

"So am I," said Elaine.

"You thought it was all right before."

"I think so now—but I'm sorry."

Bromel walked back toward her.

"You are surer than ever that you won't marry me?"

"Much surer."

"Then I know what's happened!"

"Do you?"

"You've met some one else."

She took her embroidery—made an attempt at two or three stitches—put it down again. Bromel was looking at her. She looked back as hard as she could.

"I suppose I haven't the right to ask the question," said Bromel at last.

"Which one?"

"Whether you haven't met some one else."

"Oh, was that a question? I thought you made a statement. You are quite right, of course."

"It's Lancelot, then!"

"Who else?"

"And he loves you?"

"Now, that question should not be asked. What could I say if he didn't? You ought to assume that he does. As a matter of fact, he doesn't."

"Nonsense!" said Bromel. "If he loved you, he'd tell you, but how would you know if he didn't love you?"

"He told me," said Elaine. "It seemed best, on the whole, to ask him."

"Asked him if he loved you?"

"I could think of no other way to find out."

Bromel stared as if life had gone from him.

"Don't look at me so, Bromel. I started to be sorry for you, but you'll make me laugh. I'm sorry for myself, too. Shall I tell you the whole story?"

"I should think no woman would care to spread such news about herself," said Bromel.

"My mistake—I thought the secret would stay with you," said Elaine. "You're right again. Good-by, Bromel. . . . Aren't you going?" The tone of her voice roused the fat spaniel by her side. He got up and moved over toward Bromel. "Come back here, Arthur—lie down!" said Elaine. The spaniel lay down.

"I don't want to go," said Bromel, "and I'd like to hear whatever you care to tell me."

"There's less pleasure in it now," said Elaine. "The moment has passed. Oh, well, I won't make a mystery of it. It's very simple. A few days ago I loved nobody— now I love Lancelot. I told him so, and naturally he said it was impossible. He gave no reason, but of course I can guess. Yet I believe I shall have him, in the end. As Guinevere can't have him."

"I don't understand you at all."

"Lancelot says nobody really loves who doesn't want children."

"What has that to do with it?"

"Everything."

"I'm shocked beyond measure!"

"You would be, Bromel."

"Fortunately there's no danger. Only one kind of woman would do such a thing."

"Those with the maternal instinct."

"Absurd! You haven't the maternal instinct. You just want Lancelot."

"Well, I promise you this—I shan't propose to him unless I know he will accept. Don't worry about me, Bromel—I shall manage somehow."

Again Bromel walked slowly up and down the room, with his eyes on the floor.

"You take it awfully well," she said, "and I can't forget the hours you've spent on me. We've become good companions, just diagnosing my heart. I'm afraid I'm selfish."

He stopped and looked at her.

"It won't make you happy."

"What won't?"

"Having a child."

"Bromel! What shocking words from your lips!"

"It won't make you happy, Elaine."

"It would make him happy."

"It wouldn't! The misery that would come to you both from such an experiment!"

"It's not an experiment. Remember how often it has happened before. Men and women have been here a long time."

"It has happened before, but it never came out well. Lancelot will remember that. Do you mind telling me— does he know anything yet about your designs?"

"Not a word. I've trusted you, Bromel. You could spoil the whole thing by warning him."

"There's no point in warning him. He might think it none of my business, anyway. But as an old friend I suppose I ought to tell your father enough to put him on his guard."

Elaine laid both hands on the arms of her chair, then sank back and looked at him.

"Tell my father if you like! Warn him of his coming grandchildren! You probably can't keep the secret anyway. He'll be surprised at the solicitude you show for his family fortunes! Tell him that as the rejected suitor you feel his descendants are in your care! Really, Bromel, you have much misplaced courage. When father gets through with you, do you think I shall respect you more for betraying my confidence?"

"You needn't accuse me," said Bromel. "Lancelot has stolen the love I should have had. I shan't warn him—no doubt he's aware of what he's doing, and he has flattered you somehow into thinking that you are capturing him. You are to be his victim, I can see. I'll explain it to your father, and then I'll find Lancelot and challenge him."

"I hoped you would enjoy a longer life! Just tell Lancelot you know he's my lover, and see what happens to you. He belongs to Guinevere, I told you. But do what you like. Our friendship is at an end, and you'll have no more confidences from me."

"I don't wish to quarrel with you, Elaine—"

"No quarrel at all. We have just ceased to be friends. Before parting I've told you what you now think you had better blab to the neighbors."

"I shall warn your father that Lancelot is stealing you away," said Bromel, "and then I'll take my place by the bridge down there, where Lancelot must pass when he comes to you. I'll have it out with him."

Elaine laughed. "But, Bromel, he isn't coming. I may never see him again. You don't mean you'll be waiting out there, day after day?"

"When I've spoken with your father, I'll deal with your lover."

As it turned out, he did not wait long. Late the next afternoon Sir Bors came riding that way and made for the bridge. Bromel stopped him.

"You are a tall man," he said, "and rather dangerous-looking; I suspect you are the man I'm waiting for."

"That may be," said Bors. "Has your friend any particular name?"

"It's no use being facetious, Sir Lancelot," said Bromel.

"I'm not Sir Lancelot," said Bors, "but if I can be of any service to you, I'm a relative of his."

"He is the biggest rascal in his family," said Bromel.

"I'd rather meet him, but meanwhile you'll do well enough."

Sir Bors looked at him in silence for a moment. "Lancelot is no rascal, and the rest of his family, if you count the cousins like myself, are too numerous to discuss in detail. I'm sorry you have listened to lies about him."

"I haven't," said Bromel. "He has stolen the heart of an inexperienced young woman here—I might almost say unprotected, except for what I can do. He intends to bring her to shame, unless I stop him. Don't shake your head at me that way! Unless you wish to fight."

"I never saw less need of fighting," said Bors. "The whole thing is silly. I don't know who you are, nor who the lady is, if she exists. I suspect you are out of your wits."

"I am Sir Bromel—the lady is Elaine, in the castle there."

"You don't mean King Pelles' daughter?"

"I thought you knew her," said Bromel.

"I know King Pelles," said Bors. "Suppose we go in together and find out what the trouble is?"

"Go where together?" cried Bromel. "You don't cross this bridge unless you first take my life! You are false as Lancelot himself. I wouldn't trust one of you."

"I'm sorry you feel so," said Bors, "but if you will have it—"

He drew back a few yards and then rode hard at Sir Bromel, whose chivalry was out of practise, except in the spiritual sense. Bors was inclined to laugh. A few passes and he had Bromel at his mercy.

"I'm sorry to kill you," he said, "but it's that or you take back the slander."

"I'll take it back, but it's probably true."

"As I said, I'm sorry," repeated Bors, unlacing Bromel's helmet.

"I take it back," said Bromel.

"That's better," said Sir Bors, and let him up.

"I don't see anything to laugh at," said Bromel.

"Correct," said Bors. "There's nothing for you to laugh at. You have your life on one condition—go directly to the Court, find Lancelot, and apologize to him for what you have said."

Bromel promised—in fact, offered to swear on the hilt of his sword.

"That's all right," said Bors. "Now you start looking for Lancelot, right across that bridge."

He watched Bromel well down the road, then turned toward King Pelles' castle.

Pelles received him in the great hall, where Lancelot had been entertained. Elaine heard it was Lancelot's cousin, and joined them.

"A pleasure to see you, Sir Bors," said the king. "And looking so well. You had no interruption on the road, I hope?"

"None to speak of," said Bors.

"You found the bridge easy to cross?" said the king.

"Perfectly. There isn't anything wrong with the bridge, is there?"

"No," said the king. "The bridge is satisfactory. Have you seen your distinguished cousin recently?"

"Not very—I didn't go to Lonazep," said Bors. "I understand he and Tristram did well. They always do."

"Was Iseult there?" asked Elaine. "I was going with father, but didn't after all."

"You should have gone. Yes, I believe Iseult was there."

"Sir Lancelot admires her, doesn't he? When he was here he spoke of her."

"Now don't let us get on that subject," said Pelles. "My daughter, Sir Bors, is infatuated with him. I might as well tell you, before she does. If you'd do me a kindness, persuade your cousin not to come here again. I don't want her to compromise herself further with so splendid a man—compromise him, I mean."

"If you cared for the family reputation, father, you wouldn't introduce me to Sir Bors in these terms. I do admire Sir Lancelot, but who doesn't?"

"Quite right," said Bors. "We are all devoted to him."

"That's not it—you don't know," said King Pelles. "When he was here a while ago my daughter talked to him with most daring frankness about the relations—I should say the intimate relations—of men and women, and before he left she made what I believe are called overtures. No doubt the whole Court has heard of my disgrace."

"If you think Lancelot would talk about a woman," said Bors, "you don't know him. In this case he has had no occasion to be discreet. You are unjust to your daughter."

"I'm sorry," said Pelles. "I wish I were."

"Sir Bors," said Elaine, "I thank you for your trust in me. It's a pity to bother you with our family disputes, but since my father has gone so far, I think he ought to lay before you what he thinks is the conclusive evidence. It's at least amusing, and it does me no harm."

"We'll leave that to Sir Bors," said the king. "There's an admirable young man in the neighborhood who has been seeking my daughter's hand. Yesterday he came to me with a story which I must believe, partly because I trust him, chiefly because his conduct supports it. He said Elaine had just told him she was desperately in love with Sir Lancelot, that she had declared her passion, and—I blush to add this essential detail—she had hopes of bearing him a child. My daughter now declares that Sir Bromel grossly misunderstood her or misrepresents her—that Lancelot does not love her, and never did—but Bromel is convinced that your cousin has somehow played false. He waits at the bridge to challenge Lancelot. Would he do that if he hadn't good reason for what he told me?"

"He might be convinced and yet be wrong," said Bors. "I don't attach much weight myself to his judgment."

"You know him?" said Pelles.

"We've met. I think I know him. He means well."

"Since you know him," said the king, "we might send for him to dinner. He's probably down at the bridge."

"Wouldn't that be a happy reunion!" said Elaine. "When you put your mind on it, father, you certainly—"

"I've just come by the bridge," said Bors. "He isn't there."

"Perhaps it's as well," said Pelles. "He feels strongly about this matter—as I do myself. Elaine, will you give orders for dinner, or shall I?"

"You, father. You do it much better."

"I'll be with you again in three minutes, Sir Bors," said Pelles, and disappeared through the door.

"I suppose you understand," said Elaine, "my father's a fool."

"I never thought that of him."

"Think it now. I hope you didn't kill Bromel."

"Oh, no," said Bors. "He tried to stop me—nothing more serious. There's something on his mind."

"I should say there was. What did you do with him, Sir Bors?"

"Sent him to beg Lancelot's pardon for the charges he made."

"Concerning me?"

"Yes."

"Then the whole Court will hear of it!"

"I never thought of that," said Bors. "It was a mistake to send him."

"Oh, well, Lancelot will know I haven't forgotten him," said Elaine. "I really do love him, Sir Bors—that's why Bromel and my father embarrass me. Lancelot is innocent of everything but his own charm."

"I've seen this happen before," said Bors. "Lancelot will understand. Let's hope Sir Bromel doesn't get to talk with Guinevere."

VII

ILL though she had been, Guinevere kept her beauty. Hers was the kind of loveliness that owed less to outer form and coloring, less to a tall, proud body, to a chiseled face, to a miraculous aureole of hair, than to some excitement of spirit within. Even in health, you felt, that woman would never be at peace—no more than any other flame. Her controlled dignity was an achievement.

She was seated in a corner of her garden, sheltered by the castle wall. Too feeble as yet for much walking, she could at least spend the summer day near roses and marigolds, with knights and ladies to talk to, or—when the talk failed—with the spread of country to look at, the meadows and the forest beyond. Lady Anglides, friend of her girlhood, stood beside her, Sir Ector observed a respectful distance, Sir Gawaine rested himself on the grass at her feet. Under a cherry tree Agravaine and Meliagrance were playing chess. Agravaine was winning. Meliagrance had placed himself where he could keep his eyes on Guinevere.

"Altogether," said Gawaine, "the tournament may be considered a failure."

"A failure?"

"You were not there, madam."

"If I had the strength," she said, "I'd laugh. Will you never be subtle?"

"I can't say that," interrupted Sir Ector.

"Are you talking about my subtlety?" said Gawaine.

"I'm talking about the jousts. The queen's absence grieved us, but it was a wonderful tournament."

"Was it? That first day, when Palomides killed Lancelot's horse—I didn't think much of that."

Guinevere looked at him.

"Lancelot's horse was killed?"

"It wasn't his best horse," said Ector.

"Well, the Saracen killed it, anyway."

"Palomides killed it?"

"Yes, madam, the one who follows Iseult around—her honorary lover. He has it in for Lancelot. He was vicious from the start."

"But Lancelot is far too strong for him," said Guinevere.

"Exactly. It had just turned out so, but Palomides dropped his lance, drew his sword, shaved Lancelot's spear as though it were an asparagus stem, and sliced the horse's head nearly off."

"Those eastern swords are sharp," said Ector.

"I didn't know that sort of thing was allowed in tournaments," said Guinevere.

"It's not. You may kill the man but not the horse. They explained the rules to Palomides. Meanwhile the horse died."

"A small matter at that," said Ector. "It was a great tournament. Lancelot never did better, the king of course did finely, and Tristram was there. God, what a man!"

"I'm interested in your report of the king's performance," said Gawaine. "You think he did well, except for being unhorsed?"

Agravaine and Meliagrance stopped playing and

looked at the queen. She kept her manner, but it seemed a long moment before she spoke.

"Gawaine, are you annoyed at Sir Ector because he didn't flatter me, or because he is more generous than you? Never mind, Sir Ector. If Arthur were here he would be the first to admit that most of you ride better than he."

"I ought to be crushed by your rebuke, madam, but I'm not. Essentially we agree. Ector is generous. In fact, too generous. He knows as well as I do, the king fell off his horse."

"Not in the tournament," said Ector.

"Well, just before it. It's the same thing. That Saracen again, madam. He's angry with Arthur, too."

"He isn't," said Ector.

"He is, I tell you. Agravaine had the news from a man who heard Palomides talking about it."

"Gawaine," said Guinevere, "I doubt if you would enjoy a more direct contact with facts."

"Anyway," said Ector, "the second day was more worth while. Tristram changed his armor and came in disguised, and one by one the men tried what they could do with the stranger, and found out. That was lively work."

"Yes," said Gawaine, "but then Palomides changed his armor, too, and went at him for life and death. How do you understand that? Then Lancelot came in, cool as you please—don't you remember?—and Palomides stepped aside and let him take on Tristram. I thought they'd kill each other before they found out who they were."

"Why, Lancelot admires Tristram," said Guinevere. "He'd be sorry to lift his hand against him, even by mistake. I thought he liked Palomides, too."

"He might have a grudge against him for unseating the king," said Gawaine.

"But why should Palomides quarrel with both Lancelot and Arthur?" said Guinevere.

"The story Agravaine heard throws light on that."

"Gawaine," she said, "I see you want me to ask what the story was. Tell it, if you'd feel happier."

"Oh, no, it's not important—and as you say, it may not be true. Too bad there's no way to find out."

"But there is! When Arthur returns, I'll ask him. He will tell me."

"I had forgotten how easily you could get your contacts with truth, madam," said Gawaine. "Why don't you ask Lancelot about his relations with Iseult? That might explain why Palomides is jealous."

Meliagrance left his chess game and moved over where he could hear better. Agravaine joined him. Guinevere seemed not to notice them.

"Gawaine," she said, "I did not realize what a mischievous tongue you have. I never before thought you a coward. Ask that question of Lancelot, yourself, to his face. Ask him when we are all here together, to enjoy the interview!"

"At your command, madam, I shall ask him," said Gawaine. "May I tell him it is at your command?"

Meliagrance started to laugh, but stopped when the queen looked up at him.

"I don't know how we got on this subject," said Ector. "It was a fine tournament. Gawaine makes a mystery out of an accident. The king met them on the way to the tournament—"

"Who was it he met?"

"Tristram, Iseult and Palomides, madam. Palomides, not knowing who it was, ran at the king. Arthur wouldn't have fallen if he hadn't been off his guard. The night after the tournament the king and Lancelot went to Tristram's tent. I followed them. On the way Agravaine joined me. We found them in the friendliest sort of talk."

Meliagrance cleared his throat. "Was Palomides there?"

"No—just Tristram and Iseult."

"How friendly was the talk when you left?" said Meliagrance.

Ector hesitated a moment and turned toward Agravaine.

"I can't judge," said Agravaine. "I wasn't paying attention. Iseult is so beautiful I couldn't keep my mind on anything else."

Meliagrance made a gesture with both hands, palm up, as though the case were proved.

"Neither could Arthur and Lancelot. Especially Lancelot. That's the whole story."

Guinevere's lips tightened for a second, but then her tired face broke into a smile, as though she liked the remark.

"Iseult is evidently a person to look at," she said. "As soon as I am strong again we must have her here for us all to see in spite of Palomides."

"But will the king want them here?" persisted Meliagrance. "It won't be a comfortable visit, after what has happened."

"What has happened? I am ready to listen, if any of you will explain what you are hinting at."

No one spoke. Guinevere looked so worn and feverish

that the Lady Anglides leaned over her and said something in a low tone.

"Not now!" cried the queen. "I will stay till I get to the bottom of this. Never in Arthur's court have I listened to such insinuations. Are they really talking about the king? Is it his wife they are entertaining?"

"For myself," said Meliagrance, "I'm talking about Lancelot. The rumor is that he admires Iseult. There is nothing unnatural or scandalous in that. No one suggests that Iseult would take him instead of Tristram."

"And I," said Gawaine, getting up from the grass and dusting himself off—"I was talking about the king. I doubt if he and Tristram are good friends now. That night in the tent Tristram was discourteous to my brother here—said Agravaine was the murderer of Lamorak, or at least an accomplice. If Agravaine is a murderer, so am I, and so is the king for holding us innocent."

"Why can't you give a fair account of what happened?" cried Ector. "Tristram was Lamorak's friend, and he says Lamorak was killed not in fair fight but in ambush, greatly outnumbered. He says the ambush was unknightly, and Lancelot agrees with him. So does the king, I'm sure. Did you really expect to get through this tournament without hearing an opinion of what you did a year ago? No doubt Tristram is worried for Iseult and himself; in a country where one ambush has been laid, how can he be sure what may happen?"

"I see you are right, Sir Ector," said Guinevere. "It was certainly a remarkable tournament."

"What are you men thinking of?" said Lady Anglides. "Did you come to inquire after the queen's health? To cheer her up?"

"That's what we came for," said Ector, "but we've gone at it the wrong way. It's poor taste, madam, to repeat this gossip. You'll be glad to have us take our leave."

"The only thing I don't like," said the queen, "is to hear you quarrel, or seem to quarrel. Whatever Arthur does is well done—you all know that—and Lancelot is— what he always is. Gawaine, you owe too much to both of them to be disloyal."

"I'm not disloyal, madam. I'm one of the truest friends the king has. I have reported only the facts."

"Do you call that being a true friend?" said Meliagrance. "Have you considered whether the facts will stand reporting?"

"Have you considered the queen—that's what I'd like to know!" said Anglides. "Your talk would sicken a strong person, not to speak of an invalid."

"I'm no longer an invalid, Anglides," said Guinevere. "The conversation has brought back more energy than I thought I had. . . . Who was that you were speaking with, Sir Ector?"

"Madam, there's a young stranger at the gate who is looking for Sir Lancelot. He has some message for him which he won't leave with any one else. He insists on knowing when Lancelot will return, or where he can be found now."

"We'd like the answer to those questions ourselves," said Guinevere.

"Perhaps he comes from Iseult," said Meliagrance. "Or from Tristram."

Guinevere seemed not to hear him. "What is the young man's name, Sir Ector?"

"He calls himself Sir Bromel. I'll find out where he comes from."

"It's not necessary. I've a notion to find out for myself, if you men will permit me. Tell him to come in, Anglides. You needn't stay."

VIII

Guinevere was quite herself again by the time Arthur came home. She heard his hearty laugh in the courtyard, and listened for his quick step on the great stairway. When he knocked at her door she was prepared to welcome him.

"You can't tell how happy I am to see you again, Guinevere. And you're looking better, so much better!"

"Oh, I'm entirely well now! You had a great tournament, I understand."

"Very exciting," said Arthur, and settled himself in the end of the couch. "Tristram and Palomides brought novelty to it."

"I'm glad it turned out as you wished. What did they do that was novel?"

"Oh, without them there would have been only the familiar oppositions. But I didn't enjoy it altogether."

"Why not, Arthur?"

"We missed you."

He looked sharply at her as he spoke, and when she smiled he seemed pleased.

"And besides, Tristram told me right out he bears a grudge for Lamorak's death last year. Agravaine was present when he spoke."

"I'm sorry about Lamorak," said Guinevere, "and sorry Tristram is resentful. I wish the tournament had been altogether happy."

"It was more than satisfactory, for the most part. I exaggerate the difficulties by speaking of them."

He sat watching her for a moment, apparently enjoying what he saw, and with the air of being content in his own house. She looked up and returned his smile.

"Arthur, don't you think these tournaments have served their purpose? The men take them so seriously. Won't they always breed trouble?"

"You've spoken of this before, of course. No, I believe they are useful."

"For what, Arthur? When you were settling the country you had real things to fight for, and the jousts were good training, but now—"

"They still are, Guinevere. I know your opinion, and I'm sorry I can't agree. I'm glad we are at peace. We never should have been if we hadn't known how to fight."

"I'm glad of the peace, too," she said, "but can't we go on to more important business now we are through with wars? Peace isn't the end, is it? Isn't there something else to proceed to?"

"I believe, Guinevere, that peace is itself progress. If the tournaments serve no other purpose, they keep the men in health—they are fine exercise."

"Exercise! Men get killed in them."

"Yes, they are rough at times—but men get killed accidentally even though they never enter a tournament."

"When you speak of health, you refer to their bodies, I suppose," said the queen. "Your men are sinking into habits of gossip and irritability."

"Some will gossip and some will be irritable," he replied. "There are always a few small people. It's no use minding them."

"Not even when they talk against you—your own men?"

"They don't."

"Don't they! When I was in the garden the other day Gawaine and Meliagrance came with some others to ask after my health. For sheer lack of anything important to talk about they told me you were unhorsed by Palomides. There was a time when none of your men would have admitted that to themselves, not even if it were true. Now they tell it to me."

"They told the truth."

"I was hoping they lied."

"No, I wanted to see what Iseult looked like, without letting her know who I was, so I rode by with my visor down. When Palomides came up I wasn't ready, but perhaps it would have made no difference. He's a powerful man."

"I'm very, very sorry, Arthur."

"Oh, I'm not. It's of no consequence."

"On the contrary. You discredit yourself by silly behavior."

"Silly or not, I'm glad I did it. A man should let himself go once in a while. If I were such a stickler for the proprieties as you are, I'd be equally a victim of nerves. You're too repressed."

She waited a moment, too, before she spoke again.

"So that was when Tristram talked about Lamorak. He might well feel uneasy."

"I didn't speak to Tristram then—not till the next day."

"Was Lancelot with you?"

"Dear me, yes. He was right behind me. He unseated Tristram and we got away before Palomides could trouble us again."

"If Lancelot got away, as you call it," said Guinevere, "it wasn't from danger. He must have been ashamed."

"He disapproved of my riding by. He says I should have addressed Tristram. He opposed my seeing them again the next evening, though he went along to protect me—or perhaps to protect you. He fears I'm losing my heart to Iseult."

"Gawaine says you both are."

"I see. That's what upset you."

"No," said Guinevere. "If you and Lancelot admire Iseult, you ought to do so openly. I told the men that as soon as I was well enough I should have Tristram and Iseult here, where we could all see them. I was hoping you had invited them already."

"Better think twice about that," said Arthur. "Iseult is all right—a very fine stately woman—very much like you, Guinevere, except that her hair is black, and I imagine she's not so intense. But Tristram is extremely blunt. He wouldn't get on well with our men."

"Isn't there something wrong if our men can't behave properly toward a visitor? Do have them both here! Don't deny me!"

"He won't come, I'm sure, Guinevere. He's afraid of something. Not Lancelot, I think."

"Why did you look him up that second time?"

"To apologize—and I wanted to see Iseult. Riding by, the day before, I really couldn't judge. She's a beautiful woman. I told her so, and Lancelot added firmly that you are still more beautiful."

"Well, you both seem to have tried hard to make Tristram happy," said Guinevere.

"It was a blunder, and my fault," said Arthur. "Let's talk of pleasanter matters. Has anything amusing happened?"

"I've got on very well—there's been nothing unusual. Arthur, you ought to have Tristram here, just to quiet these rumors."

"Let's think it over. He won't come, but we might ask him, to show good will. When Lancelot gets back the gossip will stop."

"Why not when you get back?" said Guinevere. "Are you the king, or is he? When I married you, you had a high spirit. Am I the cause of the change? You give orders, not always sensible ones, and Lancelot carries them out. Young though you are, you don't exercise; you can't sit your horse as you used to. You ask if anything amusing has helped pass the time. Such thoughts as these. When you order Lancelot to do your work, or allow him to protect you, doesn't it occur to you that he may—"

"Guinevere, I had no idea you were jealous of Lancelot. I thought you were as fond of him as I believe he is of you. Don't poison my friendship for him. He is my superior, and always was. If I were as bad as you say, would he remain loyal?"

"If he is loyal by nature, he will be loyal," said Guinevere. "Perhaps he remembers old times, not so long ago."

"You are still weak, Guinevere; I've tired you out. We'd better talk no more of this now. Before I go I want to tell you some happy news about Lancelot."

"You spoke of waiting for Tristram till Lancelot returned. Where is Lancelot?"

"He's here—we came back together—but I'm sending him on another errand to King Pelles."

Guinevere started at the name, but Arthur did not notice.

"You can't guess what the news is."

"How could I?"

"Lancelot has fallen in love. At last. I always hoped he would, but there seemed to be no romance in him. It's Elaine, King Pelles' daughter."

"That's interesting," said Guinevere. "When did he tell you?"

"He didn't tell me himself—it came from a young man named Bromel, who met Gawaine. I can't make out whether the affair has been going on a long time, or whether it began when he went there just before the tournament. It ought to be of long standing, the way Bromel takes it. He wanted Elaine himself, and accused Lancelot of stealing the girl, and Bors thrashed him for the slander. Now he's looking for Lancelot to apologize. Incidentally he has confided his story to Gawaine. If Lancelot was trying to keep it a secret, Bromel has his revenge."

"You haven't seen Bromel yourself?"

"No—Gawaine told me."

"It's probably not true. Gawaine likes to belittle you and Lancelot these days."

"When has he belittled me?"

"He told that story about Palomides."

"But that was true," said Arthur. "No doubt this is true, too. You don't care to hear good news of Lancelot. I entirely misunderstood your feeling toward him."

"No you don't," said Guinevere. "I'm glad, for his

sake, if he is to be happy. He ought to have married long ago. But there's something about this report—if he loves Elaine, why doesn't he tell us—tell you, at least?"

"He probably will," said Arthur. "The match would be creditable to both. Pelles is a gentleman, though he lacks a sense of humor. His wife, I've heard, was a brilliant woman. She died young. There's no reason why the girl shouldn't be the right wife for him."

"No reason at all," said Guinevere, "if he loves her."

"Of course," said Arthur, "I always thought Lancelot would fall in love with a woman of unusual place in the world, some unique beauty. Like Iseult perhaps. His destiny would seem to go that way. But if he's in love, that settles it."

Guinevere sat with her head leaning back against the deep chair. Her eyes were closed. Arthur realized how ill she must be. He got up to leave her. She opened her eyes.

"Have you seen this girl Elaine?" she said.

"I'm trying to remember. Probably not. She stays mostly at home."

"Has Bors returned? I'd like to hear his version."

"So should I. He'll be here in a week or so. He can tell us—unless we'd rather ask Lancelot himself."

"I intend to ask him," she said. She closed her eyes again. Arthur moved toward the door.

"Did you say you are sending him on another errand?"

"Yes. If he has an affair with Elaine I'll help it along. He probably wants to be there. The business could wait, but I'll give him his chance. Isn't that the thing to do?"

"I suppose it is," said Guinevere.   "I haven't thought of him in such a relation—I can't say."

"If you think I'd better not send him, there's still time."

"No, let him go. If he loves the woman, nothing will keep him away from her, and if any one is to aid him, it should be you."

"I'm afraid we've been talking too long," said Arthur. "I've been thoughtless, as usual."

"Before Lancelot goes I'd like to see him."

"I hope he'll confide in you," said Arthur.

"Does he know about Bors and Bromel?"

"How could he?"

"Gawaine may have told him—or Meliagrance."

"You still worry about Meliagrance?"

"Not worry—but I cling to my opinion," said Guinevere.   "That man is no friend to me—nor to you, if I judge correctly."

IX

"ELAINE," said King Pelles, "this ill-advised behavior of yours is beginning to have results. Sir Lancelot, I believe, has heard from Bromel."

"I'm not responsible for Bromel, father—he's not part of my conduct."

"Perhaps he is, after all. Very much a part of it. He represents or misrepresents you, running through the country with his version of your wild talk. I have just received from Sir Lancelot a message which seems to refer to you. He's to be here in two days on another errand, and he begs that we may meet alone."

"Private business, obviously," said Elaine.

"Perhaps—but I strongly suspect he doesn't wish to be further—I may say implicated or entangled."

"Poor man!" said Elaine. "Why does he run into this peril?"

"The king sends him. The business is not private—the trouble is with you, Elaine. It's an extraordinary message; they never send word in advance."

"The last time he came, you knew in advance—you got the castle ready."

"Only by accident. I happened to hear of it."

"Well," said Elaine, "there's no use guessing. I'll ask him why he wanted to meet you alone."

"On the contrary," said her father, "I take his wish as a command. To-morrow you will go to our castle at

Case. It's not far, and I'll send a few of the servants over to make you comfortable. Amuse yourself there till Lancelot is gone, and if he asks for you I'll say you are traveling at some distance. Bromel will have no further occasion to talk."

"He wouldn't, in any case," said Elaine. "Thank you for the prudent arrangement, father."

"You'd better go in the morning," said Pelles.

"I'm not going at all," said Elaine. "It wouldn't be safe. I'd behave much better here, with you to watch me."

"I've watched you for some time, with deplorable results," said Pelles. "Be ready to-morrow morning."

"You don't mean you will turn me out of the house, just because Lancelot is coming?"

"That's what I mean."

"Well, I won't go!"

"As you prefer," said Pelles. "In that event I will entertain Lancelot at the other castle myself. This is more comfortable, but the other is possible."

"You intend to send me away every time he comes here?"

"I'm discussing this particular visit. You go or I go."

"If you respect the family reputation so much," said Elaine, "can't you see that your precautions are ridiculous? I'll make a bargain with you, father—let me stay, and I promise not to say a word to him."

"Impossible! If he were here he would speak to you."

"Do you think he really would?"

"Now don't make me angry, daughter. He'd have to address you, out of courtesy, and once you got started, I couldn't stop you."

"If you were my mother," said Elaine, "I could tell you everything that's in my heart. You'd see that I ought not to go away."

"I'm not your mother," said Pelles. "But stay if you wish. I'll go."

"I get down on my knees to you," she cried. "Let me stay and see him, with you beside me. I know better than you how much safer I'd be that way."

"To-morrow morning, I said." He looked down at her. "You might as well get off your knees. I've made up my mind."

She got up quite cheerfully. "You've made up my mind, too. I was in some doubt, but now I know what I want. I'll go. You really should have let me stay to redeem myself by good behavior in Lancelot's presence. But now I don't wish to behave myself. I want to be as different as possible from you. I dare say I can manage it. I want—"

"Stop talking to me that way," said Pelles. "You have lost your self-control absolutely."

"Oh no, not entirely," said Elaine. "But it wouldn't matter. You are going to control me, if I understand you."

"I am."

"By force. Your wits against mine."

"Exactly."

"My poor mother!" said Elaine. "Well, it's not such a bad prospect, after all."

X

"GUINEVERE!" cried Lancelot.

She was seated in a tall chair, such as they had carried into the garden for her. He started across the room with his arms outstretched, but she made no motion to greet him. He stopped. She looked paler now than that day out-of-doors.

"I had no idea you were still so sick," he began.

"I am quite well."

"Guinevere—we have been parted so long—"

"It has been a long time, and we have missed you here. Arthur has told me about the tournament. Did it satisfy you?"

"No," he said.

"I'm sorry. Why not?"

"You were not there."

"They all say that. No, I wasn't."

He wondered what she meant. She leaned her head back in the chair—that trick of hers—with her eyes half closed.

"Nothing went quite right," he said.

"I gathered as much."

"What do you mean, Guinevere?"

She raised herself suddenly in the tall chair, and looked straight at him.

"If you fail me, our love is at an end. I think you have failed me."

"Failed you? What are you saying?"

"You know well enough. You understand what our

love means. If you go the same way as Arthur, I've absolutely no use for you."

He sat down on a bench near the wall.

"Guinevere, what have I done, or haven't done?"

"You don't know, of course!"

"I don't."

"Well, for example, your encounters with Tristram
and Iseult—you and Arthur waylaying them on the road
and haunting them in their tent."

"I went with the king both times. Why are you
angry?"

"Would you have gone either time if you had been
alone?"

"Certainly not."

"That's why I'm angry. Both incidents were dis-
creditable. You did what you knew was unworthy."

"Guinevere, I had to follow him. I've no wish to excuse myself at his expense, but he was resolved to go."

"Lancelot, we had to reach this moment, sooner or
later, and I'm glad we've got to it while we are still
young. You must choose between Arthur and me. Our
relation is queer enough already—you are my lover, yet
you pride yourself on loyalty to him. You can't be true
to both. If you still feel our love justifies itself, then get
up your courage, man, and accept its consequences. If
you prefer to be loyal to Arthur—well, it was an error
to begin by making love to his wife."

"I declare, this is an unexpected greeting," said Lancelot. "You're not telling me all that's in your mind.
What has happened? Make love to his wife! That was
not the way it began."

"You mean I made love to you?"

"Our hearts needed no courtship," he said. "And what are these consequences of our love which you ask me to live out, except my worship of you?"

"Those phrases are unusually good," said Guinevere. "It's a bad sign. In your natural moods you are not eloquent. You know why I gave myself to you. I could love only one kind of man—the kind that makes a difference in the world, who builds something, who always goes on. I once thought Arthur was that."

"For my part," said Lancelot, "I never admitted he wasn't. You'll bear me witness. I loved you for yourself, not to improve you, as you seem to have loved me, and not by way of expressing a criticism of your husband."

"What you loved me for is of little importance now," said Guinevere. "You two seemed to be different, but you are much alike. As well have remained unhappy with Arthur! When I found he was satisfied with himself, and couldn't imagine a career, not even when I pointed it out, there was nothing for me to help him in. I turned to you for the chance to live. I thought I could find life through you—I could dream, you could act out the vision— together we could—even in spite of Arthur, we could bestow on him a kingdom and a name. Oh, Lancelot, do you think I'd have given myself to you if this had not been the one hope for our souls?"

"This certainly was your idea of it," said Lancelot.

"Exactly—my idea, which you have ceased to share."

"Why, I always came at it differently, Guinevere. I simply wanted you so much that I was false to my best friend, and I don't like to think of it, but I've hoped you were finding what you talk of so much—outlet for your

energies through whatever I've accomplished. I owe
you everything. If you hadn't loved me, I shouldn't have
done so much. I've tried to follow your idea. When I told
you once what a yearning I had—still have, in fact—for
a son to bear my name, you said that good deeds must be
our children, and that even children are begotten in vain
unless they grow to excel their parents. Always something higher, you said."

"You understood me a while ago," said Guinevere.
"Why have you changed?"

"I haven't."

"Absurd—you know you have. You now follow
Arthur into scrapes where your name and your influence
are sure to be lost. If he wants to look at Iseult, why
must you go too?"

"If you think he's in love with Iseult—"

"Tristram probably thinks so, but I don't," said
Guinevere. "Arthur is in love with nobody. He needs
to be amused—he's an absolute boy. I don't suspect you
of loving Iseult, either. That's not the point. But when
he does foolish things, you follow him and do them too.
You let him decide whether your behavior shall be noble
or quite insignificant."

"Guinevere, if I hadn't gone along that first time,
Palomides or Tristram would have killed him before
they found out who he was. After that I felt bound to
watch him. Let me tell you this—just because I have your
love—his wife's love—I can't stand by and let him be
hurt. I must protect him even at some cost to myself, for
if I didn't, and he were killed, I'd have to consider how
far I had willed his death."

"I don't want Arthur to die," said Guinevere. "What

are you talking about? But I, too, have a conscience. My one excuse is that through our love you became the best of living men—or so I thought. With this result, our life together might be said to have a reason, to be almost holy. Otherwise, we are only two traitors, concealing a sin, and I'll have no more to do with you."

"But I first tried to dissuade Arthur, and then I saved him. Wasn't that all right?"

"You may judge by what men think of you," said Guinevere. "They class you now with Arthur. They say you were pursuing Iseult, two vulgar gallants, and that Tristram has grown suspicious. Why should you protect Arthur from himself? You can't, anyway. Let him be what he is. You, also, be yourself. Then the difference between you and him would be clear. Perhaps he might be shamed into wisdom. As it is, you encourage his folly."

"If I stay in his kingdom I must obey him."

"Did he command you to go with him to see Iseult? I dare say he didn't. In any case you must choose. Our love, our dream of creating something—or obedience to Arthur and his self-satisfaction."

"If he commands me, I must obey."

"Even against your judgment?"

"Yes."

"Then we part now. If he directs your life, I know what sort of end it will come to."

"Not a bad one."

"Not a great one, either. I'll remember what I thought you could be, and pretend that's what you still are. But I shan't care to see you again."

Lancelot paused a moment before he answered her.

"You expect too much of me, Guinevere—that's the whole trouble. If you hadn't expected too much of Arthur you would still love him. You are tired of me already—it doesn't matter much what I do or don't do."

"I expected more," she said, "than either of you lived up to, if that is expecting too much. When I married Arthur I thought he would become a great man, but—"

"He was a great man."

"So you have remarked before. We differ, as usual. Perhaps we can agree that our love began in the hope of a career for you."

"Guinevere, our love began because I loved you—that's all I know. You had an idea of making something out of me, and I was afraid you might be disappointed."

"Well, I am."

He paused again for a moment.

"Guinevere, suppose I agree with you, essentially. After what we have thought of, a mediocre life can't be a happy one. But you've shown me no way out."

"It's I who have failed, you mean—I haven't inspired you. As you will."

"You're hasty—let me say what I mean. You advise me to stand aside while he does foolish things. But when he commands me also to do foolish things—no, I won't say that—his commands have never been foolish. But when he commands something I've a reason not to wish to do—"

"Such as?"

"I needn't give examples, Guinevere."

"I command you to—Arthur's wife—consider it one of his sacred commands!"

"I can't think of an instance just now."

"Well—I suppose you can't. I was hoping you could. I was hoping you'd say you were unwilling to revisit King Pelles' daughter. Arthur has just told you to do so."

"King Pelles' daughter?"

"Arthur knows the story, and so do I. He's glad you have at last found some one to love. He sends you on this journey so that you may see her again."

"That's very far from my understanding of his orders," said Lancelot.

"The orders are of no importance. You are on your way to visit her."

"I don't know what you've heard," said Lancelot, "but I tell you this—I don't love Elaine."

"Yes, that's the name. The story's true."

"If I took this seriously, it would drive me out of my mind," said Lancelot. "Some nonsense has come to your ears, you are jealous, you blame me for being loyal to Arthur, and you say our love is at an end. Won't you understand my side of it? The story of Elaine is unusual."

"Oh, no."

"But it's perfectly innocent."

"I prefer not to hear it."

He stood and looked at her, but she had nothing more to say. He turned his back and walked toward the door.

"I hope you'll continue this affair more discreetly than you've begun it."

"It's not an affair—it never will be. I've seen the girl but once in my life—no, twice—on my first visit to her father. I expect never to see her again."

"You swear you will not see her on this next visit?"

"I swear."

"Don't, Lancelot. Save something from the wreck.
Whatever else, you mustn't be a liar. Arthur has no other
purpose in sending you there than to let you see her."

"Guinevere, so far as he has told me, so far as I've
any right to think, he is sending me there on an errand
which doesn't concern Elaine. I shall be there only a short
time, and I've sent word to her father that I must see him
alone. She will keep to her room, no doubt."

"Most extraordinary!" said Guinevere. "Why did
you do that?"

"So far from loving the daughter, I'd rather not meet
her."

"Is she so unattractive?"

"She is attractive, I suppose."

"Then you must be afraid of her. Do you fear you
will lose your heart?"

"Well, it sounds foolish, but she's in love with me,
and since I don't share her sentiments, I'd rather keep
out of the way just now. In time she'll get over it."

Guinevere laughed. Then she looked at him in a long
silence. "Of course I can't express surprise that she loves
you. It wouldn't be courteous. But I do wonder how
you know it so positively, after two casual meetings."

"She told me herself."

"What?"

"She asked me for my love—not marriage, but love.
I told her it couldn't be."

"That was all?"

"Yes."

"I should have expected her to say she'd have you
sooner or later, in spite of everything."

"She did say something of that sort."

"They always do," said Guinevere. "And frequently it turns out so. There's a kind of man who succumbs to the appeal of women he doesn't love. He's exalted by the sense of his own generosity. . . . She will be immensely flattered by your message to her father."

"I don't see that."

"Why, she'll know you have her on your mind, and you're afraid to meet her. You wouldn't be afraid if you didn't suspect your own resolution to say no."

"It won't come about so," said Lancelot. "When I return you will have recovered more of your health, trifles won't bother you, and you will have ceased to believe evil of me. I'll tell you all that happened, on this visit as well as the first, and you'll see there's no occasion to be jealous."

"When you come back I shall not listen to your history—we shan't meet. No, Lancelot, we part here. If you go on this errand to King Pelles, I will never speak to you again. And if you annoy me by arguments or pleas, I will ask Arthur to send you out of the kingdom. Lancelot, decline this compromising visit, if you still love me—explain to Arthur what you have just told me. If he can't see the point, refuse to undertake any further adventures which you know will be unworthy! Unworthy of you, or—it might occur to you—of me."

"I told Arthur I'd do as he asked, and I've already sent that message to King Pelles."

"Arthur can find some one else. He doesn't depend on his best knight for small errands."

"But, Guinevere, you say Elaine will be flattered by my letter to her father. How much more will she think of my staying away altogether!"

"If you stay away," said Guinevere, "it won't matter what she thinks. But now do what you like."

"Guinevere," he said, "if you were not very tired, if you were quite yourself, you wouldn't take such a tone."

"If you still loved me, the tone would not be needed."

"Guinevere—"

"Well?"

"If you force me to choose between obeying you and obeying Arthur in matters which you consider insignificant—"

"This is not an insignificant matter."

"Then in any matter. If I must choose between your orders and his, I obey the king. He has commanded this errand, and I shall go, though it happens to be quite against my own wish. I have told you nothing but the truth."

Guinevere stood up and faced him, her eyes blazing. She bowed slightly and waved him to the door.

"Until you send for me, I shall not return," he said. "But you will send—you will repent this unreasonable mood. At the first word from you I will come. I love you only—and always."

She looked at him steadily till he had left the room. Then her strength went out of her, and she fell back, limp and pale, in the tall chair. Lady Anglides came in.

"Sir Lancelot prays to see you for a moment more."

"I will not see him, not now, nor again, ever," said the queen. She did not open her eyes.

"Madam," said Anglides, "he is standing at the outer door, with considerable company."

"Give him my message clearly," said Guinevere, "before them all."

XI

WHEN Lancelot rode up for the second time to King Pelles' castle, he had the earlier visit on his mind. The castle, he noticed, was not changed, but the reception was different. His arrival seemed to attract no attention. He was annoyed at himself for being sensitive about it. The servants took his horse, of course, but with a portentous solemnity. He was sorry he had come.

Pelles stood in the doorway. Lancelot fancied he was a little stiffer than usual, but consoled himself remembering it wasn't possible.

"Very kind of you to send that message in advance," said the king. "It gave us a moment to prepare at least a modest welcome. In this remote district the service is inadequate—every year it's harder to maintain the house with any flexibility. At least since my wife died. I miss her."

"In the housekeeping, as in other things, your daughter, I'm sure, is a great help."

"Come in and sit down, Sir Lancelot," said Pelles. "The journey must have worn you out."

They sat down in the large window.

"On second thoughts," said the king, "I'd like to ask you, if you don't mind, how you made that mistake."

"Which?" said Lancelot.

"Your supposition that Elaine is a help. You're a bachelor, I understand, but even so you ought to be a

better judge of housekeeping. Would you mind telling
me, did Elaine try to persuade you she was competent in
that direction?"

"Your daughter is almost a stranger to me—"

"So I hoped—thought!" said Pelles.

"But I imagine she has ability, where she cares to apply
it, and I assumed she would exert herself to help you."

"I see," said Pelles. "Thanks very much! Let's get
at once to business—Arthur's message. You are in a
hurry, I believe. I wish you'd stay the night with me, but
from your letter I fear you can't."

"I ought to be in Camelot again as soon as possible."

"But you must sleep somewhere," said the king. "Why
not here? You'd be a companion for an old man in an
empty house."

"Elaine isn't at home?"

"No, Sir Lancelot, she is not at home. She's on a
visit to some distant relatives of ours. I mean, she's at a
distance."

"I'm disappointed," said Lancelot. "I really am."

"Are you? When I received your message I thought
to myself you couldn't ask for a lonelier spot to meet in
than this house when she is absent."

"But when I asked to meet you alone," said Lancelot,
"I had no such discourtesy in mind as to suggest that she
leave the building."

"Hadn't you?" said Pelles. "No, you intended no discourtesy, but I did think that was just what you wanted.
As I was reading your letter, it was a satisfaction to know
she was already out of the way. I don't blame you at all,
Sir Lancelot. My daughter is very dear to me, but she's
eccentric, and I'm sorry she has annoyed you."

"Annoyed me! She hasn't. Not in the slightest."

"I was afraid she had. From her own lips I gathered—I am quite certain about this—that she had forced her admiration upon you. She does admire you. I tell her she hasn't much self-control."

"So far as I am concerned," said Lancelot, "she needs none. I think of her as a charming young woman, who made my stay here most enjoyable. She is outspoken, and since she praises too generously, I can see she might be misunderstood. But more often by other women than by men, I should say. So far as her admiration was personal, I wasn't foolish enough to take it seriously."

"If you don't take Elaine seriously," said the king, "I must warn you to do so at the earliest opportunity. She is strong-willed, and in this matter she has made up her mind. If there were any way for her to engage your interest, she would. What worries me is that she's a reckless talker, and some day some speech of hers may embarrass you."

"I shan't think ill of her till I have to," said Lancelot. "I don't love her—"

"Thank God, Sir Lancelot! I feared you did."

"I don't, and she knows I don't!"

"Does she?"

"Well, she has no reason to think I do."

"From what she said, I almost believed at one time—"

"What, King Pelles?"

"It's very difficult to put into words—I understood that she hoped to have—no, I can't say it! It must have been my mistake. You didn't give her any occasion?—no, of course you didn't."

"Upon my word," said Lancelot, "this is a queer business. What do you mean by an occasion? I didn't give her anything—I haven't had two dozen words with her alone in my life—and those were in your garden, when the breakfast was late."

"Don't be offended—forgive me," said Pelles. "Whatever I have on my mind is Elaine's fault, not yours. I shouldn't have mentioned it."

Lancelot looked at him. The king was showing his years that afternoon.

"I'm sorry you worried about her, King Pelles. If I don't love Elaine, at least I can say truthfully I admire her—she has a fine brain and a warm heart—she'll be happy, one of these days, and a credit to you, when the right man comes along."

"To me the prospect seems remote," said Pelles, "but I hope you're right. You don't happen to have an idea as to the right man?"

"No, I haven't."

"That's just it—neither have I. . . . Well, we've got off the subject. You'll stay to-night, I hope?"

"Perhaps I can get back to Camelot as well from here—yes, with pleasure."

"Good! Now let's talk about King Arthur's affairs. What message has he sent to me?"

"It's about hay," said Lancelot.

"What have I to do with hay?" said Pelles.

"Hay and oats both, but principally hay," said Lancelot. "Our stables at Camelot depend largely on your land for fodder—"

"Oh, certainly," said Pelles. "I didn't get the connection. What about my hay?"

"This summer it is coming to us rather below the standard."

"Impossible!" said Pelles.

"Arthur is sorry, but the stablemen complain, and he wants to know if there is any justice in what they say."

"The stablemen say, do they? Arthur is conveying a message from his stablemen to me, is he? And through you, Sir Lancelot? Doesn't he examine the hay himself? I dare say you wouldn't take another man's word for what your horse gets."

"They complain that the hay is dusty—some of the horses are getting the heaves."

"I sent you no dusty hay, Sir Lancelot—I had none. There was just enough rain all the early summer. We couldn't hope for a finer stand of grass."

"Well, that's the complaint," said Lancelot.

"You've seen this dusty hay yourself?" said Pelles.

"I can't say I have."

"Hasn't your horse got the heaves?"

"Of course he hasn't!"

"Well, it's a queer way to make a complaint. . . . Just between ourselves, Sir Lancelot, what does the king mean by sending me such a message?"

"Nothing unfriendly," said Lancelot. "He has been worried recently over the performance of his own horse. The animal isn't so steady, he says, nor so sound as it used to be. When he talked to his men, they blamed the hay. He told me to find out the facts."

"We send it to Sir Kay. Does he find it dusty?"

"I am bound to say he does not. He is quite firm about the quality."

"Then it lies between Arthur and his horse," said Pelles. "It really has the heaves?"

"It has failed him on one or two occasions lately," said Lancelot. "He told me to tell you so. That's what worries him, I suppose."

"Well," said Pelles, "his horse gets the same hay as yours is eating at this minute. Shall we see for ourselves what it is like?"

"Hardly necessary," said Lancelot.

"We'd better. Then you can examine the hay at Camelot, and decide if there's a difference."

They walked through the castle yard to the stables, and Pelles had a man pitch down a fair-sized bundle. Pelles took up handfuls of it. Lancelot turned it over with his foot.

"What's the matter with that, now?" said Pelles.

"Nothing," said Lancelot. "If Arthur's horse eats that, there should be no complaint."

"Tell them that's what I sent, and if the horse eats anything else, it's Arthur's affair, not mine. I'm not flattered to have the question raised, Sir Lancelot. Almost a reflection on my integrity. I've the best grass lands in the realm, field after field of that quality from here to Case."

"To where?" said Lancelot.

"My other house, Case Castle, five miles up the road. It belonged to my mother."

"Ah, I've never passed that way—I didn't know of it," said Lancelot.

"Didn't you?" said Pelles. "Why, yes you did—until this moment I had quite forgotten about it—but when you were bringing Queen Guinevere to her wedding, your whole party stopped there. I offered it to the king. You must remember."

"I do now," said Lancelot. "Indeed I remember! But I failed to connect the place in any way with you."

"I wasn't there at the time," said Pelles, "and I couldn't ask you here because of our grief . . . My wife's recent death . . . Dear me, what a coincidence! That's where my hay ends."

Lancelot said nothing more, and they walked back to the hall.

"I'll have them bring the candles and we'll dine shortly," said Pelles.

Lancelot watched them bring in the tall slender lights and set the food on the spacious and lonely table.

"We might as well be seated now," said Pelles.

"When I was here before," said Lancelot, "we waited for her."

"I beg pardon?" said Pelles.

"Elaine came to mind," said Lancelot.

"Ah, yes, she does that," said her father. . . . "Oh, you'd better take more than that, Sir Lancelot—it's goose, remember, not a real meat. I thought of a peacock for ... u, but after looking them over I decided not to starve , ou. But goose isn't much better for a fighting man."

"I'm not fighting at present," said Lancelot, "and the goose is remarkably tender."

"On my estate," said Pelles, "we pride ourselves on other things besides hay. Our game is excellent, and the fowl we serve—well, we have at least the raw materials for housekeeping."

"Don't you think she'll show her ability at it when she grows older?" said Lancelot.

"Who? At what?" said Pelles.

"You were saying that your daughter is not a devoted housekeeper."

"Very well put. Did I use that phrase?"

"The idea struck my attention," said Lancelot. "Character expands with time, I believe, in the proper circumstances."

"I don't know that expansion is desirable," said Pelles. "A little discipline, if one could be sure of the right kind. Don't you care for the beans, Sir Lancelot? Or a little more stuffing with the goose? Sir Lancelot will have some more—"

"Thank you, no," said Lancelot. "I've plenty. You have an excellent cook, King Pelles."

"Not bad. In fact, I make a point of keeping up the tone of the place, Sir Lancelot. You can understand my feelings at this suspicion cast upon my hay."

"It's a trivial matter, I assure you," said Lancelot. "I'm sorry I brought the message. The whole episode has been unfortunate."

Pelles did not contradict him.

"If by any chance you should have occasion to mention my visit when your daughter returns, I trust she will not think my request for a private talk with you was—with reference to her—personal?"

King Pelles was occupied with a stubborn joint of his goose.

"I hope you don't find me irritable, Sir Lancelot."

"Not irritable—silent, perhaps. But this talk about the fodder annoys you. Don't let it."

"May I ask you a question?" said Pelles. "When you were here before my daughter made some slighting remarks about King Arthur. You recall? I promptly stopped her. But quite between ourselves, I begin to suspect Arthur is changing."

"For the better, if at all," said Lancelot.

"You'll forgive the suggestion, won't you?" said Pelles. "I feel antiquated when I talk to you young men who rule us nowadays, but I assume the privilege. Hitherto the words I have heard Arthur speak—not many, I regret to say—and the occasional messages I have received from him, have been full of sense. Now he is very busy, they tell me, and certainly he grows remote from us. Since his messages become rarer, they ought to be more important. They aren't."

"He is busy," said Lancelot. "Not with the heavy problems he had at first, but still busy. There are enough simple duties to use up all his time."

"Of course," said Pelles. "But simple duties don't need elaborate execution. His stablemen ought to have settled it with my steward. You know I'm delighted to have you here, Sir Lancelot, but I should think your time and Arthur's much too valuable for this detail."

"In itself a detail," said Lancelot, "but if it rises from some dishonesty in his service—"

"Ah, do you think so?"

"No, I don't," said Lancelot. "I just threw out the suggestion for what it is worth."

They finished the meal with few words more. At the end Pelles came back to his fixed idea.

"Am I right in supposing the king is very busy?"

"Very."

"Would it be indiscreet to ask what enterprise engages him just now?"

"No special one, I should say."

"Nothing involving fodder—unusual attention to the quality?"

"I'd tell you if I knew," said Lancelot. "I don't. He may have all sorts of plans without mentioning them to me."

"Really?" said Pelles.

Lancelot strode up and down his room, taking in the sense of his loneliness. Guinevere, Elaine, Bromel, Pelles—these were his thoughts. He was angry at the queen, much angrier than he had realized when he had set out on the errand. What right had she to humiliate him? When he returned to Camelot to-morrow, what would he return to? Was she right, jealous or not, in saying that Arthur had contrived this journey to bring Elaine and him together? Pelles wasn't such a fool, after all. Did he suspect some hidden purpose in the visit? Could the old man possibly believe he was Elaine's lover? Not after the letter. That was for Guinevere's sake—and how much good had it done him? She had poked fun at his diplomacy, and he had passed a stupid evening.

Well, it wasn't wise to think too much, about this or anything else. He would get some sleep.

He heard a soft knock at his door. Probably the king, he thought, with some later reflections on horse-feed. He drew the bolt, looked out, and saw a dust-covered man, fresh from a long ride.

"Sir Lancelot," he said, "I bring you a secret message, for you alone."

"Come in and shut the door," said Lancelot. "Nobody can hear us, so far as I know. What's your message?"

"Your lady is at Case Castle. She wishes to see you at once."

"Very interesting," said Lancelot. "Who is this mysterious person who sends me invitations at midnight?"

"Sir Lancelot," said the man, "I have brought the message."

"It might very well be a trap."

"It might," said the man.

Lancelot tried to imagine how Guinevere could have got to Case Castle so quickly.

"I shan't go now," he said. "To-morrow I will stop at the castle and pay my respects to the lady."

"As you will," said the man. "To-morrow she won't be there."

"How do you reach the castle?" said Lancelot.

"The road to the left, after you cross the bridge. It's straight ahead five miles or so. I'll guide you."

"Not to-night," said Lancelot.

"To save time," said the man, "I had your horse saddled. You'll find him ready in the courtyard."

"Have him put back in his stable! What right had you to disturb him? Who let you get at him? Who are you?"

But the man was gone.

Lancelot sat down in his silent room and tried to think. It wasn't like Guinevere to send messages. But what if she had determined to test his promise, or in sincere regret wished to end their quarrel? He knew the very room in Case Castle—

But she couldn't travel so far—almost as fast as he had ridden. She must have repented only a minute or two after he had left her. Then who could be luring him

out? That fellow Bromel they talked of? Or had he
another enemy in this part of the world? To-morrow he
would look into it.

But before he slept he must see what that rascal had
done to his horse. He made his way down the castle
stairs. The door was unbolted into the yard—the horse
was still there, ready for him. No stable hands to be
found—all asleep, probably. He might call the guards
from the outer gate, but it would wake the household.
The moon was clouded—not much light to find your way
by.

He went into the hall, where his armor had been laid,
put it on, mounted his horse, and sat listening in the
gloom. Then he started slowly toward the gate. His
horse had never been so noisy, but the guards watched
him out as though they were used to midnight departures.
He crossed the bridge and turned toward the left.

This way of leaving a house where he was a guest
made him feel guilty, somehow. Besides, he didn't know
how he would get back, or whether the morning sentinels
would let him in, or how he could explain the adventure
to Pelles. Undoubtedly he was making what Guinevere
would call a decision. When he got there she might tell
him his ride was a silly prank, more in Arthur's line than
in his. But this time it was her command. What would
she say if he had refused to come?

He put his horse to a gallop.

The woods seemed fresh for so late in the year. He
noticed how the dampness brought out the wood smell.
There was not enough light to see the road—he trusted
the horse to find the good parts and avoid the holes. Of
course no one trusts a horse that way in daylight. What

an effort we make to guide ourselves, he thought. His
own life—how he had tried to fit it to a plan, because
Guinevere wanted it so. Perhaps she would have liked
him better if he hadn't tried so hard.

His horse seemed willing to slow down to a trot. Not
surprising after the long journey. Certainly nothing
wrong with his fodder. Pelles must give some definite
answer to-morrow. Would he have the spirit to send Arthur the sort of word he had spoken at dinner? After
all, the arrangements in Pelles' household were too slack.
Unpardonable to let that stranger get at the horses.

Case Castle loomed up, not far off. He pushed into
a gallop once more. Now that he was here, could he
say he was her lover? Had he come for passion—for
curiosity—or for pride? Their quarrel was too recent.
The wound was still open. Poisoned, perhaps. Her
public rebuke of him—what would happen when it came
to Arthur's ears?

The gates were raised—he had only to ride in. Here,
too, they took him for granted. A man led away the tired
horse, and Lancelot entered the hall. There were still
a few lights burning, and a lady rose from a chair to greet
him.

"We hoped you would come, Sir Lancelot," she said.

"I am told the queen wishes to see me."

"The queen? Oh, indeed she does."

He couldn't place the woman, but she had a familiar
look. She helped him out of his armor.

"Where is she?"

"The large room at the end of the corridor, at the
top of the stairs."

That was the room. It was Guinevere, to be sure.

The familiar steps—the long corridor—the door slightly
open. He knocked. He could see a light inside. He
opened the door and entered. Just as it was before—
heavy chairs and tables, rich hangings on the walls—and
now two candles burned beside the curtained bed.

"Guinevere!"

The curtain was drawn back, and a white hand, up-
turned, reached out to him. The appeal made something
catch in his throat. He walked over to her and bent down.

He might have known, of course, all along.

XII

"Now don't go till I have a chance to explain!"

She sat up in the bed, and in spite of his wrath he saw how beautiful she was.

"There's nothing to explain," he said. "I came here through a mistake. You must forgive me—I will leave at once."

"Not till I've told you," she cried. "It wasn't easy to get you here, and I can't let you go without a word. If you went now, I'd never have another chance to tell you."

"You got me here, did you? Very well—I was tricked into coming. There's no reason why I should stay."

"Oh, isn't there?" said Elaine. "It was no more a trick than you played on me!"

"I never did!" said Lancelot.

"Didn't you write a letter to my father, saying you wished to see him alone?"

"There was no trick in that."

"It was one way of getting me out of the house. Father sent me off at once—out of my own home—just because I had told you I loved you, and you were afraid of me, Sir Lancelot, you were afraid of me!"

"Your father said you were already on a visit when my letter reached him—a visit to distant relatives."

"Well, you see what you've done to father's character, too. There was a time when he wouldn't have told fibs."

"Elaine," said Lancelot, "this is all very pretty, but as

I see it, here I am decoyed to a strange house at one o'clock in the morning, and—and—"

"Yes," said Elaine, "in the bedroom of a wild young woman who has retired for the night. Sir Lancelot, you're seriously compromised."

"You have harmed me more than you suspect, Elaine. You deceived me by what you knew I— That man said it was Guinevere."

"He's cleverer than I dared hope. I told him to say it was your lady."

"Perhaps that was his phrase."

"Then I didn't deceive you, Sir Lancelot—you tricked yourself."

"You have no reason to call yourself my lady. You have no claim on me."

"True, Sir Lancelot, but if I had said Elaine you wouldn't have come."

"In any case I needn't stay. I should have liked to see you at your father's house, but you'll understand why I can't accept your hospitality here."

"I'm not sure you are such a wonderful man after all," she said. "You're timid, and you're not quite truthful. Glad to see me at my father's house! Why did you send him that letter?"

"I'll be frank about the letter. I considered it wise not to see you on this visit, not because I disliked you, but because I feared you might—well, you might—"

"Of course," said Elaine. "It might go to my head."

"But I wanted to see you, as a friend, even when I wrote the letter."

"Did you really? As a matter of fact, I'm glad you wrote it. Father immediately thought of this place, and

I saw what a chance it gave me—I never could have got it at home."

"What chance is that?"

"My one chance to have your love—for this night."

"You are mad, Elaine! So am I, to stay here."

Before he could leave her, she was out of the bed and standing before him, white and slender. She reached up to put her arms about him.

"Listen," she said, "I have risked more than I ask you to risk, all I have in the world—my father's good opinion, what my friends may judge of me. It's not because I'm reckless, nor because I don't know. And I risk what you may think of me—that's what I care most about. But for this one night I want as much of your love as you can spare me. I shall come no nearer to happiness. That's all I ask of you, Sir Lancelot. If you prefer, I'll swear not to see you again, as long as I live. I'll promise anything else—only don't say no!"

"I can't pretend to love you, Elaine, in the way you mean. Surely you won't wreck your life for—what shall we call it? It isn't even the shadow of love. You said you wanted passion, but this isn't it. The real thing will come. It's worth waiting for."

"So far as I'm concerned," she said, "it has come. Don't I know? I shall never love again. Oh, I dare say you think I will, many times—but when you met Guinevere, didn't you know it was once and for all? You will never love me—she came first—but I think you like me, and you can understand what—how it feels—and you might be kind."

"I do like you, Elaine. For that very reason I can't do what you ask. Your good name—"

"That's all considered, as I told you. But you can have more than one kind of good name, can't you? Guinevere has a good name."

"You mentioned the queen before. What are you trying to say about her?"

"No make-believe, Sir Lancelot! You and I are face to face—"

"You'd better get back into that bed. We can talk just as well."

"Sit here, then, and listen. Even if you refuse me, you'll have the grace to be as sincere with me as I've been with you. You are Guinevere's lover, and she is your mistress. I believe it, or I wouldn't have brought you here to-night. If your heart were free, I'd try to win it all for myself. I don't blame you, Sir Lancelot—I envy her. But don't talk of propriety. You've thrown that over for something you believe is more intensely real. I shall follow your example, if you'll let me."

"Elaine, do you understand how grave the charge is you're making against the queen?"

She looked at him intently as one might look again at a page, to be sure of a word.

"Grave charges?" she said. "I didn't mean them as charges. But if you and she are not lovers, tell me so on your honor. I shall believe you."

He said nothing.

"Of course. She's a happy woman. But in one respect I have the best of it—I owe no loyalty to any one else, and if you take me, Sir Lancelot, you can do so with an easy mind—no one else will be harmed."

"No," he said, "you wouldn't be happy. You think you would be, but afterward you'd see the episode in a

rather drab light. That is, if you were fortunate. At
the worst, though you don't seem to have thought of it,
you might find yourself with a child to rear in an unkind
and critical world."

"You speak from experience," she said, "and perhaps
you'll tell me a little more. Do you regret your love for
Guinevere? I mean, if it were to do again, would you be
her lover?"

"I don't regret it," said Lancelot. "I would make the
same choice again."

"Are you entirely happy?"

"Perhaps not entirely—but who is?"

"Exactly, Sir Lancelot,—who is? That's the way I
thought it out. You are not entirely happy, nor Guinevere, nor Arthur, I dare say. My father is propriety in-
carnate, but he doesn't seem happy either. He loved my
mother, but I doubt if he made her happy. As for reputation, men honor you more than Arthur—they can't help it.
My father, who never does an incorrect thing, has no reputation at all. Don't let's fool ourselves with words, Sir
Lancelot. You've had a deeper share of life than some
other men, and you wouldn't exchange your fate for
theirs. If you'll be kind to me now, I shall have more
than I can hope for otherwise—not more than I'd like,
but more than is possible in any other way. It is fine to go
about the world relieving wants and miseries, but have
you ever made a truer rescue than to give a little more
meaning to another person's life?"

"Elaine," he said, "you've stopped me from urging you
to obey the usual convention, but I don't doubt the convention is right. If I had to choose again, I'd choose what
I've been fortunate enough to have, but I could imagine

something more completely happy. To say that a life is justified is to confess, obviously, that it wasn't innocent. And you would never get from loving me what I have had from loving Guinevere. In the first place, she is an extraordinary character, and in the second place, she loved me."

"Doesn't she any more?" said Elaine.

"I was going to say," Lancelot went on, "I could easily do what you ask, but it would be for a very low reason. You stood before me here and I saw your body. There's something beastly in us, which isn't love. This minute, as I speak, I could take you in my arms, but afterward I might hate you."

"Take me!" she said. "I don't care about afterward."

"But you would care."

"I've only one more argument," she said. "Then if you wish to leave me you may. The people I've grown up with are all good, but they are all uninteresting. You're the only interesting man I've ever met, Sir Lancelot. The good ones ought to be fascinating, and I've asked myself why they aren't. I think I know. The priest says you must restrain the strong impulses every healthy person has, in order to turn them into some higher force. Isn't that it? Well, all the good people I know are so occupied restraining their impulses that they never get to developing a higher force. If they had it, they wouldn't know what to do with it. You say you have low impulses. Well, you are the one man in your time who accomplishes noble things. If you refuse me, I shall lead a correct life, with my soul stifled. Do you really want me to be—like my father? But if you take me, knowing that I love you unselfishly, if you give me back one hour of the deep emotion all my good people put out of the family heart long ago, I shall pray for you, Lancelot, for saving me—it will stand against your sins, when all's done."

Lancelot looked down at the pleading face and the lovely body. He laid his hand on hers.

"After all," he thought—

XIII

In the morning light he stood at the narrow window, and looked out at the strange country. Elaine opened her eyes, and watched him.

"To think that Sir Lancelot has loved me!"

"I've been thinking about it," he said. "I told you I might hate you afterward."

"Do you?"

"I could kill you!"

She rose from the bed and came over to him.

"You may kill me, if you wish. You gave me what I asked for. I have had at least so much of your love. If you've been disloyal to yourself, if you dread what Guinevere may say, if for any other reason you'd like to get rid of me, kill me now."

He bent down and kissed her.

"Be happy if you can. But this is a great wrong. No good will come of it."

PART TWO
ELAINE AND GUINEVERE

ELAINE AND GUINEVERE

I

"HAVEN'T I been hospitable?" said Guinevere. "When she came I asked her to stay here, in a room near me, and I've made a point of seeing something of her every day. If there's anything I've left undone, tell me and I'll do it. But I've the right to know how it's to end. Do you wish her to join my household permanently? Now don't be irritated."

"You've asked that question before," said Arthur. "I think she wants to stay only till Lancelot returns. We know her story—we might as well help her."

"She is King Pelles' daughter," said Guinevere, "and if you are correct, she's more eager to see Lancelot than he is to see her. That's all of her story I know."

"Not quite all—you know about the child—I told you myself. She'd make Lancelot a good wife, and he's growing toward middle age alone. It's for his sake I'm keeping her here till he gets back. If a little courtesy to the girl would help on their marriage and my friend's happiness, it would be worth the trouble, wouldn't it?"

"Arthur, you told me she came on affairs of the kingdom—you said she had to come herself because her father is dead and she has no men folk. Now she seems to be here on a different mission—we are to aid her in capturing Lancelot. He won't agree with you as to what is his happiness. He has his horse, and she doesn't live so far away; he can decide such things for himself."

"He ought to," said Arthur, "but I'm not sure he can. Perhaps he doesn't quite know what he wants. If she has borne him a child, as they say, and if he cares for her as she seems to care for him, I wish they'd marry. Why they haven't already, I don't know. Entertain her till he comes back, and we'll find out, perhaps."

"You ask too many favors of this kind, Arthur. I had to entertain Iseult here, after you and Lancelot compromised yourselves. You had reasons for that, too—why she should be asked. I've forgotten what they were."

"It was four years ago," he said. "No wonder you've forgotten. Once in four years, you see, no oftener, I ask you to do what you call a favor."

"The calendar is not involved," said Guinevere. "You should never ask such favors. Once to mend your reputation I had to appear ridiculous. Now it's to mend Lancelot's. I won't do it."

"Guinevere, sometimes I think you have a prejudice against the people I like. Yes, I'd be glad to mend his reputation; still gladder to put a little color into his life, which seems a bit too self-sacrificing and monotonous."

"How self-sacrificing has he been in the matter of this woman, I'd like to know," said Guinevere. Her hand played with the long braid of her hair. She pushed the footstool away and leaned forward, as though about to rise. "If she remains with us till he comes back, I suppose you will ask me to keep her till they are married."

Arthur did not reply, and after a second or two she put her foot on the stool again and settled back in her chair.

"Perhaps you are right," she said. "I think I'd like to see them together. We can tell then. But if Lancelot says the story you heard is not true—"

"It is true, Guinevere—you have no more doubt of it than I have. Everybody knows about the child."

"If he doesn't love her, she needn't stay," said Guinevere. "If he does, he needn't stay."

"What's that?" said Arthur.

"Must I say it in words of one syllable?" said Guinevere. "If he loves her, they'll marry. If they marry, he will take her to live in his own country, or she may take him to live at Corbin. They won't live here."

"I hadn't thought of that," said Arthur. "It would seem strange with Lancelot living elsewhere."

"We shall have to get used to it," said Guinevere.

Arthur stirred uneasily, got up, looked out of the window, turned suddenly and looked at his wife. She was watching all his movements, and she met his eye steadily.

"Is there anything else you wanted to ask of me?"

"If you are busy, I'll leave the room now," said Arthur, "and take up the matter again, at your leisure."

"Finish it now," said Guinevere. "I'm sick of it."

"I'd like to know," said Arthur, "what has come between you and Lancelot. There's a story about you two. When he went to King Pelles' that time—when I told you I wanted to help him along—they say you sent him off with a public rebuke of some sort. You and he are talked of now, quite as much as he and Elaine."

"Ask him what's wrong," said Guinevere. "I told him he was wasting his life in small things—that he had had the promise of a career, and I had tried to inspire him in it, but I was a fool to try."

"He shouldn't have paid much attention to that," said Arthur. "No worse than you say to me, every so often."

"He took it harder than you do," said Guinevere, "perhaps because I told him your characters are much the same, after all, though I did think at first there was something in him. I told him he had ruined his life by following you into unworthy situations."

"That was rather strong," said Arthur. "If you wanted to insult a friend, couldn't you do it without dragging me in?"

"I didn't drag you in—you came in quite naturally. I married you because I thought you would be a great man. Being a woman—"

"Haven't I heard this before?" said Arthur.

"It is still true. Since I'm a woman, I can't do stirring things myself, but I'd like to aid the man who can and will. When I saw you had given up your career—I shall always believe it was your career—I hoped Lancelot would carry out your work, and I encouraged him—all I could. Naturally, when he followed you into that imbecile adventure with Iseult and Tristram, I told him what I thought. His excuse was loyalty to you. I don't mean he laid the blame on you—he took your part."

"That's what you couldn't forgive, I suppose."

"Precisely."

"Even so, I don't see why you are wrought up over Elaine. She shows no disposition to imitate me."

"That woman is bent on ruining his life."

"I thought it was ruined already. Why can't you let her enjoy what's left of it in peace?"

"She can enjoy it anywhere she likes," said Guinevere, "except in my house."

Arthur did not reply at once. He looked at her several times as though he were about to, but she kept her eyes on the floor. "I'm more interested in you and me," he said, "than in Lancelot and this woman."

"Yes?" said Guinevere.

"Yes," he said. "If you talk as you've been doing, I'm not surprised there are scandals in the Court. I don't claim to be perfect. Do you?"

"What you started out to do was a sort of claim. The world expected you to keep it up."

"Keep what up?"

"Oh, it's no use talking about it, Arthur. Neither you nor Lancelot will do anything more of importance. I'm caught in a sort of trap."

"Well, it's not of my making. When we married, you started in to change me—what I did then you said was obsolete. Now you are disappointed because I'm not as I used to be. . . . You may have been right the first time. The world in which I made my place is already passing—and I don't regret it."

"Why don't you?"

"It's served its time. We did a lot of fighting—Lancelot got his name for that sort of thing. But now we have new problems. At least, he has one with this girl. I used to think that men must marry the women they love, or else not love them, and that no good woman would love a man she wasn't married to. I suppose you still think so?"

"Go on," said Guinevere.

"Well, it now seems to be more complicated than that. Such ideas don't affect me, but they're in the world and must be reckoned with. That's why I'm friends with

Iseult and Tristram. There was a day when I wouldn't
have had them in the house. So with Lancelot. If he
and this girl have had an affair—if they've a child living
at this moment, as people say, I shan't condemn him or her
till I know more than I do."

"I'm familiar with these ideas," said Guinevere.
"Would you hold them if you were King Mark?"

"Mark isn't very intelligent," said Arthur.

"In his situation few husbands are."

"The problem would be there, whatever I did," said
Arthur. "When a country is wild, as mine was at first,
people have to fight for their lives, against hunger if not
against enemies—women are satisfied then to have a pro-
tector and a good provider. When things get settled,
they ask their husbands to make them happy. That's a
large order."

"It does seem a good deal to ask of a man," said Guinevere. Arthur got up to go.

"Just how does it stand? Shall I send Lancelot to
talk it out with you? He's expected to-morrow?"

"Certainly not. Why should I talk it out with him?
Send him to his informal wife. You didn't tell me he was
coming back so soon."

"You didn't give me a chance. When I came in the
room you demanded that I send her away this afternoon.
I asked to keep her till he returned. If you weren't so
hasty, Guinevere!"

"Then she goes to-morrow?"

"I doubt if either, or both together, will leave the moment he sees her. And I won't promise to send him to
her, as you ask. I'll let them meet naturally."

"I doubt if I was over-hasty," said Guinevere. "I
know just how it will be."

II

WHEN Lancelot got back, he had a word with Arthur, and then started to find Guinevere. Arthur had not mentioned the visitor. Elaine was walking on the terrace he had to cross to reach Guinevere's tower. When he saw her he stood transfixed.

"You seem surprised to see me," she said. "I hope it's with pleasure."

"I'd no idea you were here," he said.

She smiled at him.

"I haven't heard from you—not in a long time."

"I haven't heard from you, either," she said, "not once."

He made no answer.

"You did get my messages—as long as I sent them?"

"Yes," he said.

"Then you know I have a son. I don't say we have. You never came to see him."

"He is my son," said Lancelot, "and I wanted to see him. But I knew I'd better stay away."

"I beg pardon?" said Elaine.

"You understand perfectly—don't pretend. You asked me to come back to you, but you must have known I wouldn't. Then you sent word it was not for yourself, but for the child. You evidently think I'm quite simple. You know I don't love you. You had your way that one

night, and I dare say I shall pay for it. But there's no
sense in making it worse. If I went to you now, even to
see the boy, you'd imagine it was to see you."

"You're not kind," she said, "nor fair. You liked me,
though you didn't love me, and you've no excuse for being
rude now."

"I'm not rude. It isn't a matter one can be polite
about. I warned you. I didn't love you, and I knew
I'd hate you afterward. Or it might have been you who
hated me."

"Then you still hate me, Lancelot?"

"Perhaps not hate—but I don't like you. May I go as
far as that? When I think how much of my happiness
you took away from me—well, I don't like you. You
probably didn't know any better."

"I knew what I was about," said Elaine.

"I've hoped you didn't. I've tried to think I ought
to take the blame."

"Have you?" she said.

"Yes, I have. But I shan't try any more. And don't
expect me to feel cordial to you, after that trick."

"Even if you have no use for me, you might take an
interest in the child. Lancelot, I give up. I'm here only
for the boy's sake. I came in person because you wouldn't
reply to my messages. I've always been truthful with
you—it's a fact that I did what I could to capture you,
and I said I'd ask nothing more. I thought I could keep
my part of the bargain—I thought I could get what I
wanted without asking. If I bore you a child, I thought
you would come back to me. Of course I was mistaken.
But now the boy needs you, Lancelot, and I hadn't thought
of that. He's a fine child, I believe, but living alone with

me he is rather self-centered—I dare say he's spoiled. He
has the most astounding energy, Lancelot—I can't do a
thing with him. That's why I came here and waited for
you. Will you help me? No, not that—will you do something for your own son?"

Lancelot leaned against the terrace railing and thought
a moment.

"I'll be truthful, too. My nature is poisoned, I suppose, so far as you are concerned. I can't pretend to be
just—I suspect you at this very minute. If I go to see
my child, I must have something to do with—with his
mother—and you might win your point even yet. You
knew from the first, I love one woman, and though you
have spoiled that happiness, I shall save as much of it as
I can. When you stopped me here I was on my way to
see the queen—that door at the end of the terrace leads
to her rooms. You know it, of course. Do you think I
could go to her now, as I still intend to do, if you had first
got a promise out of me to visit Corbin? I have no
secrets from her, I warn you—what we talk of, I'll tell
her, if she cares to know. Between you and me there can
be no companionship."

"Have you told her about your child?" said Elaine.
"Or is that one of the things she doesn't care to know
about?"

"Before I went away," he said, "the queen was angry
with me because of rumors of you. This has happened
once in so often, the last few years. I dare say I've lost
her love. She didn't ask about the child, but if she does,
I'll tell her."

She was so slow to reply that he looked at her
sharply.

"I think I'm telling you the truth—I think I am," she said. "I think it's entirely for the boy I'm pleading now. I'd like to see you often for myself, Lancelot, I won't pretend the contrary, but I know you don't love me. I speak for the boy. If you can think of a way to bring him under your influence without exposing you to my malign contagion, I'll accept the arrangement, whatever it is. I can't pretend to be a good mother to him, but I do want to give him his chance. Won't you do as much?"

"What is he like?" said Lancelot.

"In looks? The image of you. He's healthy and strong—too energetic, really. He plays with the stablemen, and loves the dogs and horses, but he won't learn his letters nor stay indoors long enough to be washed, and he has no manners at all."

"I hope he tells the truth," said Lancelot.

"I think a subterfuge would be impossible for him," said Elaine. "He takes after his father."

"Where's he now? Here at Camelot?"

"At home," said Elaine. "I didn't bring him."

"Why not?"

"If you ask, I must confess I lost my courage. As you know, I have no husband. At home it makes no difference, but I've never traveled with him among strangers, and this would be the hardest place to begin—your true love keeping her eye on me."

"You've met Guinevere, of course," said Lancelot. "I forgot for a moment just where we are."

"I've met her," said Elaine. "Yes indeed! I'm her guest. Didn't you know that?"

"I didn't know you were here. Her guest, eh? She realizes who you are?"

"That remark is discourteous to her—or to me. I'm not sure which. She realizes who I am. She knows all about us. I can tell by the politeness she puts on. We smile at each other—with our faces. Lancelot, it's been charming, waiting here for you."

"Through no fault of mine," he said. "You came because you wanted to, as you do everything, and you shouldn't have come. If there had been any real need of me, you could have sent word."

"Again? Would you have answered this time?"

He had nothing to say. He tried not to meet her eye.

"You see," he began at last, "the way you've acted, I can't do anything at present. The queen will want to know why you are here. She's too clever to ask that question before, but now I'm back, she'll expect your motive to show itself. If I begin to visit you at your home, just imagine how easy it would be to persuade her, or any one else, that it's only to see the boy. And when I've told her it's my own child—"

"Very well, Lancelot, don't come to my home—see the boy somewhere else. I'll send him wherever you say. Would there be a place for him here at Court?"

"Not now—later, perhaps. It wouldn't be comfortable for a child to hear the things they'd say. Perhaps not even the queen would be kind to him."

"She certainly wouldn't be," said Elaine, "and I shouldn't want her to. I ask no favors of her."

"Well, in that case you'd better do what you can for him where he is, and when he's fourteen or fifteen, I'll bring him here. That's the best I can promise."

"I suppose I may now go home," said Elaine. "Don't you sound to yourself a little selfish?"

Instead of answering, Lancelot moved slightly in the direction of Guinevere's tower.

"You knew my father died, I suppose," said Elaine.

Lancelot turned back toward her.

"I heard something," he said. "I hoped it wasn't so."

"He died before Galahad was born, I'm glad to say. He wasn't very observing, and I never told him. It wouldn't have surprised him, about me, but he admired you—thought you quite perfect. He always corrected me when I called you Lancelot. 'Sir Lancelot, daughter.'"

"He was a generous man," said Lancelot. "Against my will I did him a wrong."

"Can't you think of it except as right and wrong?" she said.

"How else could I think of it?"

"Why, as something which couldn't very well be helped—something which, if embarrassing, at least was natural."

"But anything of that sort can be helped," said Lancelot. "I won't disclaim responsibility."

"Then why did you come that night when I sent for you? It wasn't for love, you say."

"I didn't know it was you—I thought it might be Guinevere, and if it was, I had to come."

"Exactly, you had to. But of course when I sent the message I didn't know you and she were in the thick of a quarrel. Call it luck, if you wish—I say it was fate. Take it step by step. If you had loved me you wouldn't have been angry at my message—but I sent it only to find out if you cared. Was there anything else for me to do? When you got there you didn't wish to stay, but it was awfully late, and it wasn't easy to go, was it? And you did want me a little, didn't you? Afterward you hated me. That wasn't what I wished—nor you either, perhaps. But there it is. I don't regret any of it, Lancelot, and I'm sorry you do. It was part of our lives, and it had to be."

"I don't admit that," said Lancelot. "If I did, I'd have to let any one who wanted to, interfere with my life and say she was a destined part of it. You didn't play fair. After I had come to your room at midnight, the harm was done—your people knew I was there, and I never could explain it was an innocent errand."

"It wasn't," said Elaine, "but it was more innocent than you intended. You thought it was to be another woman, your friend's wife."

"The only point that concerns you," said Lancelot, "is that I wouldn't have come if you had sent the message in your own name. There were plenty of ways, all honorable, to find out if I loved you. As a matter of fact, you shouldn't have asked—that's for the men to do. Or if the women are to take a hand in it now, they ought to give us the privilege a decent man gives a woman—the privilege of saying no."

"You might as well go on in and make your peace with Guinevere," said Elaine. "One of us at least had better be happy. When I risked everything to win you, I knew I probably couldn't do it, and failure gives me no surprise. What I'm amazed at is your hardness. You talk as though you were quite outside the whole affair, a passer-by telling a naughty little girl to behave herself. No one would imagine you had ever shared with me that—that wonderful passion. I'll tell you now, Guinevere never loved you as I did, and as I do—loved you just for yourself, not for your name. Even if you despise me, you

ought to see how I love you, and it ought to affect your
manners. You were generous enough to have pity on me
once. It's strange you should forget now what we are,
you and I, what everybody is—how little happiness we
reach in this world. You aren't interested—or are you?—
to know what my sufferings have been; you rode away,
and left me to explain everything and live out the consequences. It was I who had to face the world with the
child. I've brought him up, so far, without your aid. Not
a word from you, not even when he was born. If I had
died, I dare say you wouldn't have come to the funeral—it
would have been too compromising. Now I've had a taste
of hell in the society of your mistress here, and I've put
up with the talk of this Court, just for the chance, knowing I couldn't have it otherwise, of asking you to help
make a man of your boy. As I understand your response,
you consent to meet the child some time in the future,
when he is grown up. In your view of things, it must be
perilous for a father to associate with his son. Isn't
there a drop of kindness in you, Lancelot?"

She tried to keep the tears back, but could not. When
her protest stopped, it was because she no longer controlled her voice.

"Just what do you wish me to do, Elaine?"

She turned away from him, and tried to dry her eyes,
but her body still shook. When she grew quiet she stood
looking out over the city and the fields beyond. Her
hand nearest him rested on the terrace wall. He covered
it with his own hand.

"What do you want me to do?"

"I've told you—it's quite simple—I can't say it
clearer."

"I'm naturally stupid, and you'll continue to think me hard-hearted," said Lancelot, "but I still have the impression, Elaine, that what you want is not simple at all. If it's only to do my part in making the boy what he should be, well and good—that at least I ought to do. But when I decline your proposals, I'm not thinking of the child. I have you on my mind, a very beautiful and alert woman, who was too much for me once, and might be so again, if I'm not careful. In our talk I feel I'm skirmishing with an adroit opponent—no wonder you feel no sympathy in my remarks. Plainly, I think you are not speaking for the child."

She turned and looked up at him with a bright smile.

"Lancelot," she said, "if we engage in any more of these skirmishes you'll become too acute for me. You are almost right. I am pleading for the child, but I want you for myself more than you will know, no matter how much you guess. Even though you are unkind, to talk with you is a reward after lonely years. I brought tragedy into your life—I suppose because I was selfish. If you brought it into mine, it was because you were so splendid. I'm sorry for us both."

She was close to him, her face was open and glowing; their destinies, obscurely tangled, for the moment seemed clear; he took her to his heart and held her there, his lips on hers.

"We must go," he said at last.

"I must—you don't have to. Or not far. Guinevere has come down to look for you."

He turned quickly. She was standing in the doorway at the end of the terrace.

"Lancelot," said Elaine, "she knows. I saw her face when you kissed me."

III

Sir Bromel rode toward Corbin Castle. His thoughts must have been profound, for he noticed nothing by the roadside till he was almost at the gates. Then a flying stone struck his horse and made the animal bound. Sir Bromel reined in, and looked back to see where it came from. In the tall grass, within ten feet of where he had ridden, stood a small boy, not more than an infant.

"What did you do that for, son?" said Bromel.

The boy stared calmly at him, still rubbing the dust of the pebble from his hands. Bromel turned his horse, and the boy waited for him, apparently pleased.

"Did you throw that stone?"

The child nodded.

"Well, what for?"

The child's face broke into a happy smile.

"Make 'em jump!"

"Oh, you wanted to make my horse jump, did you?"

The child nodded again, delighted at so much understanding.

"All horses," he said.

"If I get the idea," said Bromel, "you are throwing stones at every horse that goes by. You are a precious young rascal. I've more than half a mind to get down and thrash you now before you are any worse."

"Get down!" said the child.

"Upon my word!" said Bromel. "Come over here, young man, where I can put my hands on you."

The child came at once.

"Get down!" he said. "Gimme a ride."

Bromel looked at the small, eager face. A certain clearness in the eyes and a boldness of manner made him guess who it was.

"Do you live there?"

The child looked at the castle and nodded.

"Well, take hold of my hand and climb up. We'll ride together."

"Get down," said the child. "Ride alone!"

"If you think I'll give you the horse to break your neck on, while I go on foot, you've something to learn. Come on, climb up!"

"I won't!"

"You're right this time—you won't," said Bromel, turning the horse once more toward the castle. He rather expected the boy to cry, but he was disappointed. The child settled back in the grass, to wait for another traveler.

Bromel rode into the courtyard slightly ruffled. Even without this particular kind of meeting, the sight of that child would have bothered him.

"I've come to see the Lady Elaine," he said to the porter.

"She isn't here, Sir Bromel—she's at the Court," said the man.

"At the Court! She's there now, is she?"

"On a visit," said the man. "She's been gone quite a while, and we don't know when she's to come back, but it's soon, I think."

"She didn't take her son with her, did she?"

"Dear me, no, it's a mere child yet. We look after him here."

"Oh, you do?" said Bromel. "I'd like to see the child, if you don't mind."

"Alice! Alice!" called the man. "Bring down Master Galahad for Sir Bromel to see!"

There was a rather halting step down the stairs and a frightened woman appeared. Something had recently happened to one of her eyes—there was a black ring around it.

"I can't find him, and that's the truth," she said. "I've searched the house."

"Does he run away often?"

"All the time, sir. It's mostly to the stables, but he's not there now."

"No, you'll find him in the grass beside the road, just outside the gate," said Bromel.

"Heaven be praised!" said the woman, running toward the gate.

"Alice is devoted to him," said the porter. "The worse he is, the more they like him."

"He's a difficult child, is he?" said Bromel.

"My God!" said the porter.

They stopped to listen to the sound of trouble outside the gate. In a moment Galahad came sauntering into the courtyard, with the nurse vainly urging a quicker pace. The boy came straight for Bromel, as if to greet an old comrade.

"Want to see the new dog-house?"

"I don't, as a matter of fact," said Bromel. "I want to know how you get out on the road there, when your mother's people are supposed to be watching the gate."

"I'd like to know that, too," said the porter. "It's not the first time. I wonder if he's found a hole in the wall."

"Went through the gate," said Galahad.

"You're a naughty boy," said Alice. "Sir Bromel has seen all he wants of you, and now you'll come upstairs with me. I won't let you out of my sight till your mother gets back."

"Won't go!" said Galahad.

"Won't you now!" said the nurse, and picked him up bodily. As they disappeared through the door, Bromel saw Galahad making a good fight of it, every part of him wriggling except the area around the waist where the woman had her grip of him. They must have been halfway up the stairs when Bromel heard a sharp cry. It was Alice's voice, not Galahad's.

"That would be the other eye, now," said the porter.

"You don't mean he strikes the nurse?"

"When he's in a temper, he'll strike anything he can reach, sir."

"Not his mother, I hope," said Bromel.

The man seemed not to hear.

"You may tell your lady I called," said Bromel. "It's a long time since I've seen her, and I'm sorry she's away. I've observed her son at his worst."

"Oh, no, you haven't, sir," said the man.

"Tell me this," said Bromel. "Doesn't anybody bring him up? Isn't there some one on the place to give him the whipping he deserves?"

"I doubt if you'd like to try it yourself, sir. And his mother thinks you should use persuasion."

"Well, I hope he won't kill somebody, or put out the nurse's eye. . . . Look at that, now!"

Galahad was standing in the door, where he had been
listening for several seconds.

"Want to see the new dog-house?"

The porter laughed.

"You shouldn't laugh," said Bromel; "that spoils a
child, to laugh at his naughty remarks. And you shouldn't
let that kind of child know you're paying so much attention to him."

"New dog-house?" said Galahad.

"What's he talking about?"

"We're building a good sized kennel for the new bloodhound," said the porter.

"What on earth does Elaine need with bloodhounds?"
said Bromel.

"Master Galahad saw one and wants it," said the man.
"His mother is against having so fierce a dog around.
Perhaps he'll forget about it, and we shan't have to have
it on the place. Meanwhile there's no great harm in
building the kennel."

Galahad came over to the horse and took a great interest in the toe of Bromel's mail-clad foot.

"I suppose the nurse is still bandaging her face,"
Bromel said to the porter. "You'll have to watch him.
. . . When I come again, Master Galahad, if I ever do,
I hope to see some improvement in you. If there's a
naughtier boy in this end of Arthur's kingdom—"

Galahad let go of Bromel's foot with a vigorous push,
which sent the spur in the horse's side.

"G'wan home!" he said.

IV

"I CONSENTED to see you merely to say farewell. If I were more generous I should congratulate you."

"If you'd only be patient a moment, Guinevere—"

"No explanations! My eyesight is reliable. In that respect I've nothing to say against your choice. Of course you two won't stay here. Please go where I shall never see you again."

Lancelot was standing near the door, and she sat by a window at the other end of the room. She spoke without looking at him.

"Why do you stand there? I told you to go."

"Guinevere, won't you listen to me? I've loved no one but you. Elaine has meant to me nothing but embarrassment and annoyance. If she had such a claim on me as you think she has, would I bring her here, or wish her to stay? She came of her own will, to make trouble for me, as she made it once before. Say what you please, but don't call me her lover. My disposition toward her is anything but tender."

"It was because of your dislike, I suppose, that you were embracing her on my terrace."

"You needn't be sarcastic—that was the reason, partly. I had just said some hard but true things about her coming here, and she broke down and cried. When I thought of her loneliness, and of the failure she thinks her life to be,

121

and of my own sharp words, I very foolishly took her in
my arms—"

"Don't say foolishly, Lancelot—it's not polite, and it's
not fair, after availing yourself of her favors."

"Fair or not, it's true! What I did, what you saw,
misrepresented my attitude, misrepresented it to her, no
doubt, and I think I was a fool. She met me by accident
as I was—"

"You're sure it was by accident?"

"Oh, she may have been waiting for me, but when I
came to your terrace, to present myself to you, I had no
idea she was at the Court, much less in that very spot."

"Where did you think she was?"

"Where I've been careful not to go, these four years—
I thought she was at her home."

Guinevere laughed.

"So she makes you as nervous as that! You're afraid
to meet her, you don't like her, but when she finds you,
you feel sorry and have to kiss her. Lancelot, I didn't
know a character could collapse this way. You might
have thrown me over for a woman you thought finer or
more beautiful, but to be false for a person you despise!"

"I have not been false!" said Lancelot. "I have not
been false!"

"Well, if this is being true, you must stop it. Find
a more secluded place to cultivate your antipathies!"

"Guinevere, I can't stand this—you'll drive me out of
my mind!"

She didn't answer for a moment. He was twisting
one of his hands in the other, like an embarrassed boy.
She looked at the hands, and he dropped them, limp and
quiet.

"I can lose my mind, too, so far as that goes. What have you and I done? We found fine words for it, but I've been your mistress—I see now, I've been nothing more to you. It's useless to say again what you were to me; if you could understand, we should still be happy. Merely to exist, like an animal—I'd rather be dead. I've no excuse now, nothing to show for my life, not a vestige of self-respect. Twice I've given myself to a man I over-rated."

"If you mean our love was better for me than for you," said Lancelot, "of course you're right. Without you I might have been really as bad as you now think I am. But you're not just. You began to blame me for loyalty to Arthur—God knows how little we've been loyal to him! It's curious, but without your love and what it taught me, I shouldn't have felt troubled about him, probably, any more than Tristram about Mark. But even the slightest loyalty to him annoyed you, so you sent me away. That was the beginning of my troubles. If you knew every step of it, you could see a straight line from that hard message you gave me at this very door, to the kiss you witnessed a while ago."

"Stop there," said Guinevere. "It wasn't I who kissed Elaine. I've no curiosity to know every step of your innocent and inevitable life, but if you will, you may tell me one episode in it. We've heard that she has a child, and you are its father. Is that true?"

"It is."

"I supposed it was. Yet I'm amazed to hear you admit it. I'm learning something about the extent of human impudence. You don't love Elaine, not the slightest, you avoid her society and kiss her in public only out of ex-

treme pity, but it's true that you and she have had a
child. Really, Lancelot! . . . Well, this is a waste of
time. . . . Will you go?"

"If you wish it. But I'd like to tell you about the
child."

"Lancelot, have you no idea how preposterous you are?
The details could hardly interest any one but you and
Elaine."

"Some of the details concern you. You've got to listen,
Guinevere! You weren't yourself, I suppose—you in-
sulted me, you put me out of here like a dog. Yet I said
then, what was true, that I still loved you, that I'd come
back when you called. That night at Corbin a message
arrived, from you as I thought; you were at Case. I
couldn't quite believe you were there, but I had
promised—so I rode out. Beyond that, I can't say much
for myself. You may smile, but the girl was lost in passion, she seemed bound to be wretched except for what
happiness she could snatch out of such an adventure—and
you had been cruel. If I was weak, it was partly your
doing."

"I shouldn't have believed it," said Guinevere, "if I
hadn't heard it from your own lips. Is that the kind of
mind I mistook for intelligence? If I hadn't sent you
away with hard words! Do you remember what the hard
words were about? I was urging you not to go at all.
You can't say you weren't warned. Be a liar if you want
to, but be a good one—give me a real excuse—not just
that she was wretched without you and wanted a child as
a sort of souvenir. I could have no child—not Arthur's,
because I loved you—and you and I thought we had no
right to call a soul into a doubtful world, perhaps into

shame. With this woman you had less delicacy. I can imagine the kind he will be. Later on, when he behaves as you may expect him to, people will whisper he is Lancelot's son. Over against every fine thing you once did, he will contrive something mean or gross, to wear off the honor from your name. You'll have no right to rebuke him—it won't be his fault. Quite aside from my affections—I mean from the hurt you have done me—you can see why I don't care to have my name mentioned with yours. I shall live on in some fashion with Arthur. You must go your way with this woman. Perhaps, when you've got deeper into the tangle, you'll marry her, for the child's sake. I rather think you ought to, and it will make no difference to me. But you must leave the Court at once, and never return. I won't risk seeing you or her again."

"Where shall I go? My life has been here, with you."

Guinevere laughed again.

"Do you wish my advice—in these minor matters? Why don't you go to your own country? It has the advantage of being a long way off. Take the woman with you, and do what you can for the child. . . . There's another way, of course—you can go live with her at Corbin. She has a rich estate, they say, and no doubt she will take excellent care of you."

She did not notice the expression coming over his face—it might have been a stroke of some sort.

"But in that event, please be careful I don't have to see you. As for your career, you needn't worry about it—it is over. I warned you what would come of your drifting, from day to day. It's too late now. . . . I expect you to go at once. I mean, to-day. And your woman too."

"Guinevere, do you think she wishes to stay?"

His voice was so husky and weak, she turned to look at him.

"Not after you go. But there will be no question of her going. I can attend to it—only it would be simpler if you told her yourself. Not on the terrace, please."

Lancelot stood and twisted his hands. He had not heard, it seemed.

"There is nothing more, I believe. I really shall be grateful if you go at once."

He looked a little hurt, as though she had said something thoughtless.

"Whenever you send for me—" he began.

"Oh, good God! Is there to be another woman?"

"There is none but you."

She turned white.

"Leave this room! If you say another word to me, I will call Arthur, tell him the whole story, and ask him in mercy to kill me."

She walked past him and opened the door. He turned to see what she was doing. Then as though he suddenly remembered something, he went away, without looking at her, and without a word.

V

When Arthur came to her room, at the end of the afternoon, Guinevere was still seated at the window looking out across the field to the edge of the forest, where the slanting sun fell. At the sound of his step she rose and hurried toward him. He had not seen such a smile of greeting for many a day. She flung her arms about his neck and kissed her astonished husband.

"I wanted you to come," she said. "I've been lonely."

"I always come about this time," he said. "I'm glad you wanted me more than usual."

"Not more than usual, Arthur."

"Well—we'll leave well enough alone. I'm glad you wanted me."

"I always want you," she said, "but I haven't always realized it so much."

"You aren't sick again, are you?"

"Never better."

He sat down near her.

"Draw the chair here—we can both watch that wonderful light."

When his chair was beside hers, she reached for his hand and held it.

"I've been thinking it all out, Arthur."

"Thinking what out?"

"I'm going to start over again—I've criticized you too much, and what I've said has come between us. I've

assumed it was your fault, but now I see some of it was
my mistake."

"I don't mind being criticized," said Arthur. "I've
taken it pretty well, haven't I?"

"That's partly why I'm sorry I talked so much."

"Oh, such things happen. I'm not surprised I haven't
given satisfaction. You were probably right."

"At the time, of course, I thought I was."

"So I gathered."

She continued to look out the window, but the landscape did not interest him.

"I want to ask you a favor," he said, "and I've brought
some news. Elaine is going home—a sudden decision of
hers, and I want you to say good-by to her."

"Why not?" said Guinevere. "Of course."

"I'm glad to know it's of course. She came to take
her leave and asked if I thought you would be free
about this hour—she naturally can't go without thanking
you for your hospitality."

"She was really your guest, after all," said Guinevere.
"You asked her here, I suspect, and you saw to it she
stayed. But that's ancient history. Tell her I'll see her."

"I've already told her so," said Arthur. "I couldn't
say less, and I came right over to explain to you. It's
very fortunate you—feel as you do."

"Yes, it's fortunate," said Guinevere.

"Well, she'll be here presently."

They were both silent a moment.

"Lancelot goes with her, I suppose," she said.

"It doesn't seem so—I wanted to ask you about that.
Did you see him?"

"I did."

"I was hoping he told you something about his relations with the girl."

"He told me something."

"In confidence, or may I know too? Is he her lover?"

"He says he cares nothing for her—in fact, she pursues him."

"Guinevere, that surprises me. Then there's nothing to that rumor about her child?"

"He says it's his child."

"That's the strangest thing I ever heard!"

"Isn't it!" said Guinevere.

"I'd like to know what's happened to him."

"She probably can tell—but I shan't ask her, Arthur. If you wish to know, ask her yourself."

"She doesn't know—I've asked her."

"What?"

"She has no idea where he's gone. That's the news I was going to tell you—he has disappeared. We're looking for him. Some of the men suspect foul play."

"He has ridden off somewhere," said Guinevere. "No doubt he'll be heard from in good time. I shan't worry—whatever his faults may be, Lancelot can take care of himself."

"But his horse and his arms are here. He seems to have gone lightly dressed—no cloak, no helmet, no sword, no spear!"

Guinevere looked up.

"You were the last to see him, we think," said Arthur. "Did he seem quite—well, like his usual self?"

"What do you mean?"

"There's a report he went hurrying through the town on foot, bareheaded, like a crazy man. I haven't found the person who saw him, if any one did, but the story is spreading that he is insane. Bors and Ector are trying to find him, but as Ector just said to me, if he's out of his mind, he may have thrown himself in the river."

"He wasn't insane when he left me," said Guinevere, "but he wasn't his usual self. Elaine has bothered him. In a way she's on his conscience. He confesses to the child, yet he doesn't love her, nor intend to live with her."

"I wouldn't mention it to Elaine," said Arthur. "If she speaks, try to comfort her."

Lady Anglides entered.

"There's some one to take leave of you, madam, when you are at liberty."

Arthur looked at his wife.

"If it's Elaine, she may come in now."

"I'll go see if there's any news," said Arthur.

When the door had closed behind him, Guinevere arranged her silken skirt, smoothed down her long braids, and brought the footstool nearer. She did not raise her head when Elaine came in—perhaps because she came in so quietly.

"I'm going home, Queen Guinevere—I wanted to say good-by, and to thank you."

"I wish you a safe return," said the queen. "You've nothing to thank me for."

"Your hospitality," said Elaine. "I should have been proud to have your friendship, too, if you had cared to give it to me."

Guinevere said nothing, and Elaine turned to go, but the queen called her back.

"You mustn't think me unkind. I understand you are a very clever woman. You know why we are not friends."

"I don't know. Why aren't we?"

"If you give me that answer," said Guinevere, "I made a mistake in speaking so frankly. You know perfectly well. We needn't discuss it—we can be frank in silence. Only don't pretend surprise that I'm not cordial. You were daring to come here at all—to force me, of all people, to entertain you, so that you could see him."

"You might say severe things of me, madam, and be within the truth, but I'm not quite so bold as that. I never wanted you to entertain me. King Arthur suggested it—I suppose to honor my father's memory by the kindness—but it has been torment to me."

"Consider how agreeable I've found it," said Guinevere. "I should have preferred—well, as I said, you have nothing to thank me for."

She made a gesture of dismissal, and Elaine half turned—then suddenly changed her mind.

"Do you know, what you said is entirely true—I have to thank you for nothing. You've made me as wretched as you could all the time I was under your roof, and your selfishness, before I ever saw you, has spoiled my life."

"Really, I miss that point," said Guinevere.

"Oh, no, you understand it perfectly. You are the king's wife, but you must have Lancelot, too. If you had left him alone, he would have found a true woman to love him and give him the children he longs for. But no, you must keep him your devoted servant, must rob his soul to feed your own conceit!"

"You forget yourself," said Guinevere. "I can forgive you, fortunately, out of pity—I know what makes you lose your temper. Though you have got him into a predicament, he isn't yours."

"I don't need your pity," said Elaine. "You need mine. He did love you once, even if you're afraid to admit it, but now he begins to see how selfish you are, and what you have kept him from. Don't say he still loves you—say what you are much surer of, that he is loyal to you. If he were free, don't I know which of us would have him? That night he came to me, he wanted to come. He never thought it was really you at Case, so soon after he had left you here. On the terrace yesterday, when he kissed me—you saw him—it was because he shares my trouble. He knows we understand each other best. I'd be sorry for you, Queen Guinevere, if you didn't go out of your way to make him miserable. I can't forgive you for that."

Guinevere smiled.

"I might borrow your phrase," she said. "If you hadn't been selfish and treacherous, my own life would have been happier. But others before you have known what love is. You'll learn the truth as you live on. As you grow older it won't be easy for you to contemplate your conduct."

"Well, I have his child—that's something."

"You have—a reminder and a reproach."

"Do you think so?" said Elaine. "So far he's been a great comfort. It's as if he knew he was my compensation—he's strangely affectionate. When I'm rather down in spirits, I remember my happiness—to have given Lancelot what no other woman gave him. As to the embarrassment, I thought of that beforehand. I'm proud I had the generosity to do it. But then, I owed no loyalty to any one else—I dare say that made a difference. I could give myself completely."

"You were saying," said Guinevere, "you have his child. Are you sure of that? You don't think the boy will leave you, when he knows more? How will he feel when he discovers the shadow on his birth? Where will he lay the blame?"

"On you, I think," said Elaine. "I'll explain it to him."

Guinevere laughed.

"I shall be interested to see that boy, when you've made a man of him."

"Queen Guinevere, your bitterness does you no honor. You drove Lancelot away. If his mind is ruined, as they are whispering, you did it. If he is found dead, you killed him. He was always loyal to you, even that night at Case—he never forgave me for luring him there. When I stopped him yesterday, he was on his way to you. I waylaid him because I knew, for your sake, he wouldn't come to me anywhere again of his free will. I wanted to ask his help in bringing up our child. I asked Lancelot to have him here, to make him what his son ought to be. I promised, if he would do this, to keep absolutely out of his way. Because he is loyal to you, and knows you wouldn't like to have my child around, he refused. Then you rewarded him by saying something unkind, and he is lost. They can't find a trace of him. Sir Ector thinks he's killed in ambush. You did it all—and you sit there making up sarcastic remarks. Be just, Queen Guinevere— so far as honor is concerned and generosity and loyalty, look at the difference between us! Do you think anything you could say would weigh with me?"

"If you say I'm unkind," said Guinevere, "I suppose I am, but I didn't mean to be. I was trying to tell you

the very mildest part of the truth. Whether Lancelot has
gone insane, I don't know, but I think the rumor is false.
Even if it is true, I decline to accept any responsibility
for his condition. Since you came into his life I've seen
little of him. From what he said yesterday I judged it
was you he had on his mind."

"I don't know what he said, Queen Guinevere, but
unless his nature has changed, he spoke courteously of
me, as he always speaks of you."

"He spoke courteously," said Guinevere. "But you
see, what you have done is to block the happiness of us
all, yourself included. My happiness, I confess. I loved
him. You've hinted at it—it's true."

"You don't have to be so brave," said Elaine, "I shan't
tell Arthur."

"You make it hard to be as open with you as I'd like,"
said Guinevere. "Don't think you're the only one to feel
lonely, to want children, and all that! Don't say you
couldn't help loving him—as though that meant anything!
I couldn't help loving him, either. The few years before
he met you were the best in his life—he did wonderful
things. People used to say he spread a kind of light
where he came. It was our happiness. We, too, wanted
children—but there's more than one kind of child, as
you'll find out. My children were Lancelot's noble work
and his splendid name. You can say it another way—
there's more than one kind of mother. One woman may
give you life, another may give what makes life worth
while. I'm not so childless as you think. Perhaps you
will envy me."

"For only one thing I envy you," said Elaine. "If
you called him, even now, and if he were alive, he'd come

back. You think it would be for love—I say, for loyalty.
But for whatever reason, I confess I'd be glad if I could
call him to me. Beyond that, I've nothing to regret, and
no cause to envy anybody."

"My congratulations!" said the queen. "I know few
people so happy. Most of us have much to regret, from
our faults or from the mistakes of our friends."

"I'm going now," said Elaine. "The sad thing, after
this plain talk of ours, is that we haven't come to an
understanding."

"We understand each other perfectly," said Guinevere.

"I doubt it—but I mean, supposing Lancelot should
return, and in his right mind, what's to become of you
and me?"

"Now I don't understand you at all," said the queen.

"Well, do you expect to give him up to me, for the
sake of the child, or me to give him up to you, for your
sake?"

"I never heard a question so cold-blooded!" said
Guinevere. "He will do what he likes. You and I shall
let him follow his choice."

"Shall we?" said Elaine. "If he's to decide, I fancy
we'll each do our best. I know I shall. But he'll choose
you, out of loyalty."

"I shan't lift a finger," said Guinevere. "If he wants
you, he may have you. I've told him so."

Elaine hesitated a moment. "When he chooses you,"
she said, "will you be gentle to my boy, for Lancelot's
sake? I shan't come here again, but I want his father to
bring him up among his own kind, and give him his chance
in the world. It might be in your power, one of these
days, to make him happy or wretched."

"How old is the child?" said Guinevere. "It's rather far off. Lancelot may not come back, you know—and I'm not supposing him dead. Many things may happen. As for your son, he doesn't interest me. Strictly speaking, he's your affair."

VI

THERE were some at Court who persisted in believing Lancelot had met his death. Half of them maintained he had gone mad and so had come to an accidental end—the others whispered that he and Guinevere had quarreled. A few more profound observers were sure he still lived, no matter how long he stayed away, and they foretold his reappearance at some dramatic moment. For this last idea Bors was responsible, without intending it. When he came back, from time to time, he declined to talk, and the Court was free to guess. If any one said Lancelot had gone mad from grief, Bors let the remark pass uncontradicted. If some one hoped for a brilliant return, he never said Lancelot was in his grave—from all of which you might conclude that Lancelot was hiding, and Bors knew where. Guinevere asked no questions. For a year or so she lost some of her bloom, she was irritable with her ladies and sarcastic with the men. Then she changed suddenly, recovered her zest in life, developed a taste for splendid pleasures, encouraged the Court to be gay. Arthur seemed to like the change.

Gawaine was talking it over with his brother one day, as they rode toward Camelot.

"She has heard from him—that's what it means," said Agravaine. "She knows where he is."

"I doubt it," said Gawaine. "There would be other

reasons, in a woman like Guinevere. She's not so young—
she begins to catch sight of middle age. It's pride, perhaps—she won't be through with life yet."

"What I don't understand," said Agravaine, "is
Arthur's blindness. Even if he couldn't see it before,
he ought to have known when Elaine brought the affair
to a crisis."

"Are you sure he's blind? I've an idea he knows
more than people suppose."

"Then he's a poor fool to put up with it."

"I don't know about that, either," said Gawaine. "If
he sees that Guinevere has transferred her love—well,
what if he has grown tired of her? In spite of her
beauty, she must be a trial. No one doubts his affection
for Lancelot. My opinion is, if you went to him now
with proofs of his wife's infidelity, he would drive you
out of the land as a public nuisance."

"If that's the sort of person he is," said Agravaine,
"you've given me an idea—do you think he brought
Elaine here to end it, by making them quarrel?"

"Guinevere might," said Gawaine, "but not Arthur.
He's not subtle enough—or perhaps he's too subtle."

"Do you think she's found another lover?"

"No," said Gawaine. "She loved Lancelot."

"There's Meliagrance, of course."

"Nonsense!"

It did seem to be nonsense. Meliagrance was victor
in a tournament, a few days after these words—in a
minor tournament, so to speak, with no Palomides, no
Tristram, no Lancelot. In the great days Lancelot had
always brought his trophies to lay publicly at the queen's
feet. Meliagrance now brought his prize.

"It's of no value in itself," he began, "but your acceptance will render it memorable. I won it only to do you honor—my best, however humble."

Guinevere had her ladies about her, Anglides and her newest friend, the young Ettard. Some of the men were standing by. Perhaps they all compared it with other scenes. Guinevere played her part well. She took the offering with a gracious smile.

"It isn't a humble gift," she said. "I prize nothing more than the courtesy of my husband's friends."

Something seemed to go wrong with Meliagrance. He got to his feet and rubbed off his knees.

"Of your husband's best friend," he said.

They looked at him aghast, and he retired in complete silence.

"What made you say that?" said Gawaine.

"Didn't you see? She was laughing at me!"

"No, she wasn't."

"Do you think I don't know? She deserves harder words than that!"

"Possibly," said Gawaine. "It depends on what effect you wish to produce. If it's to shame her, you need no help—you have a very happy inspiration as you go along. But if you're after her good will, you ought to take lessons. One more touching appeal like that, and she'll persuade Arthur to hang you!"

So Lancelot's absence made nobody happy. When he ran down the narrow street that afternoon, unarmed and bareheaded, he disappeared from the knowledge of his fellows, but something of him stayed behind, to color their thoughts and affect their conduct.

What happened to him next they never learned, not

even after he was a sane man again and back in his
familiar place, for he had no memory of those days. We
are told that for two years or more he ran wild, quite
mad, from one remote region to another, living on fruit he
could gather in the woods, and on anything else he could
get, and he had nothing over him but his shirt and his
breeches. But though this sounds specific, we don't
know. The story begins to be reliable where he crossed
the path of those who still had the use of their minds,
or at least were saner than he.

Sir Bliant, for example. Sir Bliant and his lady were
riding one day not far from their castle, and because
of the heat they rested a while in a pavilion the squires
had pitched for them. Sir Bliant had left sword and
shield hanging near by on a small tree; he talked with
his squires while his lady took her ease on a cot in the
corner of the tent.

Sir Bliant says he heard the most astounding noise,
as of a sudden battle—he thought at least ten men were
fighting, he says. One of his squires got to the door of
the tent first, and saw a tall man, bearded and almost
naked, lashing at the shield with the sword. Clearly the
sword would soon break, the way he was going at it, or
the shield be cut in two. Perhaps the pavilion had started
a flicker in his poor brain, or the sight of weapons had
stirred his old passion.

"Put down that sword, man!" shouted the squire,
as you would order a servant. Lancelot looked at him
in a dazed way, and then very gently laid the sword on
the grass, and walked over to the squire. Before Sir
Bliant could interfere, he saw his attendant lifted by
the shoulders, shaken like a carpet, and dropped limp on

the ground. Lancelot took up the sword again with infinite tenderness, and before letting drive at the shield once more, ran his finger along the blade, to see how much edge was left. Bliant, being unarmed, thought he would try diplomacy.

"Good fellow," he said, "wouldn't you like to put down that sword for a while? It's sleep and fresh garments you need, rather than exercise."

"As for that," said Lancelot, "the first sign of them you give me, I'll kill you."

Bliant says he retired to the pavilion without any false shame for his speed, and the surviving squire lent him a suit of armor, a sword and a shield. So he came stepping out to finish the madman. When Lancelot saw him coming so armed, he ran at him, and with one stroke broke Sir Bliant's sword across Sir Bliant's head. Bliant was grateful for that preliminary smithy work on his own good shield, which had spoiled the edge and cracked the blade, but even with such good fortune he fell unconscious, and he would say the stroke permanently interfered with his brains, if ever his head was muddled in after life. Lancelot paid no further attention to him, but having started to run, kept on to the door of the pavilion and right into the tent. The lady and the squire retired through another door on the farther side. Then by happy chance Lancelot caught sight of the cot, walked over and felt it, as though he had stopped in with the idea of purchasing a bed. It was softer than the ground he had recently been lying on, and he gave a sigh of satisfaction, stretched himself out, and went to sleep.

The lady meanwhile had hastened to what she supposed was the corpse of her husband. At the noise of her weeping Sir Bliant opened his eyes.

"Where is that madman? I never felt such an arm."

"He's asleep," said the squire who remained sound.

"You don't mean you killed him?"

"I don't. He decided to take a nap on your cot."

Sir Bliant, with his head still throbbing, had to laugh.

"Well, don't let's wake him. We'll bind the poor fellow hand and foot, and then you must get a horse-litter from the castle—we'll carry him home, cot and all. I dare say he was a man of parts, while he had the use of his wits."

"He put me in mind of Sir Lancelot," said the squire. "I saw him once at Lonazep."

"He felt like Lancelot," said Bliant.

They were careful not to disturb his slumber, and got him to the castle without mishap. When he woke at last he was patient with them, childishly gentle. It was sad to see him bow his head over his bound hands, but they dared not release him till he showed some promise of a mind. Even after his health came back, thanks to good food and shelter, no one had the courage to shave him. He would sit all day, rough and silent, looking through the narrow window at the open fields and the strange road that wound across them from the castle door.

So it was, Bliant says, for a year and a half. Then he got into a small war with some of his neighbors, he says, and one afternoon as he was riding through his own lands two brothers attacked him, Sir Breuse and Sir Bertelot. They set on him both at once, and he fled for his life. Lancelot at his window, fettered as usual, saw Bliant coming and two men after him. The old instinct awoke, he snapped his fetters, at sad cost to his skin, and when the two brothers chased Bliant through the gate, there was Lancelot ready for them. He pulled Bertelot off his horse and wrenched his sword away, and then gave Breuse one of those famous salutes on the head, such as Bliant had tasted. Breuse wilted from the saddle, and was saved only by Bertelot—and by Bliant's willingness to have them escape. Once they were gone, Bliant says he was ashamed of himself, seeing Lancelot's fetters broken, and the state of his wrists. After that the madman went free, like one of the family.

Another year went by, Bliant says, till one day they were starting out to hunt the wild boar. Lancelot had no glimmer of what it all meant, so far as they could see, but he stood watching them make ready. One of the men had tied a fine horse to a tree and stuck his spear in the ground while he helped one of his fellows. They say Lancelot stood looking at the horse as though he were trying to grasp a difficult idea. He must have mounted suddenly, when their attention was elsewhere, for the last they saw of him was a funnel of dust down the road. The spear was gone. He must have taken that, too.

So much for Bliant's testimony. Next we have the story of the hermit, but that bears few marks of truth. It is said a devout hermit found him in a forest, terribly wounded by a wild boar. Lancelot had killed the beast, but not till the mischief was done—a fearful gash and the blood flowing in torrents. The hermit saw there was no time to lose, but Lancelot threw his sword at him, from where he lay. The hermit persisted in his kindness.

"How did you get this hurt?" said he.

"I never met such a fool," said Lancelot. "Don't you see that boar?"

"I can heal you," said the holy man. "Let me help you as a friend."

"I couldn't stand another friend," said Lancelot. "Touch me once, and I will twist the head off your neck."

The hermit left him temporarily, till he met a fellow with a dung cart. They turned back and, finding Lancelot already unconscious and manageable, they loaded him and the boar on the wagon and brought them to the hermitage. There after many weeks the hermit was able to cure Lancelot's body, but not his mind. In fact, there was something about the treatment that made him crazier than before.

But that is the way old stories are multiplied and embroidered. This episode is suspiciously like the bringing of Lancelot to Bliant's castle. In one version they brought the bed along, in the other the boar.

We really know nothing of his adventures between his leaving Bliant and his appearance in the village of Corbin, of all places—the cluster of houses near Pelles' castle, Elaine's home. He came running up the road, his hair disheveled, his clothes torn. The small boys threw stones and sods at him, and the dirt soiled his face, but he kept on running, till some of the castle men came out and rescued him. They, too, guessed what he might have been, before his mind went, and out of pity they shut him up in Galahad's new dog-house. It had a strong grating in front of it, and they could look in on him as he strode up and down. In one part of the grating there was a place for pushing in food and drink, without danger from his violence.

"Do you know we've got a madman on the place,

madam?" said Alice. "The men caught him a few hours ago, and they've put him in the new kennel."

"My bloodhound died just in time," said Galahad. "I'll go see him."

"You'll do nothing of the kind," said Elaine. "You'll stay here."

"You ought to go see him yourself, madam," said Alice. "He's as big as a giant."

"I don't care to see such misfortune, if I can help it," said Elaine. "Poor man! Is the dog-house comfortable enough for him?"

"It's strong, and he would be dangerous anywhere else," said Alice. "His hair hasn't been trimmed for ages."

"I've never seen a real madman," said Galahad. "Is he like a mad dog?"

"Not exactly," said Elaine.

"This one is quiet enough in the kennel," said Alice.

"I'll go see," said Galahad.

"You will not," said Elaine. "I positively forbid you."

So Galahad went down and saw his father for the first time. Lancelot was crouched in one corner, hiding his face from the curious household. Galahad threw stones at him until one good-sized missile hit the back of his head. Lancelot got up and came over to the grating, and the little crowd stepped back—all but Galahad. Lancelot took hold of the bars of his prison, and gazed long at his son's bright eyes and golden hair.

"Madam," said Alice, "young master has made friends with the madman."

"I told Galahad not to go near him."

"Well, they're good friends," said Alice. "They stand and look at each other by the hour, and the madman seems as gentle as a dog, even when Master Galahad hits him with a stone."

"Galahad! You don't throw stones at him?" said Elaine.

"To stir him up," said Galahad. "And not always stones. Sometimes sticks."

"At your age, not to know better—a big boy nearly seven!"

"I don't hit him in the eye, or anywhere dangerous," said Galahad. "I'm careful. Only on the head."

"Only on the head!" said Elaine. "What if you cracked his skull?"

"He's mad anyway, isn't he? Mother, you're always spoiling things!"

"I'd like you to be kind, Galahad. That's all I want. Vulgar boys throw stones at madmen, but you ought to be gentle."

"Mother, why do people go mad?"

"If we knew, we might cure them."

"Alice said it's from love, didn't you, Alice?"

"Alice may be right. I've heard of people who went mad from love."

"This one didn't," said Galahad. "He must have been a real man."

In time they let Galahad feed the prisoner, as a bribe not to throw any more stones. Every day he pushed the food through the little door in the grating, and Lancelot would look out at the boy. The household got used to it, and paid no more attention, grew careless, in fact—or Lancelot may have discovered how to climb the bars. But one quiet evening he slipped across the yard and into Elaine's garden, where she had told him of her passion, that morning long ago. He found a spot to his liking under a pear tree, near the well, and stretched himself out to sleep.

There, walking alone, Elaine found him. She knew the face under the wild beard, and her happiness blinded her for a moment; she thought he had come back for love, after all those years. When she spoke to him, he sprang up, and she saw that he was mad.

SEVEN long winters came and went, and Lancelot's name ceased to be mentioned at Camelot. One afternoon toward the end of spring Guinevere was walking on the terrace with Lady Anglides and Lady Ettard, looking at the beauty of the year. The forest had still its first green, and the orchards were cloudy with blossoms.

"When I was a girl, we went to the woods for May-flowers," said Guinevere. "Up before full daylight, while the dampness was sweet in the sun, and we brought the blooms home with the dew undried. I'd like to gather them once more."

"Oh, but that's a pastime for young lovers," said Anglides. "No other adventure thrills like those simple errands, when the heart is as green as the year, and very tender to the motions of beauty—to every light on the leaf, to every bird singing. That is, with one you love beside you."

"That's the way to explain poets," said Ettard. "The winter is so dreary and the house so damp, we always forget how good life is. In the spring we remember."

"I suppose you mean," said Guinevere, "that poems and May-parties have to do with much more than the loves of boys and girls. They are a lost part of life coming back to us."

"No use talking of it now," said Anglides. "We are past our youth and the secret is gone. It's too late for us to be anything but philosophers."

148

"Too late? Never!" said Guinevere. "I intend to be young again. We'll go Maying to-morrow morning."

"But it's not the first of May, madam," said Anglides.

"Neither with us nor with the year, but what are dates? The heart sets the age, and I'm going."

When she spoke to Arthur about it later, he took a different view.

"You women can't go riding off into the forest alone," he said. "Take some of the men along."

"Aren't the woods entirely safe?" she asked. "I thought you had nothing more to do, they were in such good order."

"They're safe," he said, "but it would look very queer for you to ride unattended. The men will be glad to go."

"They would spoil it, Arthur. It's a whim of mine to go Maying as I used to. We shall have to make believe, to recover past times, and we couldn't do that with the men around. I'll go with Anglides and Ettard; we can protect one another, and I shan't ride far."

"I don't like it," said Arthur. "You will probably get home safely, but it's the wrong thing to do. It's not like your common sense."

"Not common sense," said Guinevere, "something far higher."

"What time shall you return?"

"The middle of the afternoon, not later."

"Well, on the low plane of common sense," said Arthur, "if you're not back then I'll send for you."

They rode out of the castle next morning before Camelot was awake. The masquerading spirit was on Guinevere; she had found a girlish dress in an old trunk, and her eyes sparkled with adventure. Anglides and

Ettard were sympathetic but sleepy. The morning air made them shiver. From the castle tower the watchman saw the three dwindle away across the plain, as they took the straightest road to the forest. On the edge of the shadows he saw them pause a moment, as though to consider their path. Then they vanished among the trees.

The woods were damp, as Guinevere had said they would be, but it seemed to be dampness, not dew. Some glamour was missing. Perhaps they all were too conscious. Certainly they were nervous, and made the horses so—the three fine heads were up, with ears alert, looking for a surprise. They were well into the forest before Guinevere broke the silence.

"I never could make up my mind about woods," she said.

"About what, madam?" asked Anglides.

"Woods, like these—forests."

"Is there a problem about forests?"

"Yes," said Guinevere, "I never know whether I like them or not."

"Why, I thought we came here to-day just because you love forests!"

"Oh, I'm not speaking of May-parties now," said Guinevere. "You know, we might very well cut down all these trees and have bright fields and clear roads. Every one says we ought to have fields and roads. But then we want the trees, too. Arthur is always proud of having let the light into his forests, but always angry if any one else cuts down the wood. Do you remember how the old stories make people get lost in forests? When I was a girl I heard a priest say they were the image of human error. He was for clearing them out. When I first knew Arthur, I thought he was going to cut them all down."

"Then the priest wouldn't have approved of May-parties," said Ettard.

"He could find no fault with this one," said Guinevere. "There are no men with us."

Perhaps she regretted the remark. For some time they went in silence.

"Arthur has made these woods very tame," said Guinevere. "He has cut all the brush, and lopped off the branches as high as your head—see how far through the trees you can look—and the ground between them is as smooth as a carpet."

"But it's wonderful," said Anglides. "I'd never call it tame. Isn't this as a forest should be? I was just thinking, it's as perfect as the woven trees in your great tapestry, at home."

"There's something to be said for woods before you clear them," said Guinevere. "They haunt me. Have you ever noticed how much stronger they look, how much bigger the trees are, what a sense of power they give? That's where the most terrific giants live, and the bitterest dragons, isn't it? When we clear the forests we get rid of such inconveniences, but unfortunately we get rid of the trees, too."

"I don't believe in giants and dragons, madam, and neither do you. We've never seen one."

"That's why we must believe in them," said Guinevere. "If we should see one, they would be no better than any other fact—we should be convinced, and lose our faith."

They rode once more without words, till they came

on a patch of flowers in a glade, and remembering why
they had ridden out, they got down, tied the horses to
young trees, and gathered the blossoms.

"They are beautiful as ever," said Guinevere. "I am
still young."

"When I ask a question about forests," said Ettard,
"I wonder why they and the flowers and the world about
us are so many images of men and women. The flowers
we have gathered made you think of youth, the woods
made the preacher think of human error. We live in a
room of mirrors; everywhere we turn, we see ourselves."

Guinevere held up a large cluster, and arranged the
blooms, one by one. Her gown was a light green, a match
for the grass, and she wore her braids over her shoulders.

"It's not altogether so with me," she said. "When I
look at men and women, it's often the other way about.
They make me think of morning and evening, high moun-
tains and deep forests—and other things. Man is a mirror, too, of something—I don't know what. In all the
men I have known I've sought the mystery of the un-
touched forest, the immense life which might be trained
instead of tamed. That's why there's something wrong
for me in stories where the giant or the dragon is killed.
They might have been so useful, and they are always more
interesting than the hero who cuts them down. It isn't
fair—he couldn't do it without a special kind of sword,
and after they are gone, we've nothing left but safety."

"May I say a word for safety? It's not a bad thing,
on the whole," said Anglides. "If I had to make my way
among these trees after dark, I'd be glad the king's men
had been through here with an ax."

"Well, now that we've gathered the blooms and settled these questions," said Ettard, "I'm ready for lunch. We must have been riding for hours!"

"Does it seem so?" said Guinevere. "I was getting on very well myself, till you mentioned food. That brought down the tone of the adventure. Well, if we must eat, these large roots will make our table."

"Just where are we, madam?" said Ettard. "I can't remember all the turns we've taken. I marvel you have such a knowledge of the forest."

"I haven't, but you can always go back the way you came," said Guinevere. "No one could miss so simple a path. I've a taste for forests, as I told you."

"I don't think I should mind the dragons and the giants myself," said Ettard, "but I wish there weren't so many bugs. Do you really enjoy your meals out here? So many years, such effort, to become civilized and comfortable—and then to go on a picnic!"

"This isn't a picnic," said Guinevere; "your remarks don't apply. This is a May-party, a spiritual occasion. I brought food only because you and Anglides wouldn't come without it. Now it gives you strength to return. We must be mounting again, if we are to reach home by mid-afternoon."

They rode briskly till they came to the first fork in the path.

"Now which way?" said Anglides.

"This—you remember that birch with the broken top," said Guinevere.

"No, I don't," said Anglides. "I think we came by the other road."

"It's in the same direction, anyway," said Ettard. "We're sure to come out on the plain."

At the next turn they all agreed which way to go, and at the next turn after that. Then Guinevere pulled up sharply. A man sat on his horse watching them from the glade by the roadside, so still, they had not seen him.

"You are far from home, Queen Guinevere," he said.

"Oh, it's Sir Meliagrance! Yes, we came a little way into the forest, and now we seem to have taken the wrong path."

"Indeed you have, if you're looking for Camelot. This will take you to Astolat. May I guide you back?"

"It won't be necessary, thank you," said Guinevere, "if you'll start us off right."

He did not move. The women found themselves drawing together somewhat nervously, waiting for him. At last he rode on ahead, without a word, and Guinevere motioned to her ladies to follow.

"Your men were curiously remiss, to be separated from you," he said.

"We came alone, Sir Meliagrance. You wouldn't guess it, but we are three country girls, on a May-party. I came out to recover my youth."

"It's late for May-parties," he said. "The season—"

"Oh, don't tell us, we know," said the queen. "Time flies, indeed it does. Is this the path we should keep on? I don't wish to put you to any trouble, Sir Meliagrance."

"No trouble, madam. This is the path, but it leads past my castle, and I was on my way home when we met."

They rode so far, they would have reached Camelot, had they been on the path they had come by. Meliagrance made no effort at conversation, and the three women lost count of roads and turnings.

"I can't understand why it takes us so long," said Guinevere. "Even though we were astray, we had ridden only a few hours. We can't possibly be going toward Camelot. And the sun begins to set."

"This is the shortest road, madam," said Meliagrance. "It's for you to say where you've ridden—and what place you were trying to reach."

"That remark I don't like, Sir Meliagrance!" Guinevere reined in her horse. "Where are you taking us? I fear we trusted you too far. Lead us right, on your peril!"

Meliagrance wheeled round and faced her in the narrow path.

"Madam, I had no wish to force my society on you— you asked to be led out of the forest. I have taken the straightest path, as King Arthur will testify, or any of his knights. What brought you here in the first place I don't know, and I'm the last one to wish any responsibility for it. You must see how embarrassing it might be for me, if any of the Court found us in this solitude, with no good reason for not being in our proper places. With your permission, I'll point out the road and leave you now. But since you can't trust me to guide you, you'll hardly care to follow my directions."

"Show us a short way, then," said Guinevere, "and we'll do by ourselves. There's no reason why I shouldn't trust you, Sir Meliagrance, but I promised to be home by mid-afternoon, and Arthur will send his men to find us. There's no time for this long circuit we've been making."

Meliagrance drew his horse into the brush, to let them pass. "Your road is simple from now on—straight ahead, and the second path to the left."

When they looked back to see if he were following, he had disappeared, and the wood seemed to have thickened with shadows.

"This is very unlucky," said Guinevere. "Almost any other would have been pleasanter to meet than Meliagrance. I wonder what he was doing out here?"

"He was on his way to his castle," said Anglides. "I didn't know his home was in this forest."

"Nor I, or I wouldn't have gone Maying within twenty miles of it," said Guinevere. "But even so, why was he riding alone, unarmed? I've an uneasy feeling he was tracking us—perhaps he is behind us still."

"Here's the second turn," said Ettard. "Don't let's miss the way again."

No more than half a mile down the path they came on a wide lawn in front of an old castle. The road went by the gate.

"That's his castle," said Ettard. "Aren't you glad he's not at home?"

"Ride on fast," said Guinevere.

But just at the portal three men stepped out of the shadow, took the horses by the bridle, and quite firmly led them inside the castle yard. They heard the gate fall. They half expected to see a band of robbers in the yard, but there was only one man there, unarmed and on foot.

"I suspected treachery, and I was right," said Guinevere. "You will pay dear for this!"

"I had to hurry, to get here before you," said Meliagrance, "and there wasn't time for a more courteous reception. You'll forgive our simple state. I'm sorry there are no women folk in the household just now, but these men will show you your rooms."

He left them standing there, and disappeared into a dark doorway in a corner of the yard. The three men helped the women from the horses, and led them up the stairway to a corridor, with cell-like chambers. Guinevere made no resistance, and the others followed her example. When they had entered the rooms, the men closed the doors. Guinevere expected to hear the locks turned, but that prison touch was not added.

The men would be gone, she thought, in a little while. She opened her door quietly. The man was still there.

"I wish to speak with my ladies."

"You may not, madam. I'm sorry."

"Will you tell Sir Meliagrance I wish to speak with him?"

He said something to one of his fellows, and then motioned Guinevere to close the door. In a moment Meliagrance entered, without knocking, shut the door behind him, and waited for her to speak.

"What do you mean by making me your prisoner?"

"Just that—you are my prisoner."

"Do you suppose for a moment you can keep this outrage from the king? Though you have me in your power now, he will hold you to a terrible reckoning."

"I've no wish to do you an outrage, as you call it. You are my prisoner for the time being, and as you say, I shan't keep it a secret."

"Sir Meliagrance, it will be better for you to kill me at once than to detain me against my will."

"You quite misunderstand me, madam—I've no thought of doing you harm, and I don't know who will object to my detaining you."

"There was a day when you wouldn't have dared!"

"You mean when Lancelot was here, madam. But there was no occasion for detaining you then."

"What occasion is there now?"

He hesitated before he replied: "You know as well as I, madam, what errand you came on, unattended. It was my duty, in faith to the king, to arrest you. I've never believed that Lancelot was dead, nor that you and he had quarreled past mending. You were overbold, coming to meet your lover in this forest, right under the king's eyes. There'll be an end to your treachery now."

"You actually believe Lancelot is my lover, and that—"

"Madam, we all know Lancelot was your lover, and I believe you came out to-day to meet him."

"If he were as near as that, Meliagrance, you know the danger you'd be in."

He smiled at her, and said nothing. Her wits left her, as she wondered whether Lancelot could be within reach. Meliagrance turned to go.

"You have some purpose in all this," said Guinevere. "What do you want of me?"

"Nothing now, madam. I did hope for your love, when you and Lancelot were said to have parted. You had cared for him, and I thought I might persuade you to care a little for me. But that was a mistake, as you made me feel."

"In plain words," said Guinevere, "because I wouldn't have you as a lover, you shut me up here—to starve me out, I suppose, or otherwise persuade me!"

"I repeat, you will suffer no harm from me."

"Will Arthur agree that you are as correct as you pretend to think yourself, Sir Meliagrance?"

"Ask him that when he comes," said Meliagrance. "I've sent for him."

"I'll tell him why you are persecuting me!"

"Tell him what you like. The men outside these doors know I've spoken to you only when you requested it. I've sent word to the king that his wife was keeping a tryst with her lover, Lancelot, and that I arrested her. That charge I'm prepared to defend with my body."

"Meliagrance, I never heard such nonsense in my life! Lancelot is not in these woods, and my ladies know our errand was harmless."

"With that I've nothing to do, madam. You came without an escort—just why, you may explain to your husband. But I found you quite out of your way, in the opposite direction from Camelot. We'll let the king decide."

"If you believed what you are saying, you'd be a fool," said Guinevere. "I suspect you are only a knave."

"Unless you have something else to say to me, madam, you'll permit me to retire."

She had her thoughts to herself, till there was a noise in the court, and she guessed that Arthur had arrived. They led her down, and brought out the three horses.

"What does this mean, Guinevere?"

"It means that Sir Meliagrance has held me and these ladies as his prisoners. We were brought into his castle by force, and kept here with a guard at the door. That man is a traitor, Arthur!"

"No traitor at all," said Meliagrance. "It has been known for some time, or so we believed—that Queen Guinevere was false to you. You would have been told earlier, if your friends had had the evidence. To-day she

came into the forest on a strange errand. If I accuse
her of treachery, King Arthur, I must be ready to
make good the charge with my life in battle against whoever cares to be her champion. Very well! I challenge
any man in your Court or elsewhere to deny that Lancelot
is the queen's lover, and that she came into the forest
to-day to meet him. Of course these ladies were ignorant
of her intention; if I hadn't broken up the plan, she
would have met him accidentally."

"It's a complete lie," said Guinevere. "Lancelot is not
in this forest, so far as I know."

"Madam, will you deny he's your lover?"

"I will tell Arthur now, as I threatened to do, that you
offered yourself for that honor—liar that you are!"

"Madam, the king can judge by my behavior whether
I love you. But do you love Lancelot? That's the question."

"I'm not sure it is," said Arthur. "You take it upon
yourself to arrest my wife and charge her with meeting
Lancelot in the forest. You must have some reason to
think he's here. What's your reason?"

"The fact that she came in so strange a way, might be
a reason," said Meliagrance. "But I'm no lawyer. I'll
fight with any one who cares to deny what I say—except
with you, King Arthur—of course I can't fight you."

"Come home, Guinevere. We will think this over."

"There's nothing to think over, King Arthur," said
Meliagrance. "I've made the charge, and I demand the
opportunity to prove it. Appoint a day, and I'll be there
to defend my word."

Arthur fixed his eyes, keen and sad, on his beautiful
wife, and on the angry man.

"Very well," he said at last, "I will appoint a day."

Guinevere sent for Sir Bors the next afternoon.

"I need your help," she said. "Can you find Lancelot?"

"Madam," he said, "I don't know if Sir Lancelot will—"

"Yes, he will," said Guinevere. "Tell him I ask his forgiveness. I am humbled. I'm in danger, perhaps of my life, and no one else can surely save me. He must be here on the tenth day from this—a week from Monday—to meet Sir Meliagrance in battle. Tell him, if he no longer loves me, he needn't come—I shan't care to live. But I'm on my knees, imploring him."

VIII

"So FAR as the riding is concerned," said Lancelot, "I doubt if I can teach you much more. You're really very good at it. But you've something to learn about the spear. That light one of yours is only a toy, remember. I was going to say you'd get the trick with experience, and when you have more weight and muscle, but that isn't all of it; you must use what weight you have. Weight does it. Your weight and the horse's, behind the spear, just as you hit your man. You aren't forward enough, for one thing."

"If you'd let me take a longer start," said Galahad. "Once I got the horse well going, I know I could do it."

"The longer the run, the weaker the blow, I've always found," said Lancelot. "Whenever I saw a man take an exaggerated start, I knew he'd slow up at the last minute, and I'd lift him off his horse with no trouble at all."

"But I wouldn't slow up."

"You think you wouldn't. No, just enough approach to get in your weight. The more skilful you are, the less run you'll need. That's where Tristram and I always had an advantage—we could get going in very little room. Some of the others, like Gawaine, needed a whole field to themselves."

"Shall I try it again?" said Galahad. "I think I have the idea."

"You're tired now. To-morrow. Put the horses

away, and we'll go up to the castle. Your mother expects us soon."

Elaine was waiting for them in the garden. She looked at her tall son, and at Lancelot, more gaunt than ever, with his hair beginning to turn gray. Sometimes, when she saw those two inseparable companions, she wondered if she were dreaming.

"What has it been this afternoon, Galahad?"

"Another try at the jousting! I'm coming on, mother—in a little while I'll begin to bother him!"

"What a way to speak of your father! If you ever know anything, he must have taught you."

"Oh, he's right," said Lancelot. "When he grows up he'll be the better man with a spear."

"I don't believe that," said Elaine, "but I'm glad he does well. You'll be making him a knight before long, I can see."

"Come on, father—will you? I want to be knighted and go on quests, like other men!"

Elaine laughed.

"You're nearly fifteen—like other men."

"That's all very well, mother—will you knight me, father? Let's go off and do something together! I don't see why you keep yourself shut up."

"Knighthood will come with time," said Lancelot. "Don't be impatient."

"I shouldn't have mentioned it, Galahad—I'm sorry," said Elaine. "You aren't ready for it yet. You wouldn't know what to do with it."

"Wouldn't I!"

"Well, what would you do if your father made you a knight this afternoon?"

"I'd go out and fight somebody."

Elaine laughed again.

"I dare say you would—almost anybody who came along."

"I'd like to rescue people, the way father used to."

"Some lady in distress, perhaps," said Elaine.

"There aren't any nowadays—father says there aren't."

"No," said Elaine. "If there were he'd rescue them himself."

"The only kind of knight I don't want to be," said Galahad, "is—well, have you met Sir Bromel, father? He just stays at home."

"Poor Bromel!" said Elaine. But she smiled.

"I had forgotten him," said Lancelot. "Here I've been—how long have I been here, Elaine? Nearly four years, isn't it?"

"Since you were well again," she said. "Before that— why talk of it, Lancelot?"

"My head is still weak, or I should have remembered Bromel. Where have you seen him, Galahad?"

"Oh, he used to come over, sometimes. He rides badly, father, and he's even more solemn than you."

"Your father isn't solemn, Galahad—he was ill a long while."

"Oh, father and I understand each other. He's all right. But no one would call you merry, would they, father?"

"They'd be mistaken if they did," said Lancelot. "Gawaine can make a joke, and Tristram can sing, but when I was your age I had to work my way up. Then I joined Arthur, and we were too busy to cultivate the lighter sides—wit and books and that sort of thing."

"It's the real work I like best, too," said Galahad, "—what you and Arthur used to do. That's why I want to be a knight."

"The trouble is," said Lancelot, "the real work has been done. Nowadays you have to go looking for dragons and giants—they don't meet you on the public roads."

"This is your father's merry vein, Galahad—he never met a dragon in his life."

"It's all in the point of view," said Lancelot.

"If there were anything to do," said Galahad, "I suppose Bromel wouldn't stay at home, either. I hadn't thought of that. . . . How does Arthur pass the time?"

"Getting on with his wife," said Elaine.

"Some day you'll see him, I hope," said Lancelot. "He was my best friend."

"Isn't he now, father?"

"Galahad, your father is tired—he has given the whole day to you. I'm going to take him up to my room to rest a while before dinner."

"I'll see how the horses have stood it," said Galahad.

In Elaine's room Lancelot sank down into a deep chair.

"Are you very tired, Lancelot?"

"Not particularly."

"I'm sorry we got talking on that subject."

Lancelot said nothing.

"And I'm sorry I spoke so of Guinevere."

He did not lift his eyes.

"In spite of all I've tried to do, you don't care for me, do you?"

"You make me unhappy with that question, Elaine. What do you expect me to say? You nursed my mind back, somehow—you've taken me in and given me shelter, though I'm a ruined man. I couldn't be grateful enough to you. . . . But you know how it all started."

"Lancelot, I'd say I was sorry, except for one thing."

"Galahad?"

"Yes. I think he begins to be fond of me, and if I can keep his love, in a way I shall have yours, Lancelot. I'm grateful to your sickness—it gave me the chance to be of use to you, and for a while at least it made you his companion. He worships you."

"His future's a problem, Elaine. When he is knighted, as he wishes, he will ride away—though where, I can't see, nor what to do. You don't want to lose him."

"I shan't. He'll come back, from time to time, and if you'll stay, even though you don't love me, I shall have a kind of happiness looking after you."

"Don't deceive yourself, Elaine—he won't come back. They never do. And I ought to have told you—I can't stay much longer—I should have gone before."

"I knew it, Lancelot! Yesterday I saw you gazing off toward Camelot. You are nearly well."

"Camelot! Elaine, that's the last place I shall go to. You need have no more jealousy of Guinevere. She wouldn't let me come near her—the best I can hope is that she has forgotten my existence. No, I shall leave Arthur's kingdom, for my own country. It's a cowardly thing, to act like a ghost, haunting my former world—I ought to be in it or out of it."

"If you will be happier away from me," said Elaine, "then you must go. But surely not till you have all your strength—you still are weak at times."

"You always say that, Elaine. But I shan't get my

strength back until I begin to use it—idleness keeps me weak."

"Take Galahad with you—the travel will do him good, and you can keep on with his training."

"We'll see," said Lancelot. "But I suspect he ought to stay here quite a while longer. I'm not the best company for him. He ought to start right—at Arthur's Court."

"Well, if you're not there to scare off the gossips, he'll hear some unkind things at Camelot."

"How much does he know?"

"He knows you are his father, of course—that's all."

"Does he think you are my wife?"

"I suppose he does—yes, he does."

"You mean you told him so?"

She did not answer.

"Well, I don't blame you much. Later he'll have to find it out."

Elaine sat watching his haggard face.

"Lancelot, is there no way I can persuade you?"

"To do what?"

"To love me—to be my husband—to lead the rest of our lives together. We have the boy—we could have everything, if you loved me."

Lancelot roused himself in his chair, and stared down at the floor.

"I can't do it, Elaine. We might have been friends—we are that now. I still think you wronged me, and wronged yourself. That rankles. On the other hand, I owe you my life, or at least my mind. But I love nobody, and never shall, as once I loved Guinevere. It's not the sort of thing you can pretend about."

"You still love her," said Elaine. "That's the whole trouble. In spite of all the indignity she has laid on you, if she said the word to-morrow, you would go back to her. You'd go back to an affair from which the glamour has been worn away. If she gave you the chance, you'd be her ignoble slave."

"She won't give me the chance," said Lancelot, "so I shan't discuss your notion of slavery. She won't send for me, and if she did, I'd probably not go. Once I would, but not now. That part of my life is over. I referred to it only as a measure of what love could be. You and I ought not to marry unless we felt such passion. I doubt if you do. I know I don't. There's no love for anybody left in my heart."

"You're altogether wrong," said Elaine. "You love Guinevere as much as ever, and some day she'll send a word, and you will go. What gives her such power? You weren't happy with her—you felt guilty. But she always could do with you as she wished. When I think how I love you, and how cruelly she treats you, yet whenever she crooks her little finger you will turn your back on me, and when you go, Galahad will soon follow, and I shall be left alone! For his sake, not mine, I wanted him to know you; now that it has happened, I shall lose him. When he sees Guinevere, one of these days, I dare say he'll come under her spell, like the rest of you. If she ever guesses how much it would hurt me, she will do her best to take him away!"

"Madam," said Alice, "Sir Bors is down-stairs, just arrived, with a message for Sir Lancelot."

"I know what Sir Bors wants," said Elaine. "Ever

since he found out where you were I've expected him to come some day and take you back to her. That is what he's here for now, I'm sure. Go down and welcome him, Lancelot. They've led his horse away—he's looking for you."

"This isn't my castle, nor my home," said Lancelot. "It's you who should go down and welcome him. Whatever he comes for, your jealousy is out of date. Guinevere doesn't want me back, and unless she did, I couldn't go."

"But you would if you could."

"I don't know that."

"Well, I do. Don't keep Bors waiting any longer."

"Elaine, I've told you, I can't welcome him, as though this were my house."

"Or as though I were your wife."

"As you please. I've no idea what Bors is here for— to see you, would be the natural guess. Either you welcome him, or he can wait in the court all night."

"Mother," said Galahad, "Sir Bors has just ridden in from Camelot, and he wants to speak with Sir Lancelot. I told him I'd call father myself."

"Of course," said Elaine. "Go on down, Lancelot. We'll follow in a few minutes, Galahad and I, to learn the worst."

Lancelot went down the stairs—the stairs Sir Bromel had descended, some years before. Galahad waited till his father was out of hearing.

"What do you mean by the worst? What has happened?"

"I fear Sir Bors has come to take your father away— probably back to the Court. If so, we shan't see him here, at least not often."

"Well, he ought to go back to the Court, whether we ever see him or not. I haven't understood why he stayed hidden away with you and me while he's needed in the world, and everybody must be wondering where he is. It was a terrible shame for such a man to stay out of it so long."

"Don't you think he has done enough?" said Elaine. "He has all the glory there is in that kind of life. If he goes back now, the best he can hope for is to do as well. I've been happy these short years just to have your father with us, even though he may have missed some addition to his fame. I still don't think his stay here was wrong. What would you have known of him, what would he have taught you, if he had been on Arthur's errands, at the end of the earth?"

"But that's the way you come at an exciting life, mother."

Something in her face checked him, and he went on with less conviction.

"Weren't you ashamed, too, that he stayed home these last years?"

"No, I wasn't ashamed at all—I was happy," she said. "Most women want their men to go out and fight for glory. When the men are brought in killed or wounded, the same women feel that life is very hard, and some of them complain it's hardest on women. Silly, I say. I never thought much of this jousting and fighting, Galahad. For a special reason, yes—to defend yourself, or something of that sort, but to fight for the sake of fighting seems absurd. And other people have some rights. We oughtn't to invent duties, and certainly not sports, which will make ourselves and others miserable. If your father is happy here, and if he has made you and me happy, then this is the right place for him to be, no matter what the Court would say. Far from being ashamed of him for staying with us, I think he owes more to you than to any king or queen."

"Mother, you've been living here very safe, as far back as I can remember, but I often imagined you weren't entirely content. I've wished I could get you out into the world somehow, to inspire brave knights, the way Queen Guinevere does. But you couldn't inspire them by that kind of talk. You don't like me to take a risk when I'm riding my horse. I'd like to know what the fun would be if I didn't take a risk. I might as well sit down by you here and learn to do embroidery."

Elaine laughed.

"When I was your age," she said, "I would have talked like that, about risks in general, but I never could see the value of the rough games you think you like. Very young people are conservative, and some old men remain very young. Your grandfather was that way. He was stately in his manners, and he thought he knew all about life, but when he died he probably knew as little as you do. He just imitated the fine men he had seen in the generation before him. It stands to reason that some things are more important, but it seems to take a peculiar temperament to be interested in the difference. I've always tried to get down to the heart and know what is essential. I wish you'd do the same, but I fear you have your father's way of looking at life."

"What seems wrong about your way of looking at it," said Galahad, "is that it sounds as though father had made his reputation in spite of you, or without your help. If men aren't to fight, nor to win fame in tournaments, how are they to be of use? Don't you want him to do anything?"

"I don't want him to leave me, Galahad. Sir Bors will take him away. From you too, of course. After he is gone, you will know whether it was worth while for him to be here."

"But I'll go, too," said Galahad. "Without him, there'd be nothing to stay for."

"Wouldn't you stay for me?"

"I hope you won't ask me to, mother. . . . Don't try to keep me all my life shut up here!"

"No, I won't," she said. "While we've been talking, I've realized that my life is a total failure. Your father never really loved me. You don't love me, either. When you were born I thought you would draw your father home, but he and you satisfy each other, and I am left out."

"I don't like to hear you say I don't love you," said Galahad, "but if loving you means wishing to stay at home all my days, of course you are right. If you've talked that way to father, I don't wonder you say he doesn't love you. He's puzzled, I suppose, that you understand him so little."

"Has he spoken about me to you?"

"Never. Not a word."

Lancelot stood at the door. They had not heard him come in.

"I'd like you to greet Sir Bors, Elaine, if you will."

"Certainly, Lancelot—but he came to see you."

"You'd better come down."

"I suppose I may as well come, too," said Galahad.

Bors was striding up and down the hall, not in a social mood, it seemed. Clearly he was on urgent business.

"You are welcome here, Sir Bors," she said.

"Am I? I was afraid you wouldn't feel so about it. Lancelot has told you, I suppose?"

"He didn't need to—when you came in, I knew it was to take him away."

"Not quite that," said Bors, "but he's badly needed at Court, and I've come at the queen's request to ask for his aid."

"Why doesn't Arthur ask for it?"

"I dare say he does, indirectly—but it was Guinevere who sent me."

"I can understand that, of course."

"Elaine," said Lancelot, "I told you the queen wouldn't send for me, or if she did I wouldn't go. That's what you are thinking of now, I suppose. I was essentially right. If this weren't an exceptional situation, she never would have sent for me."

"And you never would have gone," said Elaine. "I understand."

"The queen is in danger of her life. She has been accused of treason by Meliagrance, who insists on trying out the charge in mortal combat, and the queen asks me to defend her."

"Who is Meliagrance, father?" said Galahad.

"A powerful fighter—one of the Court," said Lancelot. "There's no one there who could surely win against him."

"Couldn't Arthur?"

"Yes, but of course Arthur can't very well defend his own wife."

"That's one of those dead ideas," said Elaine. "There you are, Galahad. Who else should defend a wife, if not her husband?"

"Perhaps," said Lancelot, "but Arthur is out of the question, and if I don't go, Meliagrance will have proved his case."

"In plain words, then," said Elaine, "Meliagrance accuses the queen of treason, and she, following the most sensitive rules of high-minded conduct, sends for you to kill him!"

Bors looked on with interest. Lancelot had nothing to say.

"When you have killed him, Lancelot, what will you have proved on your side?"

"Nothing, Elaine—no more than if a man tried to hurt you, and I killed him first. Meliagrance wants the queen's life. He wanted her love, but she wouldn't have him. This is his revenge."

"Oh, he loved her, did he? Poor man! He's as good as dead. . . . Do you go at once?"

"We ought to," said Bors.

"Galahad, help your father get ready. I will talk with Sir Bors."

Galahad went off in high spirits toward the stables, and they could hear him asking his father about the coming fight. Elaine waited for Bors to say something. He let her speak first.

"What is the treason she's accused of?"

"I'd rather not tell you, Elaine—it's immaterial, anyway—he merely wanted revenge, as Lancelot said."

"Bors, I shall hear it sometime, if not from you now, and it might be pleasanter to hear it when others aren't around. I sent Galahad away so you might tell me."

"Well," said Bors, "he accuses the queen of having been false to Arthur, and of having been Lancelot's mistress."

Apparently Elaine had not been prepared for this.

"Then it will all come out now!"

"I don't believe so," said Bors. "He said the queen was in the woods two or three days ago, keeping a tryst with Lancelot. You know Lancelot wasn't there, and the king is pretty sure he wasn't. I doubt if Meliagrance thinks he was. There won't be any scandal. Lancelot will kill him."

"You've done me a great unkindness, Sir Bors. You've taken him away."

"Oh, he'll—"

"Now, don't lie about it. He won't. He will stay with her."

"Well, I thought of that, Elaine, but if I hadn't come for him, the queen might go to her death."

"Might, but probably not. Arthur wouldn't be hard on her."

"I wasn't so willing to run the risk as perhaps you'd be, Elaine—but I'd feel the same way, in your place."

"Oh, I don't want anything bad to happen to her— that's not the kind of triumph I'd like. Yet after all, Meliagrance is telling the truth."

"If you admire him for it, you're the only person who does," said Bors.

Lancelot came in with his armor on.

"The only person who what? Are you ready, Bors?"

"I am if my horse is. Have they brought him out?"

Elaine had only a moment with Lancelot alone.

"You look like yourself," she said, "and you look happy again. She has sent for you at last."

"At last I have something to do," he said.

"Oh, I know. Tell her I give you up because I can't help myself. She has beaten me, and I might as well confess it. We are lost—Sir Meliagrance and I."

"Nonsense!" said Lancelot. "You shouldn't talk that way."

"Promise me one thing," she said. "Even though you forget me, have a thought for Galahad. He has it in him to be a great man, if some one can bring it out. I think he will be the most splendid man of all his race—except one."

"Then he will be splendid enough," said Lancelot.

When he was on his horse, he looked down at her for a moment, standing at the door.

"Lancelot," she said, "I've a feeling you will never look at me again."

PART THREE

GUINEVERE AND GALAHAD

GUINEVERE AND GALAHAD

I

Two years—and it was spring once more.

"Lancelot," said Guinevere, "I'm growing old. Not even the season makes me wish to recover my youth."

"Isn't that fortunate on the whole?" said Lancelot. "I mean, the last time you tried to be young again—"

"I got back my lover," said Guinevere. "No, Lancelot, you can't make me sorry for that. These years have been our best."

"Have they, Guinevere? I've been happy, but I've wondered about you. You haven't found fault with me for neglecting my career—but perhaps you feel it would be useless to say any more—perhaps you think my madness finished me."

"Who are those two men—there, down the road—can't you see?"

Lancelot went to the window and looked out toward the forest.

"The larger one is Bors. He's back after a long trip. The other man I don't know."

He took his seat again on the oaken bench, facing the queen in her stately chair.

"You weren't changing the subject, were you?"

"No, I heard what you said, and I don't mind replying,

Lancelot. Your career is over, but the madness had nothing to do with it. I think Arthur's career is over, too, but he isn't mad, as yet. For those two good reasons, I have no career myself. But you were generous to come back, and I've accepted my life as it is—without the work I was born to do, but still with much happiness in it. . . . Don't let's get on the subject again."

"Before we leave it, I'd like to offer a small suggestion," said Lancelot. "It's the result of careful thought, but you are free to say, if you wish, that my mind is still weak. Arthur and I aren't such failures, after all. We haven't missed our proper destiny. That's the root of your disappointment. If we hadn't succeeded, you would have had your career."

"That's what you call a suggestion, is it? You're not in a lover-like mood to-day."

"There's nothing wrong with my mood, but you said you were growing old. To be happy, you need a man around to make something out of. Pretty raw material would be best. Not having any such occasion for your skill, you think you have lost your youth."

"I'm forty," said Guinevere.

"A dangerous age," said Lancelot. "A crude person who happened your way just now would become a great man in spite of himself."

"You are developing quite a vein of wit," said Guinevere. "And your wisdom would do credit to a woman."

"It came on me quite suddenly," said Lancelot, "though I hadn't thought women very wise. I suppose they are. They're a cause of wisdom."

Guinevere looked at him a moment, then leaned forward in her chair, and stretched out her hands. He rose to his feet, but did not move toward her. Her arms fell limp.

"Lancelot, aren't we lovers still? I love you—I never wanted your love so much!"

Had they not been lost in each other, they would have seen Arthur standing in the doorway. Lancelot held the queen in his arms, and bent down for her kiss. Arthur was motionless as the tapestry on the wall.

"Guinevere," said Lancelot, "you haven't kissed me so—for how many years? It's our youth come back."

"No, it's our love," she said. "I was wicked ever to say it was less than my blessed happiness."

She raised her lips again, and Arthur drew back from the doorway without a sound.

"We have thought too much about ourselves—some of the time we might have had together has been spoiled by thinking," said Lancelot. "From now on, we'll simply enjoy our love, won't we? There aren't so many years left."

"I've always loved you—in spite of what I've said or done," said Guinevere. "I can think of nothing fine in this world without thinking of you. If I have had great dreams for you to accomplish, it was our love that brought them to mind."

"I know," said Lancelot. "Don't let's get back to that unpleasant subject. I have loved you as you are. Whenever I heard beauty mentioned, I thought of your body—and when they spoke of softness and roundness and sculptured ecstasy, it was as though you were in my arms. Other women—well, I could confess the pleasure to a priest, along with other sins, if I were in the habit of confessing, but I've given my soul for your kisses, and a good bargain, too, I'll say. I'll give all I have, to my last hour, for your love."

Guinevere kissed him, somewhat less rapturously, and disengaged herself from his arms. She smoothed her gown and took her seat again in the regal chair. Lancelot stood watching her.

"But to your last hour," she said, "will there be those possible other women—that pleasure you so easily repent of? I don't want your soul, Lancelot, but I should like you all to myself."

"I spoke of it just by way of saying how much I love you, Guinevere."

"Try to find a more graceful form of adoration," she said. "For me, Elaine never can be a figure of speech."

"Haven't you forgotten her by this time? You know I didn't love her. You know I hate the trick she played on me. I have been loyal to you always. When you were willing to have me back, I came at once, even though—"

He stopped suddenly, and Guinevere looked up at him with a smile.

"Even though you had to leave her behind."

"I left my son," he said. "But I don't regret it— once more, I wish only to tell you what a price I pay gladly for our love."

"The son hurts me, Lancelot, I don't mind saying. Your affair with Elaine I should have forgotten long ago, if she hadn't had your child. I ought to have been his mother. Oh, well . . ."

She buried her face in her hands, and began to sob. Lancelot was taken too much by surprise to know what to do. He stood by her chair, waiting for her to collect herself, and so Anglides found them, when she entered.

"Madam," she said, "King Arthur wishes to know whether Sir Lancelot is here. If he is, will he speak with the king at once in the great hall?"

Guinevere raised an absolutely impassive face.

"He is here, Anglides, and he will go at once. Our talk was quite finished."

II

Arthur was standing with a group of his knights, at the end of his great hall. As Lancelot came in they stopped talking and fell back a little to make room. He found himself face to face with Galahad.

"How did you come here, son?"

"Then he is your son," said Arthur.

"He is."

There was no reason to doubt it, as they stood there together. From that moment Court gossip, whatever there was at Galahad's expense, had a tendency to run underground. The fate of Meliagrance was not forgotten.

"What brings you here?" said Lancelot.

"I wanted to come, and asked Sir Bors to show me the way. I want to be knighted, father, if you and the king think I'm ready."

"He asked to come," said Bors, "but I suggested bringing him. The responsibility is mine, Lancelot. My errand took me past his mother's castle, and seeing how finely he grows up, I was convinced he belonged here."

Lancelot said nothing. He was proud of the boy there before him, with the build and carriage of an older man, but he would have liked to ask Bors whether Elaine had had a finger in this arrival, planning a new stratagem perhaps, or whether Bors had felt he owed her something, after bringing the message which took her lover away.

"Does she wish it?" he said.

"His mother? She didn't wish to lose him," said Bors, "but she agreed it was now or never, if he's to have a proper career."

"A career!" said Lancelot, but checked himself at once. "King Arthur, if you approve, I'll make my son one of your knights."

They turned to see what the king would say, and most of them thought he looked rather uncordial.

"You know more about this than we do, Lancelot. Your son has not shown what he is made of, but you must have ways of judging him."

"You knew his grandfather," said Lancelot.

"And I know you," said the king.

Lancelot caught a glimpse of Gawaine, standing in the group, amused and curious. He saw Galahad's handsome face, eager but a little worried.

"Kneel down," he said.

So Galahad knelt before his father, and Lancelot touched his shoulders with the sword. They said afterward that Lancelot showed greater emotion than was his habit; his voice trembled as he bade his son rise up Sir Galahad, and he added unexpectedly a sentence half a prayer and half a compliment:

"God make you a good man, for you have more than your share of beauty!"

Bors stopped to have a word with Lancelot afterward.

"He's a fine boy—I lost my heart to him on our ride, and he's handsome, as you said; he's a fair copy of you."

"Does he resemble me?" said Lancelot. "Just at that moment, and in that posture, he made me think of Elaine."

Bors wondered, but decided not to inquire, on what occasion Elaine had knelt before Lancelot and had seemed beautiful.

"I still don't know why he's here, Bors. What am I to do with him?"

"If I guess the sort of heart he has," said Bors, "he'll find something to do without your aid. When I arrived at Corbin he was straining at the leash, fretting for a chance to try his skill on any passer-by who would tilt with him. I talked it over with Elaine. Lancelot, she said you'd misunderstand if she sent him to you, yet you hadn't made a sign to show you remembered her existence or the boy's, not since you left her to rescue Guinevere. Something had to be done, she said, and I agreed. If you are annoyed, blame me."

Arthur waited for a word with him, too.

"We have been friends for many years," he said. "I should not have believed you were keeping so much of your life from me, if I hadn't seen with my own eyes."

"I wanted to tell you about it," said Lancelot, "but words don't come easy to me, least of all on that subject."

"Well, can't we have a clear understanding now?"

"If you wish—though I dare say you have guessed it all, since you've seen him. Elaine is his mother. It happened a long while ago—just before King Pelles died. The boy is seventeen now."

"I knew all that, but it's your more intimate experience I thought you might have shared with an old friend. Your love for the woman—she's your wife?"

"She's not," said Lancelot. "Had I married, I would have let you know, of course. I'm sorry to say I never loved Elaine enough to marry her, not even on the occasion which accounts for Galahad."

"When she was here she seemed a very attractive girl," said Arthur. "I hoped you loved each other and might come to some agreement. I envy you the son. She gave you a fine boy."

"That's just it," said Lancelot. "She knew I cared nothing for her, but she planned to win me through the child. Now I'm immensely fond of him, but she can't maneuver me that way. If I married her now, she would have beaten me at every point."

"That will happen to you anyway, if you marry at all," said Arthur. "But it's going to be hard on the boy, Lancelot. Gawaine and his sort will do a certain amount of talking."

"I'll put a hole through the man who raises the question—or Galahad will, if he hears of it first. He has a quick temper and a keen lance. They'll find that out before long."

"In the interest of domestic peace," said Arthur, "they'd better find it out at once. How would it be to hold a tournament in the boy's honor? We needn't say it in so many words, but they'll understand it's an opportunity to find out how hard he can hit."

"I suppose that's the best way. Except for you and me, he can manage any of them."

"We'll hold the tournament to-morrow, perhaps, if we can get ready," said Arthur, "and I'll see that the whole Court is there. I'll tell Guinevere your son is arrived. Or you may prefer to tell her yourself?"

"No," said Lancelot, "I'd rather you told her."

They looked at each other for a moment. Then Arthur held out his hand.

"I'm sorry for you, Lancelot—much more sorry than you can guess."

III

Like his father before him, Galahad found his way across the terrace to the door of the queen's tower. She had asked him to come. At the tournament she had sat with her ladies and watched the tilting—one courtier after another embarrassed by the boy's terrific energy. Lancelot sat his horse at the end of the field and looked on.

"Arthur, I should like to see the young man," Guinevere had said when it was all over. Ettard raised her eyebrows and tried to exchange a glance with Anglides.

"Tell Sir Galahad the queen wishes to congratulate him," said Arthur.

Galahad dismounted from his horse and walked toward the queen's pavilion. When they saw his manner of walking and his uncovered face, even at a distance, they all thought the same thing.

"Yes," said Guinevere, "he is Lancelot's son."

They watched him come nearer.

"Madam," said Ettard, "do you think it right, really moral, that one of his way of birth should prove so admirable?"

The queen stared at her.

Galahad stood before them, happy in his day's work, yet a little overcome with sudden and conspicuous honors.

"I'm glad to have seen the beginning of your success,"

He thought she looked even lovelier, suddenly happy, but he wondered what amused her.

"Yes," she said, "there is room for more of them, but I believe you will be greater than either, if you once see the way."

"Madam, do you see it?"

"Not for myself, Galahad, but I see it for you—a new way of being a knight."

He looked puzzled.

"Father has taught me about the horse and the weapons, and if I ride out in King Arthur's service I suppose I'll find a thing or two for myself. Father says you learn most from the difficulties as they come up."

"What is all this arming and fighting for, Galahad?"

"Why, to keep the country safe and punish wrong, I suppose," said Galahad. "Besides, it's awfully good fun."

"Good!" said the queen. "Few of them are honest enough to own up. You will keep the country safe, and punish wrong. And what then?"

"Won't that be all?"

"I hope not. If you succeed, don't you see what an idle time you'll have? Some day you may be glad if the wrong breaks out again, so that you can right it."

Galahad felt scandalized, but he could think of no good reply.

"Your father and the king made this country safe, and keep it in excellent order. No doubt you intend to go off to some wild country, and repeat the service there."

"No," said Galahad, "as a matter of fact I never thought of the wild countries. Perhaps I ought to go, but I'd rather stay here. I wanted to be at Arthur's Court."

"Worse and worse!" said Guinevere. "It's quite natural, but you must admit it's quite useless, too. I'm not advising the wild countries, but you'll waste your life if you don't accomplish something new, something entirely your own. Your father and the king really created a state and a government once. You, too, should create."

"What?"

"I haven't thought it through yet," said Guinevere, "but I feel the idea coming. Perhaps you have a glimpse of it yourself."

"My only idea was to ride out for the king—and once in a while be of service to fair ladies."

Guinevere laughed.

"Not the ladies. Perhaps that is one of the new notes we are looking for. Leave the ladies out of it."

"I don't see how you can," said Galahad.

She laughed again.

"You're getting on," she said. "It's hard, but some day it will be done, and why not be the pioneer? Don't fall in love with any of them, and especially don't let one of them make love to you. It distracts your attention."

"This puzzles me," said Galahad. "You're down on the fighting, and you say not to fall in love. What is there left?"

"That's what we must think out. . . . You aren't in love, are you?"

Galahad looked at her with considerable surprise.

"My mother asks questions like that," he said. "No, madam, I'm not, I suppose, not the way I've heard about it—but I hope to be."

"As soon as you have time, I dare say. That's the way they all do," said Guinevere. "Would you like to hear how it seems from the lady's point of view? The lover does wonderful things in her honor, and she is pleased. He keeps on doing wonderful things till they become a habit, with him and with her. Habits don't give us pleasure. She'd be sad if he stopped, but she hardly notices it if he keeps on."

"Why, I thought you, of all people—"

"Well?"

"Perhaps I oughtn't to say it."

"Say it—I'll tell you afterward."

"You've inspired more of that kind of service than most ladies—yet you don't believe in it!"

"Galahad, the men say we inspire them, but it doesn't strike very deep. They don't keep on growing. If under the spell of our beauty, as they tell us, they discover one fine thing to do, they just do it over and over again till the world won't have any more of it, and some public benefactor stops them. They've been tilting at each other and honoring their ladies for some time. That's why you ought to strike out—be sincere, be original."

Galahad was silent a moment.

"May I ask you a personal question?"

"Do!"

"I thought Sir Meliagrance did you some wrong, and you sent for my father, and he came to your rescue."

"That is true."

"Well, didn't you think my father and his skill in arms were rather useful?"

She was startled, and she had no ready answer, yet his wit seemed to please her.

"I think highly of your father, Galahad, and I owe him much—for many things. I didn't criticize him. Or

not entirely. But his skill in arms, you'll admit, was useful only because Meliagrance challenged to mortal combat.
I'd say the method Meliagrance used to establish my innocence or my guilt was silly and wicked."

"Madam! You don't mean you have lost faith in trial
by combat?"

"So far as I can remember," said Guinevere, "I never
had any faith in it."

"Why, madam, it's the climax of our profession of
arms—our belief that the innocent man can win against
one who is in the wrong!"

"I wish it were so, Galahad, but I suspect the strong-
est arm wins, and the freshest horse, and the keenest eye—
and the greatest skill and experience. Innocence and
virtue have nothing to do with it."

"You don't know how terrible that is! . . . You
can't know! . . . You oughtn't to say such things!"

"Why not, if they're true?"

"Because this means that my father, who always wins,
may sometimes have been on the wrong side—and even
when he was defending—"

"Listen to me a moment, Galahad. Your father has
taught you to fight so well that you can probably beat
any one except himself. Do you think you are perfect—I
mean, always right, except when you tilt against your
father?"

"I don't think I'm perfect."

"But you will always win, I suppose."

"This is the most terrible thing that's ever happened to
me!" said Galahad.

"It's a new idea," said Guinevere. "In spite of us,
they will come."

"Yet I don't know that it's so bad as I thought at

first," said Galahad. "My father would naturally win. He's what I should call a perfect man—or as near as you'll find. Wouldn't you say so?"

"Galahad," said the queen, "your father and I have spent almost half of our lives together, here at my husband's Court. I couldn't make an impartial judgment of him now. But what I said had no particular reference to him—that was your interpretation."

"Madam, I don't know where I stand now—I'm not sure I can fight very well again. . . . If there's nothing in it, after all, why did you congratulate me yesterday?"

"My dear boy," said Guinevere, "I was glad to see you win—I didn't say you were in the right. Was there anything to be right about yesterday? But if this idea troubles you, why not see to it that you are right anyway? There's one of the new fashions you can set! You will win I know, but be sure you are right before you start. Then perhaps the combat won't be needed."

Ettard entered the room quietly, yet with the air of an important mission. "Madam, when you are at leisure King Arthur would like to speak with you."

"In a moment, Ettard."

Ettard went out.

"Now that she's gone," said Guinevere, "let me warn you. Don't let Ettard turn your head. I see she's getting ready to do so."

"I won't," said Galahad. "I don't like her at all. She has a sharp tongue."

"She has," said the queen, "and a warm heart. And worst of all, she's much too old for you. That will probably be her chief charm. Young men like you often succumb to women twice their age. But I won't have you spoiling your life with a love affair."

IV

Lancelot found Guinevere walking in her garden.

"It's an age since I've seen you," she said. "I don't like these symptoms of indifference."

"If you disliked them to any extent, you wouldn't mention them with such satisfaction. You haven't missed me, Guinevere. My son has cut me out."

"He's an attractive boy."

"Apparently! When I've gone to your tower, these last days, Ettard has informed me that you were talking with Galahad. I looked for you here to-day, hoping to seize a spare minute of your crowded time."

He saw clearly that Guinevere was in her most radiant mood, and he knew he was not the cause of it.

"We can rest here for a moment, by the fruit trees," she said, and he took his place beside her on the garden bench.

"Yes, I've seen your boy every day since he came. I didn't wish him to come, Lancelot, but since he is here I like him. He has immense possibilities."

"That's what I wanted to talk about," said Lancelot. "His possibilities. I don't wish them spoiled."

"Why do you say that to me? I don't wish them spoiled, either."

"We differ as to what are his possibilities, and how they should be developed. For the first time, Guinevere, I, too, have some theories about another person's career."

"You needn't be insulting, however. I might very well have ignored your son, considering his informal origin, but I thought you would be grateful for kindness to him. I felt sorry for him, too. Now I begin to be fond of him for his own sake, and you seem to object. Really, Lancelot, you're exasperating!"

He drew designs on the garden walk with the toe of his shoe. Not very good designs.

"And you're hardly the best of company this afternoon," said Guinevere.

"I'm grateful to you for receiving the boy—you must know that," said Lancelot, "but I play a double part now—I'm his father, and your lover."

"There's no doubt about the paternity," said Guinevere, "but of recent years you've been my lover somewhat intermittently. At this moment you are hardly carried away by your ardor for me. I'm rather hurt, Lancelot."

"I suppose you have a right to be—though it's not what I intended. Your lover always, that's what I've been. Even when we have quarreled, I knew I was quarreling with the person I loved best in the world. I wasn't always sure you cared as much for me."

Guinevere stiffened slightly.

"Which of us has sacrificed more for the other, we shall never be able to count up. . . . Was there something you wanted to say about Galahad?"

"Yes. I gather from him that he has lost his heart to you completely. He says you inspire him. He doesn't know what's happened to him. Guinevere, you've used your arts on a mere boy. It isn't fair play."

Her radiant manner returned.

"It's perfectly fair. It's the most generous thing I've ever done. There isn't going to be a flirtation between a boy and a middle-aged woman. So delicate of you to suggest it, Lancelot. That's one of the things I shall do for him—women will become quite harmless. He's to be my masterpiece."

"Your what?"

Guinevere laughed merrily, though he thought she was putting it on.

"Don't let's go over the old ground, Lancelot. I wanted to make something out of Arthur, and—"

"And something out of me. I know. And now you've caught Galahad quite young, and this time you're going to develop a real man."

"If you like. That's practically what I mean."

"Well, when you get through with him, his own mother won't know him, his head is so upset already."

"His father won't know him, either," she said. "I'm not changing him with special reference to Elaine."

"Would you mind telling me just what the masterpiece is to be like?"

"Lancelot, I've thought of an absolutely new kind of man, an original type. In the first place, he will be spiritually strong and physically clean. He won't even have an impulse to regret or be ashamed of, and he'll never love a woman, except as your boy is fond of me."

"Well," said Lancelot, "leaving aside for a moment the possibility of changing human nature from the ground up, I'd like to know how you came to have this happy thought."

"From experience, inversely," said Guinevere. "I never met such a man. It's something quite new."

"God didn't think of it when he made us," said Lancelot. "It's original, all right. But won't he be an awful prig?"

"That will be the danger, but I think it can be avoided," said Guinevere. "His sense of humor will have to be developed. You didn't bequeath him much, Lancelot."

"He had two parents," said Lancelot. "But what's the good of it, supposing you can make such an unnatural saint of him? How is he to live in the world we know?"

"My idea is that the energy other men waste in loving and being loyal, and pretending to be, might just as well go into some real work, important and sincere. I shan't try to select the work for him. That's the mistake I made with you, Lancelot, when I tried to help you, but I wasn't so old then, and you weren't so young as Galahad. No, I'll see that his wonderful energy is stored up, not a bit of it wasted, until some day it just explodes, beautifully."

"That kind do explode, but not beautifully," said Lancelot. "I've seen it happen. Do you expect me to stand by and watch you wreck my son's life?"

"You needn't watch, and you needn't stand by," said Guinevere. "Moreover, I shan't wreck his life. If I had had my way, he wouldn't be in existence, and certainly he wouldn't have appeared at this Court. Now it's my turn, Lancelot. You ought to have got a mother for him who could bring him up. Now I shall do that office myself."

"As a bit of revenge, I can understand it," said Lancelot, "but I didn't believe you could stoop so low."

"Not revenge, Lancelot—not that at all! I'm giving the best part of me a chance it has never yet enjoyed."

"Well," said Lancelot, "I'll stand by to save him. . . . It isn't only against women you're warning him. You've taken away some of his delight in arms. When I was giving him a fencing lesson, the other day, he was asking silly questions as to how he's to know when he's fighting on the right side. I thought my head was weakening again, or I was deaf and hadn't caught what he said. I wanted to know who the fool was who proposed such difficulties, and he took offense."

"I was the fool, as you meant to convey," said Guinevere. "Yes, that's another side of my masterpiece. I hope it will seem less important to Galahad to fight, than to fight on the just side."

"I can't imagine anything nastier," said Lancelot. "I'm sorry to speak so, Guinevere, but if you teach him such sophistry, he won't be a fit companion for decent men. Imagine some one needing his help in danger, a friend, let's say, or his father or his mother, or even a stranger, and he'll be debating which side of the quarrel is more righteous! If he sees a man strike a woman, I suppose you'll want him to ascertain, before he interferes, whether the woman doesn't deserve a beating!"

"I wasn't thinking of it that way."

"But that's the way he'll think of it, once you get him started wrong."

Guinevere made no reply.

"That isn't just what I meant—but you'll be able to piece it out," he said.

He got up, as though he expected her to leave the garden, or send him away.

"Don't go," she said. "There's more to talk about. I understand at least some of the things you didn't put into words. You are wondering how I dare insist that Galahad fight only on the side of truth, when I sent for you to save me from Sir Meliagrance."

"That never entered my head—Meliagrance was a liar; he was trying to harm you because you wouldn't love him. He got no more than he deserved."

"He accused us of being lovers," she said, "and he accused me of being faithless to Arthur."

"That wasn't the point at all," said Lancelot. "The accusation grew out of that ride of yours in the wood, and Meliagrance specifically charged that you rode to meet me there. He knew I wasn't there, or he wouldn't have risked his life. He was a plain liar."

Guinevere smiled up at him from where she sat.

"Well, what's your idea of it, then? Was it wrong for me to rescue you, at your request?"

"Lancelot, I think it was my own fault that I needed the rescue. I was in too deep to get out any other way. But I don't think of that episode as an illustration of pure justice."

"Can't I save your life without illustrating something?" said Lancelot. "I don't regret our love, nor any of its consequences. Perhaps you have begun to. I suppose you'll find it hard to imagine these perfections for Galahad without being influenced by them yourself."

"Do you know," said Guinevere, "I'm just beginning to understand how we can live in a world of ideas."

"I beg pardon?" said Lancelot. "You're not going to be a mystic, or anything of that sort?"

"Perhaps I am," she said. "When you begin to think

of a perfection which you have never met, why, you're living in another world, aren't you?"

"I'm not," said Lancelot. "I never had any doubt as to which world I was in. If I get to another one, I fancy I'll know I'm there—otherwise it won't make a bit of difference. But to pretend you're somewhere else while you're here—I say it's absurd, Guinevere. Don't teach this to Galahad!"

"Will you walk with me to the castle?" she said. "Galahad is sure to have more influence on me than I on him. You can see the effect already. Ordinarily this would have been a quarrel, Lancelot. Instead, it has been an exchange of ideas."

V

THEY were walking on the terrace in the early twilight. Lancelot and Bors had gone off with Arthur to settle some question of buildings and grounds. Gawaine was exhibiting his wit to Guinevere and Anglides, with Galahad listening, impatient.

"The point is whether you want to raise fruit, like a farmer," said Gawaine, "or whether you wish a setting for the gentle life. There's a philosophy about gardens, madam, as about everything else. I'm amazed that your garden—and you so spiritual—should be, shall I say, somewhat gross? It's all running to fruit. In such a useful environment, how do you expect us to fall in love, or become poets?"

"It isn't the fruit, Gawaine, that interferes with poetry from you," said Guinevere.

"Just try me, madam. I do as well as an honest man can, so thwarted. But trim the trees a bit closer, plant a few bushes for shadow around the garden seats, give me a full moon and half an hour with any lady in your Court, and see the result!"

"Heaven help us!" said Anglides. "I'm for more fruit. Plant cabbages, madam, or squash."

"Well, leave me out," said Gawaine, "or let her have Galahad instead, for the experiment. I still maintain a garden shouldn't be an orchard."

"There are one or two places," said Guinevere, "that

have always seemed to me favorable for romantic thoughts, but I confess I never visited them with you, Gawaine."

"Come now, then, madam—but I doubt if the places exist, except in your affection for your farm."

"Oh, I couldn't trust myself, after your terrible boast."

"Of course Anglides will come, too, madam, and Galahad. You'll be wonderfully safe."

He led the way down the steps, and Guinevere laughed and followed, for want of something better to do. Anglides went with her.

"Aren't you coming, Galahad?"

"If you'll pardon me, madam, I'll stay here."

"He thinks my talk is silly," said Gawaine.

"I do," said Galahad.

"Well, you can contemplate wisdom there for a moment," said Gawaine. "We shan't be long."

Galahad listened to their voices as they wandered through the paths, below the terrace wall. The evening was golden and still, and he found it pleasant to be alone.

"A penny for your thoughts, Sir Galahad," said Ettard at his side.

Galahad turned to her, startled. This was the one who wished to fascinate him. Well, he would be firm. Remembering Guinevere's warning, he looked at the woman with considerable attention. She really had an attractive face. Something impish about it, yet kind. She wore her gown cut extremely low. He hadn't noticed before how bold she was. Nor how white her bosom. He felt uncomfortable.

"I'm waiting for the queen," he said. "She'll be back in a minute."

He thought it safer to be rude. He leaned on the terrace wall and occupied himself with the landscape.

"I'm waiting for her, too," said Ettard.

She leaned on the wall beside him, and looked out in the same direction. He wondered how soon the others would come back. He could no longer hear their voices.

"Who is with the queen, Sir Galahad?"

"Anglides and Gawaine."

"Oh, Gawaine, is he?"

Her tone suggested anything but admiration for Gawaine. Galahad was glad she had good judgment.

"I suppose you know," she said, "why your coming to Court has made us all so happy."

"No, I don't know."

"Because you are serious, and have a purpose in life. The others are nice enough, but they're like Gawaine. You really are going to do something worth while."

"I hope so," said Galahad. He wished it had sounded modest. "But you're very kind to tell me. I don't see why it should make a difference to other people."

"Ah, you don't understand," said Ettard. "Just your being here makes it easier for those of us who feel the same way. Especially for a woman. Most men think a woman is interested only in compliments, and light talk and love affairs, and that sort of thing. You appreciate how foolish and unimportant it is. No thoughtful woman would want a man like Gawaine for a friend. Perfectly frank friendship, as you can understand, Sir Galahad, man to man—just true comrades. Every one here knows you are that kind, and you're the only one. Since I've been at the Court, I've talked to no one else this way."

Galahad was deeply moved.

"Thanks ever so much for telling me," he said.

"I thought I really ought to. It helps so much to know the nice things people are saying. Praise helps us all, but usually people forget to give it, till it's too late."

She managed to suggest something autobiographic in the last words.

"But you get lots of praise, don't you?"

"Do I?"

For the life of him, he could remember nothing.

"I don't see how they could help it," he said.

He felt suddenly aged and wicked.

"I'm a good deal older than you are," said Ettard, "and I've been through a lot of experience. I don't know how you understand so well."

"It's a natural sympathy between us, don't you think?" said Galahad. "Of course I don't know as much as you do, but I feel—well, very much at home with you."

"I'm so glad," she said. "I knew a different sort of man once."

"Who was he?"

"Perhaps I oughtn't to bother you with my troubles. People should be able to keep the disagreeable things to themselves."

"When you have a friend who understands," said Galahad, "I think you might as well tell. If I could help you in any way—"

"You've helped me already," said Ettard. "There's really nothing to tell—it's likely to happen to any woman—if she has fine feelings."

"What is?" said Galahad.

"Oh, it happened long ago, but it's one of those things you don't forget easily."

"No, you don't," said Galahad.

"He said he loved me, and I suppose he did in his own fashion, and I couldn't help loving him. Not even after I found him out. That's the worst of all, don't you think—when you love somebody who isn't your ideal?"

"Yes," said Galahad. "What was the matter with him?"

"Oh, he was all right in his way—most women would have been content. But as I got to know him better, I realized he was—well, just a lover. You understand."

"Of course," said Galahad. "Not your ideal at all."

"Far from it," said Ettard. "I knew you'd see it."

They studied the landscape together.

"Just what is your ideal?" said Galahad.

"A friend," said Ettard, "a man who could sympathize without being mawkish, who wouldn't want kisses, and that sort of detestable thing. Men seem to have no idea how a fine woman feels about it. Courtly manners I like, of course, but that's different."

"It certainly is!"

"My dear father had courtly manners," she said. "He always bent over my mother's hand and kissed it, with the most reverent gesture. That's not vulgar love-making, that's a tribute. But what man could do it nowadays? Their moods are either casual or else—I suppose ignoble is the word."

"What else would your ideal man do?"

"Besides kissing my hand?" said Ettard. "I used that only as an illustration. He would honor all women, in that high way, and he would feel disgust at any one, man or woman, who surrendered to the passion they call love."

"For myself," said Galahad, "I've decided never to marry."

"Not marry? Why not?"

"For the reasons we've been discussing—friendship's so much better, so much less selfish, so much more of the spirit."

"I wouldn't exaggerate," said Ettard. "Marriage might be very spiritual. I'm sure it's possible."

"It's a concession," said Galahad. "There's something low about it."

"I can see one thing clearly. You're in love."

"I didn't say I was."

"No, but it's clear enough, when one understands. It's just the kind of love a heart like yours would feel."

Galahad adjusted himself to the idea that he was in love.

"I wish you the deepest happiness," said Ettard.

"Thanks," said he.

"Though, of course, for people of our natures, the best part of it isn't happiness."

They considered this idea in silence.

"I'm awfully good at telling fortunes from hands," she said. "Let me see your hand."

"I don't believe in that."

"Nor I, not altogether, but it sometimes turns out curiously. . . . No, the left hand, please."

She bent over his broad palm, and the white bosom could not be ignored, if he looked at her at all. When she raised her head suddenly, his face was red, and he was gazing off into space.

"Dear me—dear me!" she said. "That heart line. . . . Perhaps I'd better not tell what I see."

"What is it?"

She let go his hand.

"No, it wouldn't be fair. And as you say, there's nothing in hand-reading, anyway."

"Tell me what you see."

He thrust his hand out at her.

"I don't want to—but if you insist—and if you don't take it seriously. . . . You're in love with a woman much older than you . . . or you soon will be . . . no, you are now . . . and you can't marry her."

"I wouldn't anyway," said Galahad.

"It's a very noble love . . . dear me, here's another one . . . that's a noble one, too."

"Am I going to marry her?" said Galahad.

"I can't quite make out yet."

"Well, I won't."

"It's a queer line. . . . A great passion, I should say, and then this other woman . . . and then it goes off completely. . . . I can't see what comes next."

"That's enough," said Galahad.

"Did I read correctly?" she said.

"I don't know who that second woman is, but you're right about the first."

"I knew I was, Sir Galahad. I'm so glad such a beautiful thing has happened to such a nature as yours. You must be very happy."

"I am," said Galahad.

"Even though you are never to marry her."

"Oh, I can't marry her," he said, "but of course I don't want to."

"Of course not," she said. "If I can ever help you at all, in return for the help you've given me—"

She still held his hand—he wasn't sure whether he was holding hers. In any case he wondered how you got your hand away. He had a happy thought. He raised her hand to his lips, and printed on it a dry and bashful kiss. He was annoyed at himself for observing that the back of her hand was chapped.

He was half-way through his tribute when the garden party emerged at the other end of the terrace.

"Good for Galahad!" said Gawaine. "You see my point, madam? On the terrace here there are no fruit trees at all."

VI

ARTHUR was walking back to the castle with Lancelot and Bors.

"How's that boy of yours getting on?" he said.

"Better than I dared hope. He was rather young to come here, and he had never met many people."

"When you think he's ready, I'll send him off on some easy errand to begin with."

"He's learning a good deal just being at Court, I should think. I've no idea how much sense he'd show under responsibility."

"There's only one way to find out," said Arthur.

They walked on for a while.

"What is it you think he's learning here?"

"Manners, for one thing," said Lancelot. "How to get on with men and women."

"He ought to know how to get on with men," said Arthur.

"I think he needs a change, though he hasn't been here long," said Bors. "He hasn't the same dare-devil mood as when he rode beside me that day. Haven't you noticed how thoughtful he's growing, Lancelot?"

"He's absorbing a new life," said Lancelot. "It can't be done all at once. A few more weeks here, and he'll be well settled."

"I'm not sure that's the result we want for him," said Arthur. "I doubt if the Court is the best place for

such a boy to find himself. He needs the real world.
There are too many women in this neighborhood."

"I can't imagine a Court without women in it," said
Bors.

"You mean, you don't know of any," said Arthur.

"Well," said Bors, "I don't believe I want to. I
owe something myself to the atmosphere they create.
It's refining."

"I don't know that any one of us is valuable to the
world on the score of refinement. Gawaine is refined.
I can't trust him out of my sight."

"Gawaine has his good points," said Bors.

"I'm very fond of him," said Arthur, "but I've noticed
his refinement."

They were at the castle now, and they heard the
voices on the terrace.

"Who's out there, Bors?"

"The queen and her ladies—and Galahad, I think."

"Well, I'll go indoors. . . . There you are, Lancelot—the queen and Galahad."

"She has been very kind to him."

"Don't I know? That's why he'd better ride off for a
while. He'll be like all the rest of us in these mediocre
days. My idea of that boy is that he has something
original in him, if it isn't spoiled by bad training. He
spends a good part of his time with Guinevere, doesn't
he?"

"I believe so."

"I'll send him off the first chance I get, Lancelot.
You and I can stand being inspired better than he can."

VII

"I DON'T blame you for being disappointed in me," said Galahad.

"You are very gracious," said the queen. "I'm glad you don't blame me."

"I mean," said Galahad, "I'm mortified when I consider what I did. But still I don't think you understand, or you wouldn't be so angry."

"I saw you kiss her."

"Her hand," said Galahad.

"I've overrated your innocence," she said. "Just where do kisses begin to count with you? I saw you kiss her."

"It wasn't exactly a kiss—it was more a tribute."

Guinevere began to laugh, then stopped suddenly.

"I suppose you had been exchanging confidences."

"Yes."

"Galahad, you think I don't understand, but I know more about that conversation than you do. I know more about women. When I warned you, I knew every play in the game."

"You're not fair to Ettard, madam—she was kind and—sympathetic, and we—"

"What did she need to be sympathetic about? You weren't in trouble, were you?"

"I mean, we realized that our natures are much the same, and our ideals."

"I hope not," said Guinevere. "Let me show you how well I know what happened. She pretended to confide in you some intimate aspect of her heart."

"She did confide in me."

"Well, I shan't ask you what she said—that wouldn't be proper, but ask yourself, Galahad, whether she really confided anything at all. No matter. The point is that you then felt you must tell her something in return, and that gave her the chance to flatter you by listening to the story of your inner life. She turned you round her little finger. She made you talk too much, and kiss her, in the bargain."

"I didn't confide in her—not exactly."

"If it's not exactly, then you did," said Guinevere.

"No, she told my fortune—by my left hand—and she asked me whether she had it correct."

"If you knew how elementary that method it," said Guinevere, "you wouldn't be flattered. It must have been like drawing teeth."

"Madam," said Galahad, "if you have no opinion whatever of Ettard, I can not explain why she attends your person."

"Why not? All women are alike, my dear boy— rather, in the presence of women all men act the same way. I can play all the tricks Ettard can, but I want you to be an exceptional man, not distracted, not even by women, from the life you ought to have."

"But, madam, I don't feel I've done anything very bad. I knew you wouldn't like it, so I'm sorry I did it, but I don't see where the wickedness comes in."

"It's what it would lead to," said Guinevere. "Are you the sort of man who can be made to do anything a woman wants? That's the point. Most men, even though they think they have their independence, can be drawn this way and that by a pretty face or a graceful body—all the woman has to do is to show herself to them, and they begin imagining she's their soul-mate or a pre-destined sympathetic friend. After that anything's possible. Of course there's such a love as the most austere would envy, but it's rare, Galahad. That's the kind you ought to save yourself for. Most men have given way to—well, I've said it. That's why we feel a pity not much above contempt for the men and women who haven't loved nobly. You can say it was natural, but, after all, that's saying they merely did what nature told them."

"But, madam," said Galahad, "don't you know in practically all the stories of great knights and beautiful ladies, they fall desperately in love?"

"I've heard of it," said Guinevere.

"And you wouldn't do that?"

"I don't want you to do it. You are a rare person, Galahad—your example is going to count."

"Of course I shan't marry—I told Ettard so."

"Ettard would find that an insurmountable obstacle."

"I don't understand you," said Galahad.

"You were saying you wouldn't marry," said Guinevere.

"No, I'm not going to be a monk, nor run away from life, and I shan't condemn others for marrying—"

"I wouldn't," said Guinevere.

"But I shall try to be as little—what would you say—as little—I mean, the mind is the only part of us that will bear looking into."

"Will it?" said Guinevere. "Galahad, I don't want

you to mistake what I have said. I want you to be an extraordinary man, but not an abnormal one. I'm anxious to save you from the women who would make a fool of you, but you must love—you must have some passion and vision in your life."

"All you've said to me since I came to Court, madam, has opened my eyes to the vision. Since what people call love makes them do unkind things, and since love, in their sense, is at best rather beastly, I'll have nothing to do with it. I shall try to love beautiful conduct."

"There's danger in that, too," said Guinevere.

"Then I give up," said Galahad. "I thought you would find no objection to that."

"I know what you are feeling," said Guinevere, "the resentment against the compromises and mixtures which are our fate."

"That never came into my head—I'm not sure what it means," said Galahad. "I'm trying to live up to the idea you have of me, and all I need now is to find out what the idea is. Of course I shouldn't have kissed Ettard's hand—you wouldn't like that. But otherwise I don't feel guilty. You don't approve of women and love affairs. Very well, I'll avoid both. Yet you say it's dangerous just to try for a good life."

"You talk like your father," said Guinevere. "Let me explain. It's foolish to be led around by women, as most men are—yet so far as love is concerned, it's unwise to undervalue the common way of life, and a very fine man ought to be capable of a very noble passion."

"How is that done?" said Galahad.

"There's no recipe—you'll have to work it out yourself. But when you said you would confine yourself to

beautiful conduct, I feared you might go to pieces altogether, and merely be a safe, stupid person."

"Well, if that's stupidity—"

"Perhaps you were going to say, Ettard isn't stupid.
She isn't. Galahad, I'm advising you against two things
at once, two quite different perils. One is the vulgar en-
tanglement you might mistake for love. It's serious
enough. But the other is worse—the flagging of the
spirit, the weariness that sometimes overtakes gentle
natures. Most young men start out with dreams of all
sorts, not necessarily like yours, but dreams. They usually
end by dedicating themselves to beautiful conduct. That
is, they drop into a steady habit, one day like another,
very glad they can repeat themselves, without the pangs
or inconvenience of growth."

"They'd have to be rather ordinary at bottom," said
Galahad, "to give up so easily."

"You think so?" said Guinevere. "I've happened
in my life to be very fond of three men, each of whom
had promise of greatness. The first went just so far, and
then grew content with what he had done. The second
went much further, but then he too fell into a routine and
ceased to imagine. That's the danger for you, Galahad.
Suppose you follow this ideal of denial—though it might
save you from error and sorrow, would it produce any
positive happiness for you or for others? If you turn
your back on life, you can't grow."

"What happened to the third man?"

"You haven't answered my question," said Guinevere.

"What was it? How long I shall keep on growing?
I don't know, madam, but I'll keep on respecting the
nobler things—I can promise that—and I shan't make
others unhappy."

"Won't you indeed!" said Guinevere. "Then you will be an entirely new kind of man. Do you realize how difficult it will be? Suppose a girl loves you dearly—you will tell her you decline to return her affection for fear of making some one unhappy. She may die of a broken heart."

"They don't die of a broken heart," said Galahad. "You don't believe that yourself, do you?"

"I never died of it, but another woman might," said Guinevere. "The point is that your beautiful conduct might seem to such a woman a selfish way to protect your own feelings. A really brave man, I've always thought, would keep his ideals without retiring from life."

"Well, I begin to think it's too much for me," said Galahad. "I'm badly puzzled. I don't see how you could do both."

"I wouldn't say I had succeeded in doing it—",

"Why, madam, you're the one person who has!"

"No, Galahad—but I'm sure it's what we ought to try for. If I had a son, I'd wish for him first a strong and healthy body. That means strong passions, Galahad—strong everything the body makes you think of. I'd want him to be excited over all forms of beauty— not merely interested, but roused. I'd want this excitement in him to be so terrific and so untiring that all of his life, from one end to the other, would be like going to a fire. Ordinary men, of course, are afraid of it, or they haven't the strength to keep it up. Some of them are really glad to be weak, in order to be safe. But the kind of man I'm talking of—the excitement, unfortunately, might lead him every which way—he might try to go to all the fires at once. Choose one dream, Galahad, and be faithful to that, but don't say the things you decided not to do were necessarily bad; don't make your choice easier by pretending yours was the only good life possible. I hope you will love everything that can be loved, even though you give up most of it—keep the bodily delight in the world, yet discipline yourself."

"It sounds difficult," said Galahad, "even if I knew what to choose. You didn't say what."

"I don't know what," said Guinevere. "But I'm sure we ought to leave the world more exciting than we found it. More beautiful, with more in it to respond to."

"And more to deny ourselves of," said Galahad.

"Perhaps that's what it comes to," said Guinevere. "You wouldn't make it less beautiful, would you, so that we could have it all?"

"Well, I'll do my best," said Galahad. "I'm glad I heard this from some one I have complete faith in. If this is the way you became what you are, madam, it's the right way for me."

"Oh, don't take me for a model! But it's the right way. . . . Galahad, remember—it's the right way, even if you were disappointed in me."

Galahad laughed.

"You've been looking after your horse?" said Arthur.

"Yes, the saddle wasn't right yesterday," said Galahad. "I was afraid his back might be sore."

"Is it?"

"No, we washed it clean, and he's all sound this morning."

"Good. I want you to do an errand for me."

The boy flushed with pleasure. Arthur looked at him for a moment.

"Come over to that corner, where it's shaded."

They walked across the castle yard, and found a bench under the windows of the great hall.

"Do you think you are ready to ride out alone?"

"I think so," said Galahad.

"It's a question of more than the skill to ride and fight. On these errands you'll need courtesy and tact. You see, when we send a messenger from the Court, it's to get something done, but we should fail if we simply gave orders."

"Why would you fail?" said Galahad.

"People wouldn't obey them," said Arthur.

"You could make them, of course."

"But that's war," said Arthur. "I'm talking about government. If I give you a message for one of my lords, you must deliver it with such a tone that he won't think it's a command, yet he'll do it. You'll speak with him—I mean any one of them—in his own house, and I don't wish him to feel like a slave. On the other hand, I don't like to send a message that isn't necessary."

"I see," said Galahad. "Perhaps I could do better if I knew the man I was talking to—his peculiarities, the things I should or shouldn't mention."

"You find that out as you go along," said Arthur. "That's what I meant by tact. You've probably been learning some of it here, consorting with these women."

Galahad decided not to reply.

"My men are splendid when it comes to blows," said Arthur, "but except for your father, there isn't enough tact in the place to deliver a birthday greeting to a horse. I hope you'll be stronger on that side."

Galahad still wondered what the correct answer would be.

"Have these women spoiled you?" said Arthur.

"I think not, sir—the ladies have been kind to me."

"They would be. But I hope they haven't filled your head with ideas of how you should behave—what career you should have, and all that."

"I think I begin to see what sort of man I'd like to be," said Galahad. "I owe a great deal to the queen for her help."

"This errand I have in mind for you," said Arthur. "—I suppose you could ride at once?"

"Whenever you tell me."

"Well," said Arthur, "get your armor and your horse, and start through that gate in fifteen minutes."

He stood up, and Galahad sprang to his feet.

"I'm ready. But you haven't told me where I'm to go."

"I'll wait for you here," said Arthur. "Get on your horse. I'll tell you as you ride out."

The few minutes Galahad was gone Arthur strode up and down. A stableman passing touched his cap, but the king did not notice. He looked up sharply when he heard the hoof-beats. Galahad's armor was new and still shiny. His visor was up, and his excited face seemed particularly young.

"I'm ready for the message," he said.

"Good. You are to ride to your mother's."

"To my mother's?"

"To Corbin," said Arthur. "She'll be glad to see you. Stay a day or so—as long as seems best. Use your tact."

"Very well," said Galahad. "And what is the message?"

"You are," said Arthur.

"King Arthur, you're not sending me away from the Court, are you? Have I done anything to disappoint you?"

"Oh, no," said the king. "Come back when you like, and there'll be more errands for you to go on. But you haven't seen your mother since your arrival, and it will do you good to cheer her up and have a taste of home after your first sight of the world."

"I ought to have said good-by to the queen."

"I'll say it for you. She'll understand."

IX

"MADAM," said Anglides, "there's a man here who asks to speak with you. I told him you were occupied, but he says he thinks you will grant him this favor. His name is Bromel, Sir Bromel."

"I've heard that name somewhere," said Guinevere. "Where was it? Oh, I think I know. Yes, I'll see him, Anglides."

When she was alone Guinevere took from her cabinet a little mirror, and made sure her hair looked to advantage. When Bromel came in she was throned in her tall chair, putting golden threads through a piece of embroidery.

"You won't remember me," he said.

"Perfectly. I have often thought of our talk, so many years ago."

"I take a liberty in asking once more for your interest, madam, but you can do a service to one of your subjects, and perhaps you'll pardon my boldness when you know my errand. It concerns Sir Galahad, indirectly."

"Yes?" said the queen.

"Perhaps I should explain at once, it concerns his mother," said Bromel. "As you know, Sir Lancelot came to the Court a while ago, and he hasn't been to Corbin since. Elaine grieves deeply over his absence, so much that in the end it will affect her health, I've no doubt.

And not only that. Sir Galahad, to whom his mother is devoted, followed Sir Lancelot here, and he, too, has failed to revisit his home. I came to remind Sir Lancelot of these facts, but he is absent on some journey. Then I thought I'd talk to Sir Galahad, but he's absent, too."

"Impossible," said Guinevere. "He was here last night."

"He's not here now," said Bromel. "I'm told he rode out this morning.

"It can't be far," she said. "He'll be back during the day. He may come in while we're discussing him."

"In any event, he isn't here now, madam, and I thought of you as having some influence with Sir Lancelot, and no doubt with his son, too. If you will, you can persuade them to remedy their thoughtlessness."

Guinevere sat thinking a long while. Too long, it seemed to Bromel. He feared he had made a mistake in coming.

"Are you sure they are thoughtless?" she said.

"Madam, I wouldn't hold them so mean as to suppose the neglect was deliberate."

Guinevere seemed to take a new interest in him.

"What is your relation to this problem, Sir Bromel? I've forgotten—you are Elaine's brother?"

"No, madam, I am one of her neighbors. My home is near Corbin, and I've known Elaine all my life. In fact—"

"I remember now," said Guinevere. "What was your errand with Lancelot, if he had been here?"

"I'd have asked him to go back to Elaine, if only for a few hours. The kindness would cost him little, and it would make a vast difference to her. Her spirits are exceedingly depressed, madam, and there are moments I fear she'll destroy herself. Her father is dead, as you must have heard, and she has no interest in life except these two men. Since they have left her, she calls herself a miserable failure. Her state, in my opinion, is serious."

"She once visited the Court, years ago," said Guinevere. "I remember her as a very fascinating woman."

"She is still fascinating," said Bromel.

"Then I should think she'd have many suitors—she might have married before this."

"Madam," said Bromel, "I take it for granted you know she loves Sir Lancelot. Since he won't marry her, there could be no other man. She is of a singularly faithful disposition."

The queen's eyes narrowed rather unpleasantly.

"Why won't Sir Lancelot marry her?"

"Madam, I shouldn't presume to ask him."

Her face softened, and she relapsed for a moment into her own thoughts. "Sir Bromel," she said at last, "what do you wish me to do?"

"With your influence over Sir Lancelot, if you'd remind him that his continued absence, in the circumstances, is somewhat cruel, I believe he'd pay her the slight attention which would make her happy. She knows his duties will always keep him at Court, or take him on journeys."

"May I ask, did she send you to find him?"

"Madam, if she knew I came at all, she'd consider I had wronged her. She herself will never make another appeal to him, and she hasn't the faintest suspicion I'm doing it."

"Then you are a generous man."

"Generous, madam?"

"Sir Bromel, I've heard you were Elaine's first lover. Evidently you still care for her. You are asking me to plead with Sir Lancelot. If I do that, and if he listens to me, your chance of winning her will be small. Or perhaps you don't want her now."

"I oughtn't to bother you with my personal affairs," said Bromel, "but I've always loved her, and always shall. If she'd take me now, I'd be the happiest man in your kingdom. But she simply won't have me."

"Her affair with Lancelot was his fault, I suppose," said the queen. "I can't forgive him for betraying the girl."

"No, madam, I'm bound to say it was largely her own doing. At the time I thought otherwise, but that was because I was bitterly disappointed, and it was easy to blame him. But she herself told me what she intended to do, before she did it. That's why I fought with Sir Bors. You may have heard."

"I believe I have," said the queen. "And you still love her?"

"Yes, madam."

She looked at him, and he met her gaze steadily. He thought she had a very sad face.

"You said you tried to find Galahad, since Lancelot was absent. May I ask what your errand was with Galahad?"

"The same, madam. I wanted him to visit his mother from time to time—not to let her fear he had passed out of her life. He is so young and as yet has so little to do, there's less excuse for him if he neglects her. Not

finding him myself, I hope you'll bring your influence
on him, too, madam. It's not so complicated as with his
father—he has no possible quarrel with her, and he owes
her his duty as a son."

"Has Lancelot a quarrel with her?"

"She played some trick on him," said Bromel. "I
don't know just what, but she told me herself she had
done him a wrong. That's all past now. The main thing
is, she has more claim on Galahad than on Lancelot."

"But if I understand you, you think it would be better
for Lancelot to go?"

"It would do her more good—and I'm thinking of
her," said Bromel. "She is fond of Galahad, but the only
person she ever loved is Lancelot. Madam, she was
brought up rather selfishly—no matter how much I care
for her, I have to see that. But since her one passion has
been Lancelot, she ought to be encouraged as much as
possible. Every one ought to love somebody. I've wondered whether her interest in Galahad wasn't a hope to
reach Lancelot."

"You understand her, I dare say, better than any one
else," said Guinevere. "At least, your account of her is
the first that has convinced me. As for your errand . . .
I quite agree the men ought not to desert Elaine, but it
will be difficult for us to interfere. It was fortunate you
found neither of them. Galahad wouldn't have understood—I doubt if he has the faintest idea of his mother's
relation to his father, and I don't know what he will do
when he learns of it. If you had talked to Lancelot, I'm
sure he would have been annoyed. After all, she made
her choice."

"Did she, madam? I wonder. Of course we like to

think our lives are in our own hands, and no doubt they ought to be—they are, if we are wise. But suppose she wasn't wise? Suppose, what is a fact, that she had grown up doing just what she pleased, without suffering harm. This time, too, she did what she pleased, in a sense, but it wasn't what she expected."

"And you think we should pay for others' mistakes?"

"I don't say we should, madam, but we usually do."

"I suppose," said Guinevere, "if it were to happen again, Elaine would be wiser."

"No, she wouldn't. She loves him."

Guinevere laughed.

"You're an honest man, Sir Bromel, no matter what becomes of your argument. I think Elaine was blind to goodness in the neighborhood. As to what you ask, I'll try to help. Don't hope too much—I doubt if I could persuade Sir Lancelot, and perhaps I ought not to try. Certainly he must not know you came for this purpose—not if we can keep it from him. As it affects him, the subject is delicate. But I'll speak to Galahad. How he will take it, I don't know. What bothers me, I confess, is that your kindness, even if we succeed, will supply only a temporary cure. If they don't care for Elaine, who can make them?"

"Perfectly true," said Bromel. "I've thought of that, but it's best to do what we can at the moment and trust to the future. If Elaine died of a broken heart now, or in despair killed herself, it wouldn't be altogether just to blame Lancelot or Galahad. But they would lose credit with the world—people would say they had neglected her, and they would accuse themselves. I want to bridge over a bad moment, and let the rest take care of itself."

"She won't commit suicide," said Guinevere. "She isn't the type."

Bromel stood waiting, but the queen had no more to say.

"It would be better, of course, madam, if Sir Lancelot were the one."

"To do what?"

"To visit Corbin."

"Sir Bromel . . . I believe I made my position clear. I can't ask Lancelot or any other man to undertake a love affair, least of all with a woman he dislikes, and still less, if possible, with a woman who has injured his name. No doubt he ought to go to her. I say only, I can't ask him."

"I'm sorry to suggest what displeases you," said Bromel, "but I thought Sir Lancelot was under great obligations to you, and would listen to what you suggested."

"You amaze me, Sir Bromel! Why did you think he was under obligations to me?"

"You sent for him, madam, to defend you against Sir Meliagrance."

"I did, and he saved my life. But that puts me under obligations to him. I can't ask anything more."

"Madam, if you'll pardon me, Elaine thinks—no, I've no right to say that. But when you sent for him to defend you, you took him away from her. He was contented enough at Corbin, but after he rode off on your errand, he never came back."

"I see," said Guinevere. "Elaine thinks I broke into her happiness. If I hadn't sent for her lover, he wouldn't have left her."

"She thinks you don't approve of her, madam, and

it could hardly be expected you would. But you can see
how his duties at Court have come between him and her."

"Sir Bromel, I really see nothing of the kind. I see
a foolish girl who got herself into an unhappy tangle,
and a fine man who allowed himself to be over-persuaded
by a foolish girl, and a kind but not altogether wise friend
who thinks such matters can be patched up. We shall
have to let it work out as it will. But I'll speak to Galahad."

"You are very good," said Bromel. "I will take my
leave."

"Where do you go now?" said Guinevere. "To Corbin?"

"No, madam, to my own home. You've never seen
it. It's a small place. I don't believe the king has stopped
there."

"But you must have been here before—whenever it
was you were knighted."

"King Pelles knighted me long ago, at home. He was
over-generous, but he and my father were friends, and
he thought—well, I had his good will in my desire to
marry his daughter. But he had no more influence over
her than I have."

"I see the whole story now," said Guinevere. "You
deserve to be much happier than most of us."

"I'm doing very well, on the whole," said Bromel. "It
always comforts me to think how few of the men and
women I meet I'd change places with. In fact, none of
them."

Guinevere smiled.

"You are everything but a courtier," she said, "and
no doubt—"

Arthur was standing at the door.

"This is Sir Bromel, Arthur, a neighbor of Galahad's mother. From what he has told me about her, I think Galahad has been somewhat neglectful. He ought to visit her."

"He ought," said Arthur.

"I'll speak to him as soon as he comes in. Do you know where he is?"

"I do. He's visiting his mother."

"And he never said a word to me!"

"He wanted to say good-by, but I told him I'd convey his farewells," said Arthur. "I sent him off this morning. You and Sir Bromel are quite right. I had the same idea myself."

X

WHEN Galahad rode into the yard, Elaine was standing at the door talking with Alice and the porter. Galahad tried to come in with dignity, as he had seen other visitors arrive. He resisted the tendency toward a broad grin, and got off the horse with some deliberation.

"For the love of God!" said Alice. "They've sent him back already."

"No," he said, "they—" but remembered why he was there.

Elaine kissed him on both cheeks, and seemed unwilling to let go of him. He held her hand as they walked into the hall. Alice followed, of course, and the porter came near enough to hear the conversation.

"You are a good boy to think of me," said Elaine. "I shouldn't have been surprised if that gay life at Court had driven us all out of your head."

She helped Alice get the armor off, and pushed him down into a chair.

"We'll have steak for lunch," said Alice. "With his favorite onions."

"The steak's fine, Alice," said Galahad, "but without the onions this time, please."

"She doesn't approve of onions, that's clear," said Elaine.

"Who doesn't, mother?"

"I don't know yet. Well, Court life agrees with you, doesn't it!"

"It's great! You ought to see the way they do things, mother—and you'd love the queen. I had no idea there was such a woman."

"She is surprising," said Elaine. "I judge she has treated you well."

"Hasn't she! She says she feels as though I were her own son."

"It isn't safe to ask more than that of any woman," said Elaine. "How's your father?"

"All right, I guess. He's off somewhere—I haven't seen him the last three or four days."

"I suppose Guinevere feels like a mother to him, too."

"She likes him, I think," said Galahad, "but she doesn't seem to be intimate with him. You've no idea how distant father is at Court—not at all chummy as he was here. It's his responsibilities, I suppose."

"Who mends your laundry?" said Alice. "I've always wanted to see that done in a large place."

"Oh, the people who take care of your room carry off your things and bring them back—most of them. I've lost two of my best shirts, mother."

"I thought you were going to say the queen did the darning for you," said Elaine. "That would be the maternal touch."

Galahad detected sarcasm.

"What's new here?" he said.

"Nothing. We go on as usual. As well as we can without you."

Galahad was embarrassed to realize he had not been lonely for her.

"Haven't you done any fighting yet, Master Galahad?" said the porter. "I thought you went to Court to fight them all."

"We had one tournament," said Galahad.

"You were in it?" said his mother.

"Yes. They didn't give me any trouble."

"Your father and the king, of course, would stay out," said Elaine.

"But the king's going to send me on a real errand, if I do well on this one."

"On which?"

"He told me to come back and see you, and tell you what I had been doing, and then he will try me out on some important business."

Elaine's face saddened.

"I thought at first you had come back of yourself."

"Mother, you know I'm glad to come back. But I haven't been away long."

"It doesn't seem so to you," said Elaine. "Alice, you'd better see to that steak."

Alice took the hint, and the porter followed her out.

"You don't look well," said Galahad. "Have you been sick?"

"I've been feeling rather bad, for me," said Elaine, "but I'm all right again. In a week more I'll be myself. . . . The queen is kind to you, I understand."

"Very. Almost every day she talks to me for an hour or so?"

"Where?"

"I don't know what you mean, mother."

"Do you happen to meet her in her garden every day, or where?"

"Oh, in her room in the tower. I usually go there in the afternoon."

"She may not like that, Galahad—you must be careful not to bother her."

"She told me to come."

"Every day?"

"Yes."

"Do you think that's wise, Galahad? People might talk about you—they might say you were too fond of her, or were trying to win her favor. She doesn't see the other men every day, does she?"

"Why, mother, it's perfectly all right. Nobody would talk about her."

"I said about you."

"They'd have no reason to. I've learned a lot from her and I like to go. She's older than you are, isn't she?"

Elaine sat looking into her boy's face.

"You see the king every day, too, I suppose."

"At dinner, and sometimes around the place. He's busy. He doesn't talk much, but he's very decent to me."

"And your father?"

"When he's there, he gives me a lesson with the horse or the spear, but most of the time he's away."

"I'm glad you are with him at all," said Elaine. "He would have more to say to you than the king."

"Hardly. He says what is necessary, and asks me what I'm doing, and when I've seen the queen last—and that's about all."

"He hasn't time to speak much of Corbin, I suppose."

"Not yet."

"I see," said Elaine. "Guinevere does all the talking. . . . What does she talk to you about, Galahad?"

"My future—what I'm going to be. The reason I like her so much, mother, is that she has the noblest ideals I've ever heard of. She knows I shall do well enough as a fighter, but she wants me to be a new kind of man, she says, the kind she thinks men ought to be in a more civilized world—not just quarreling and wasting themselves on women—you know what I mean—but following some one splendid vision to the end. Until I met her, I'd no idea how mean the ordinary kind of life seemed to me—she made me realize my own tastes."

"What would you call an ordinary kind of life?"

"Why, the kind men usually follow, making love to women, and all that."

"And Guinevere helps you to rise above it, does she?"

"Mother, it's thrilling, the way she can make you see the nobility of the sort of career she wants me to have. I can understand now why they say she has inspired men, like father and the king."

"Are they samples of what she wants?" said Elaine.

"Of course—but she seems to think there might be something—I won't say better—but perhaps it ought to be easier, after their example, to go pretty far."

Elaine sat watching him. He was vaguely disturbed by her gaze.

"You'd better get ready for dinner," she said. "Your room is waiting for you—just as you left it."

At lunch Elaine asked him no questions about his life at Camelot, but occupied him with home news. She sent him off to spend the afternoon with the men on the place, who were all curious to see him, proud of the figure he was cutting in the great world. But in the evening she had him beside her in the bay window, looking out on her garden.

"How long can you stay with us?"

"The king told me to fix the time," said Galahad. "I think I'll return to-morrow. He promised to send me on an important errand, and I'm eager to get at it. I'll soon be passing this way often, mother, I hope."

"It will be pleasant to see you," she said. "I've been thinking of what you told me about the queen. Galahad, I hadn't realized you were more than a boy. How did she know you were interested in love affairs?"

"I'm not."

"But she advised you not to be like the men who make love to women. I never should have thought to speak to you about such things."

"You might, mother, if you had been at Court. I've told you how much I like it there—but I've learned some of the unpleasant things that sometimes happen among those people. There are stories of one or two brilliant men, like Gawaine, that they make love to women, if the women let them, just as though they were married. And there are women who let them. I heard one dreadful whisper about Gawaine that a few years ago he behaved that way with quite a nice girl, and she had a child. She killed herself, of course."

"How dreadful! Why did she kill herself?"

"She couldn't live, could she, after that disgrace? I don't see how Gawaine can face people. But that's what the queen was thinking of, I'm sure, when she warned me to start right."

"She might mind her own business," said Elaine. "My son needs no warning from her!"

"It was all kindness on her part—you'd know that if you heard her," said Galahad. "I tell it badly, but when she talks to me I feel ever so much stronger—I couldn't do a mean thing for quite a while afterward."

"No doubt she's kind—I spoke hastily," said Elaine. "I'm grateful for her interest in you. What does your father think of her advice?"

"I don't know."

"Haven't you talked it over with him?"

"No, I haven't. He's busy—and besides, it would be hard to discuss such problems with him, he seems so far above them."

"I dare say he has observed them, under his feet," said Elaine. "Don't get out of touch with him, Galahad."

"Now that I'm to go on errands, I may see him more frequently," said Galahad. "The queen won't approve— she thinks fighting is a vestige of savage times, and she won't have me fight at all unless I'm in the right."

"We shan't quarrel over those opinions," she said. "Fighting always seemed either cruel or funny. Your grandfather used to be greatly annoyed at me for saying so. I wonder what he would think of my son, a fighter, the size of a man!"

"Mother, I've been very selfish. Perhaps father has been, too. I've thought of it since I came home. You ought to have been at Court long ago. That's where you belong. Why don't you go back with me?"

"I've been to Court," said Elaine. "Sometime I'll go and see how you are getting on, but not now—it's too soon. When you become a very famous man. Just now you don't need me—you have the queen."

"I'd like to take you back with me."

"Galahad, I'm glad you were sorry for that poor girl Gawaine treated badly, but I must say she was foolish to kill herself. I'm worried for fear these new and noble visions of yours may lead you to be too hard on her for loving, and too lenient toward her for committing suicide."

"You mean she ought to have faced the consequences as part of her punishment?"

"Galahad, I haven't spoken to you of such questions before, but I'm not sure the girl did wrong in loving Gawaine. I don't know, of course, but I'm not sure. It sounds as though Gawaine had been cruel to desert her, but that's the only sin I have no doubt of. I want you to be a good man—remember I was your mother before Guinevere was—but I want you to be a man, willing to risk something for what you desire with your whole heart. The queen's advice sounds to me a trifle calculating and cautious."

"It isn't calculating to wish people to lead good lives, is it?" said Galahad. "I must have expressed it badly again—she is all the time saying she dislikes the men who sink into safe habits and forget to live at all."

"I dare say we mean the same thing. No matter, if you only remember to be generous. If you think of me when you are with her—"

"I often think of you, mother!"

"Well, when you do, think kindly."

"Why shouldn't I?"

"Because I belong to the elder generation. I've just found it out. I'm a little surprised at your ideas, and therefore you must be greatly out of sympathy with mine. It's always so."

Galahad was a long time getting to sleep. Something had happened to the home or to him, he didn't know which. It must be as the king said, the short experience of Court life had aged him quickly. He didn't like to admit it, but he was out of tune—he felt some discord in everything his mother had said. Had his father felt the same thing? Was that why neither of them visited Corbin?

Alice had a stupendous breakfast on the table for him, but he ate little, and in the middle of the morning he told his mother he must be riding on.

"Stay for lunch, Galahad—you can't eat on the road."

"Alice will put up something for me," he said, "and I'll reach Camelot in time for dinner."

"You know best what is expected of you," she said.

When he was about to go, he stooped from his horse and kissed her.

"Come home as often as you can."

"I'll ride over next week—I'll ask the king if I may. But I'm going to speak to father about having you at the Court."

"Later," she said.

She watched him from the doorway, and when he looked back, just before he disappeared through the gate-tower, she waved her hand and smiled.

For an hour or so he rode briskly. Then from a side path another horseman joined him, bound for the king's city. It was Gawaine.

"Hello, Galahad," he said. "How's Ettard?"

"I haven't seen her recently—I dare say she's well."

"These little quarrels and separations," said Gawaine, "are common in the early stages."

"I don't know what you are talking about," said Galahad. "I've been home, visiting my mother."

"You might easily have been doing worse things than that," said Gawaine. "Your mother is well, I hope?"

A horseman coming their way put them both on their guard. It turned out to be Sir Bromel, homeward bound. They reined in to speak with him.

"I thought you were visiting your mother, Galahad."

"I was—I've just left Corbin."

Bromel looked as though he wanted to say more, but something prevented him. His manner was a trifle less cheerful than usual.

"He lives near you, doesn't he?" said Gawaine, as they rode on.

"Yes," said Galahad.

"He doesn't look your kind," said Gawaine.

They rode a distance without speaking.

"He interrupted us," said Gawaine, "I was going to ask if you meant you and Ettard hadn't quarreled."

"Of course we haven't!"

"I'm glad to hear it. The best of luck!"

Galahad ignored the remark. Gawaine grew rather meditative.

"I wonder," he said, "why your mother never married."

"What?" said Galahad.

"The idea isn't preposterous," said Gawaine. "Bromel, I understand, is fond enough of her."

XI

"Have you deserted me?" said Guinevere. "Here it is—how many days?—since you came to pay your respects to your queen, as a proper champion should."

"I've been visiting my mother," said Galahad.

"So I heard—but not from you."

"Madam, when the king told me to go, I wanted to bid you good-by, but he said to ride at once—he would explain."

"When did you return?"

"Two days ago, madam."

"And I've seen nothing of you—had to send for you, in fact, to see you at all! No doubt Arthur can explain that."

She did not look so severe as her words sounded. She wore a new and becoming gown, and he thought how much more brilliant she seemed than his mother.

"I didn't stay away because I wanted to."

"Certainly not because I desired it! You see, Galahad, you can find no excuse at all."

"I've been very unhappy," he said.

Guinevere found something amusing in the idea.

"I suppose the charms of Ettard pursue you. No doubt you dream about her."

He got to his feet, impulsively.

"Are you like the rest?" he said.

She hid her surprise, and ignored the remark.

"Sit down. I wish to know why you're unhappy."

"With your permission I'll go now, madam. Another time I'll tell you."

"No, it's too important," she said. "Tell me now."

He sat down, reluctantly, it seemed, and showed no disposition to say more.

"What is wrong, Galahad?"

"I'd rather not say—not now, if you don't mind. It has nothing to do with the Court."

"I knew it wasn't personal, your staying away," said Guinevere. "Your father says you treat him even worse. When he was about to speak to you yesterday, he swears you turned your back and walked off."

"Yes," he said, "I turned my back on him."

He saw that his reply frightened her.

"Galahad! You haven't quarreled with Lancelot?"

"I suppose not. Not yet."

"We should all be lost, if that happened."

"I don't want to quarrel with him," said Galahad, "but it would concern nobody else if I did."

"It would concern me," said the queen. "Your father and you— Galahad, did you find your mother well?"

"She's all right, I guess. She had been sick, but nothing serious."

"But was your visit as happy as you expected?"

"Yes, the visit," he said, "but on the way back—"

"What happened then?"

"I heard something—I'll tell you another time."

"Of course, if you'd rather not tell me, I wouldn't think of urging it," said the queen.

"I'd rather tell you than any one else. In fact, you're the only person I'd breathe it to. Some other time."

"Well, I expect something worth while when you do consent to draw the veil," said Guinevere. "You've given it a notable preparation."

"It was about people I thought highly of," said Galahad, "and I can't respect them now."

"It probably wasn't true," she said. "Any gossip you hear around a Court, it's safe not to believe."

"I'm afraid it's true, madam."

She hesitated a minute.

"If it's bad, and if it's true, I hope it isn't about me. I shouldn't like you to know my faults, Galahad."

He smiled, and for the time his usual happiness seemed to return.

"It's as bad as it can be. If it were about you, it would have to be quite false."

Guinevere looked at him intently. He thought she had something on her mind and couldn't decide whether to say it.

"Galahad, I know what you've heard. I can guess the mean sort of person who would tell it to you."

"I heard it by accident, by a mistake," he said. "The man owes it to you that he's alive. If I hadn't remembered what you said, I'd have killed him then and there."

"What did I say?"

"You know—about winning even when you are wrong. I determined to be sure I was right before I struck him. Now there's nothing to do."

"It was about your mother?"

"It was."

"And your father?"

"How did you know that?"

"We all know it here, Galahad."

He seemed relieved that she knew.

"Then you can understand my feelings, madam. . . . And I had just promised my mother to visit her again next week!"

"It will be hard to go now, won't it?"

"Of course I shan't go," he said. "I shall never visit her again."

"Aren't you a little rash? You may be very glad to, some day when you have got over the shock of this information."

"I shan't get over it," said Galahad. "I won't let myself."

"And that's why you turned your back on Lancelot."

"Yes. I shall have nothing more to do with him."

"Galahad," she said, "perhaps it's because we're depraved, but we don't judge your father so harshly. It was a strange affair. He is the only one who can tell you, if he ever cares to. His friends understand it as one of those moments when even a great man may be weak. You regret it, of course, but it wasn't your fault, and I doubt if it has really handicapped you in any way. But the important thing is not to question—no one of us questions— your father's character."

"You don't question it?" said Galahad. "How do you judge my mother?"

"I don't know your mother very well," said Guinevere. "We never had any extended conversation—except once. She may have spoken of it."

"Never," he said.

"No, to be sure, she wouldn't. It was about this very subject. I expressed disapproval of what she and your father had done, and I dare say were doing."

"To think that she would talk about it!"

"If I prefer not to judge her," said Guinevere, "one reason is that I don't know enough. Around this kind of subject there's always confusion of thought. When a woman gets into trouble with a man, we blame him for wronging her, but women in general suspect she took him at some disadvantage, and women who are fond of him are sure she did. Your mother evidently wanted your father's love, even in the irregular way, if she couldn't have it otherwise. If she got what she wanted, you needn't be sorry for her."

"But they aren't married," said Galahad. "Why doesn't he marry her, even now? Why does he keep her off there by herself, as though he were ashamed? I see now why we had such a queer home."

"Perhaps he is ashamed, for one reason or another," said the queen. "But then, it wouldn't be better for either of them, and not very honorable, for your father to marry her if there's no love."

"Is there none?"

"I believe your mother cared more for Lancelot than he for her, and if she had him to herself for a time, it was only by playing some kind of trick on him. Whatever the trick was, he resents it. You can understand that."

Galahad got up and began to pace the room. He suddenly remembered where he was, and took his seat again.

"I beg your pardon, madam—but I'm more disturbed now than when I came here this afternoon. My trouble seemed beyond cure, so I didn't want to speak of it, but it never occurred to me that you wouldn't think it as bad as I do, nor that you would condemn my mother and find excuses for my father. That's the way Gawaine might talk."

"I don't excuse either of them, but they are your parents. Wouldn't it be kind to see the matter in as favorable a light as possible, since I'm talking to you?"

"But how can there be a favorable light? They ought not to have been parents—if they weren't married, it was nothing but a nasty sin for them to love each other, or pretend to love. Isn't that your own honest opinion?"

Guinevere was a little slow to answer that question.

"In that particular instance, yes, Galahad. If you had been present on various occasions when I told your father what I thought of it, you wouldn't say I excused him, nor her either. Yet as one grows older, it seems that a noble love can exist between people who are not married. They ought to be, of course, but the love is noble."

Galahad turned white.

"So you have changed too!"

"I have what?"

"Madam, not so long ago you were disappointed in me for kissing Ettard's hand. You explained what it might lead to. If I find it difficult to forgive my father, it's because of feelings you have taught me, or strengthened in me. I owe to you the vision I have of cleanness and strength. Do you want me to unlearn it now? You must have known about my parents while you were giving me the impulse to condemn them."

"You've touched the heart of the matter," said the queen. "After all, they are your parents. Would my ideals remain beautiful to you if I used them to set you against your father and your mother?"

"You don't need to set me," said Galahad. "I'm against them now—I'm through with them both."

"You are going to be perfectly logical in your scale of

right and wrong even though it condemns your own people?"

"If I'm not, how is it a scale of right and wrong?" said Galahad. "If I forgive my own people and condemn any one else, would that be any better than fighting on a side I know is untrue?"

"Yes, you are certainly logical," she said. "I haven't seen this in you before."

"Madam, I'm disturbed that you seem not to like it."

Guinevere rose and put her hands on his shoulders, and looked into his eyes. He knew well enough it was no gesture of ordinary affection, and the yearning in her face was no such appeal as his mother might have made to Lancelot.

"Tell me, Galahad," she said, "you mean that the ideal you and I have dreamt of means more to you now than father or mother?"

"That's what I mean," he said. "As I see it now, my father and my mother never gave me much, but this ideal gives me something to live for."

"I taught you the ideal," said Guinevere.

"You did. I owe it to you, madam."

"If you found out that I had done wrong, measured by our ideal, would you stick to your logic and condemn me, too?"

Galahad seemed to think the question a very theoretical one. He smiled, but something in her face made him serious again.

"Madam, I don't like to joke on such a subject."

"Which would you do? Don't fail me, Galahad!"

"I would keep the ideal," he said.

"And give me up."

"I would."

"Galahad, you said I didn't like this logic of yours. You were entirely wrong—I adore it. I have succeeded at last! If out of courtesy I said anything that would make Lancelot's sin with your mother seem less detestable, put it out of your thoughts. Hate what they did. If living with them would gradually persuade you to find excuses for them, leave them now. And if ever I do anything unworthy of me, of you and me, promise to abandon me then and there, absolutely, forever!"

"But, madam—"

"Promise, Galahad!"

"If you insist, I promise, but—"

"Now keep the promise, and you will be a greater man than your father. You ought to go away for a while—I'll ask the king about it."

"But I should like your help, madam—"

"I can teach you no more," she said. "If you keep your promise, you will have learned all I shall ever know."

PART FOUR

GALAHAD AND THE QUEST

GALAHAD AND THE QUEST

I

Arthur and his Court walked in the garden after the noon meal.

"Madam, what have you done with Galahad?" said Gawaine. "We haven't seen him since his return."

"I've no idea," said the queen. "Where is he, Sir Lancelot?"

"Galahad has his moods," said Lancelot.

"Oh, that's where he is, is he?" said Gawaine. "That boy will become a legend."

"Why so?"

"He'll be a great breaker of hearts. These serious youngsters with a high moral purpose always turn out the most dangerous."

"Is that why you are so harmless?" said the queen. She saw that the talk displeased Lancelot.

"I'd like a word with you," she said, "about this son of yours. There's a bench yonder. . . . You know what's wrong with him, of course."

"I'm not sure I do."

"Oh, yes, you are. I sent for him yesterday."

"Well?"

"He knows about you and Elaine."

"You told him, did you?"

"Lancelot!"

"Who else would dare?"

"He says he found out by accident. He wouldn't name the person, of course—I think he overheard some man talking."

"Well, there's nothing to do about it," said Lancelot. "He was bound to find out. Is he deeply hurt? That's why he won't speak to me!"

"Yes, he feels wounded. He says you and his mother are no longer his ideal."

"Really?" said Lancelot. "Is he going to judge us?"

"He has done so already."

"When he knows more of life, he'll be merciful," said Lancelot. "At present he's young. Too bad he heard so soon. You straightened him out, I suppose?"

"I think so. I said what I could for you—explained that Elaine was to blame, and almost all men have their foolish moments."

"You might have done better than that, Guinevere, and with more justice."

"I'm afraid I might. I wish I hadn't been so hard on Elaine. . . . Lancelot, why don't you marry her, for Galahad's sake?"

"You know I won't, or you wouldn't suggest it. If I did, you'd hate me."

"I'm sorry for her, Lancelot. I think I understand her now. I don't condemn her altogether."

"Not altogether, but still enough," he said. "I love you, Guinevere, but I know you."

"Do you? It would have been better if I had tried to make Galahad care more for his mother—if I had persuaded him that she wasn't to blame, that you wronged her. It would have been helpful for the boy. You wouldn't have minded, would you?"

"Wouldn't I!" said Lancelot. "I didn't wrong her. She deliberately broke into our happiness, with her eyes open."

"Lancelot, a boy like Galahad will condemn any one for wronging a woman, but he won't understand at all how a woman could have wronged you."

"While you are in your forgiving mood," said Lancelot, "you evidently don't mind taking a little revenge at my expense. Extend to me some of the generosity you shower on Elaine."

"I'm only putting it as you would, I'm sure, if you were talking with Galahad. You wouldn't blame his mother, would you?"

"I beg to point out the difference," said Lancelot, "between my taking the blame and your laying it on me."

"A fair point," said Guinevere, "but you ought to assume the blame thoroughly and at once. Galahad ought to have the best possible idea of his mother. Unfortunately, I didn't think of it in time. I gave him the other impression, that the injured party was you."

"I prize the generosity. I don't want to lose my boy's friendship."

"Lancelot, I'm very much afraid—you see, I've taught him what I tried to teach you."

"No doubt you have. I couldn't understand what it was about, and now when he talks to me, he's like a foreigner. I don't know the language."

"Well, you can see the dilemma. I tried to show him the charitable aspects of your performance with Elaine, but it was immediately clear that if I persuaded him, I should undo all I've accomplished—he would be just another sophisticated, disillusioned young man. I couldn't have that, could I? My one opportunity lost, to help a great soul develop itself! Frankly, Lancelot, his impulse was to recoil with horror from you and Elaine and your sin, and I had to choose between removing the horror, and with it his ideal, and urging him to hold to his quest of perfection, even though he shook off the dust of his feet on you and his mother. What else could I do?"

"Which?" said Lancelot.

"I told him the feeling of horror was correct—he should cultivate it," said Guinevere.

"There was a time," said Lancelot, "when I actually believed you had in you affection and kindness, and for me a certain amount of love."

"Entirely true," she said. "In one sense, I've loved no one as I love you. But for Galahad I've another kind of love, and for him only. I will sacrifice you or anybody else in the world, to make sure he becomes what he has it in him to be."

"If it were a question of sacrificing yourself, you might feel otherwise, Guinevere."

"But I shall sacrifice myself. So far as he is concerned, our position is not to be defended. I see it coming. Galahad is a sort of fate let loose. He will now find out about you and me, and then he will never speak to me again, I'm certain of that."

"He won't find it out," said Lancelot. "Nobody would dare tell him. I'll guarantee that."

"Perhaps he ought to know, don't you think?"

"See here, Guinevere, where do you and I stand? Are you back in that frame of mind where you regretted our love? Or do you agree with the priest, that from any point of view it was a sin?"

"I don't regret it, and it's not a sin for us, but for him it's going to be. I believe I have got him to a point where he will be unable to pardon us. I never dared hope I could accomplish so much. Oddly enough, it was hearing of you and Elaine that brought him on so fast."

"You want him to find out, do you? It's the craziest notion yet!"

"No, I don't want to lose him," she said, "but of course it would be a perfect end. Surely you see that."

"I'm absolutely blind to such perfection! If I could see it, I might have given you satisfaction long ago, but I never grasped the purpose of your ideals. Galahad evidently has a gift for it. He should have been your lover."

"He is my son, not my lover," said Guinevere. "We expect much more of a son."

"When I look back upon our whole story," said Lancelot, "it seems as though I should go mad. I thought I was risking my life and my name for a great love. I counted myself fortunate to do so. But now I don't know what's being done with me. I feel like a wooden chessman, moved around in a game—somebody's working out a problem, but it's not my problem. . . . If you like to have your best friends leave you, why were you so hard on me with Elaine?"

"When was I hard on you?"

"Well—that time on your balcony when she had her arms around my neck."

"Be fair, Lancelot—your arms were about her neck."

"It was her doing, anyway."

"Very likely," said Guinevere. "In her place I'd have done the same. She was trying to take you away from me. But I've outgrown jealousy now, Lancelot. She must have rare qualities, to produce such a child as Galahad. I'm sorry I was harsh with her."

"Elaine is in the background now. That's why you think you've outgrown your jealousy. For my own peace of mind I'll see that you have no recurrence of the disease."

"I'm thinking of Galahad," said Guinevere. "I'm sorry I had to take that attitude with him toward you and her—it would be very helpful if he could have the best possible idea of his mother."

"Not of his father?" said Lancelot.

"That's less important. He's probably learned all he could from you by this time, but I want to build up his ideal of a reverent and devoted life."

"You've no more heart than a fish!" said Lancelot. "Every word you say about my son is an insult to me."

"Can't you understand?" she said. "We shall always be to each other exactly what we have been."

"Just what is that?" said he.

"Lovers, wouldn't you say? Oh, Lancelot, don't be silly! Aren't you big enough to join me in planning for his good?"

"If you have any workable plan, I'll go as far as you will, Guinevere, but there's no value whatever in the kind of remark you've been making, neither for him nor for us. I won't listen to any more of them. But if there's something I can do, tell me."

"I think he had better go on a quest."

"A quest?"

"Yes—some very important errand—looking for something."

"Now you've thought up an easy task! I suppose I'm to invent the something he's to look for!"

"No, I'll invent it. But he ought to ride off, very far this time. If he's away from here, he's less likely to know about us. Of course, he might catch a rumor elsewhere, but the gossips right under our eyes are the most danger- ous. Then, too, if ever he finds out, I'm sure he will go away, and it will be less conspicuous if people are accus- tomed to his absences."

"Arthur has plenty of errands for him," said Lancelot. "His absences will take care of themselves."

"It mustn't be an ordinary errand, you know. I want something to develop his character."

"Have it your own way—I leave it to you."

"Perhaps he ought to go to some new, wild country," said Guinevere, "and put it in order, the way you and Arthur did."

"If your memory goes back so far," said Lancelot, "there was a day when you said that such work was crude and elementary—you urged me on to more spiritual enterprises. I couldn't think of any—which proved the limitations of my soul. Now you can't think of any, either—you rack your brain for the choicest occupation, the best for character, and that sort of thing, and you end up by suggesting that the boy do exactly what I did. There's progress for you!"

"You must see the difference between the two cases."

"Must I?" said Lancelot.

"We have a reason for sending him far away. He told me once that he wished to imitate you and the king, and I said he'd have to find a wilderness to put in order. Of course, I said it to discourage him, but now I'm less sure. Perhaps the vision he has can be achieved only in a new world."

"You're correct this time," said Lancelot. "Only in a new world, with a new kind of men and women in it."

"At least," said Guinevere, "we agree it can't be achieved at Camelot. We belong here, Lancelot. He doesn't."

"I've no use myself," said Lancelot, "for a goodness which has to have a special setting before it can work. The truth is, you give me a very unfavorable idea of Galahad. He seemed more promising to me before you improved him."

II

GALAHAD found Arthur on the ramparts near the gate, watching some masons repair the wall.

"Are you ready for another errand?" he said.

"Quite ready," said Galahad, "but I hope—"

"Well, what do you hope?"

"I shouldn't have said it."

"Finish it, since you began," said the king.

"I was hoping this errand would be a real one."

Arthur gave a little grunt which seemed not to indicate pleasure.

"Guinevere tells me you are rather cut up. You know your own history now."

"I know it now," said Galahad.

"And you don't approve of it, if I've heard correctly."

"I don't."

Arthur looked him over, with a rather grim smile.

"Young man," he said, "has it occurred to you that it's none of your business?"

"What isn't?"

"The behavior of your ancestors."

"Not my ancestors, of course, but it makes a difference in my feelings for my parents if they—"

"If they haven't always come up to the level of your own virtues. That's what you meant," said Arthur.

"I don't think it is," said Galahad. "I had a high opinion of my father and mother."

"So have I of mine," said Arthur. "I think so well of my father that I've spent many hours in a rather busy life wondering who he was."

Galahad looked completely dazed.

"You and I are in the same boat," said the king, "except for the difference I've just suggested. I grew up thinking my father was old Sir Ector; then I learned I was Uther's son; then that my mother at the time must have been the Duke of Cornwall's wife. Which account of my history is correct, I don't know."

"You knew your mother?" said Galahad.

"Igraine. Yes, indeed. She was a notably good woman."

"I was wondering what you thought of her."

"I think she was my mother," said Arthur. "That covers it, wouldn't you say?"

"For me it's not so simple," said Galahad. "I had a peculiar feeling for my mother."

"I had to send you home to visit her," said the king, "and you still don't look on it as a worth-while errand."

Galahad reflected for a moment.

"I was happy here," he said, "and perhaps I was selfishly forgetful, but I did think very highly of my parents."

"Of course you did, or I wouldn't have let you in," said Arthur. "And you'll think well of them again, or I'll put you out. I've no use for a man who passes judgment on his father and mother."

"I don't pretend to judge them," said Galahad.

"Don't you? I heard you had promised your mother to visit her again this week, but you've stayed away because she's not fit for you to associate with. It seems you publicly turned your back on your father, and you haven't spoken to him since."

Galahad flushed, and hung his head slightly.

"You may have acquired some virtue I don't know of," said Arthur, "which gives you the right to go through society separating the sheep from the goats, but if I had such a right, I wouldn't exercise it."

"Wouldn't you avoid people who have done wrong, and go to those who are leading a good life?"

"If we weren't talking about your parents, I'd agree," said Arthur, "provided you show me clearly who has done wrong, and who is doing right, and provided that when you join your select band of saints, they don't feel the average of goodness has been brought down. But in the case of your parents—as a child, you never gave your mother any trouble, I suppose?"

"Yes, I did," said Galahad.

"Sometimes did wrong, eh, just like a human being?"

Galahad felt a bit hurt that the catechism was so elementary.

"Well, I was going to say, your mother didn't cut your acquaintance, did she?"

"It isn't the same thing," said Galahad. "I was younger than she was."

"And your parents are older than you. That's fair. Why should forgiveness be a virtue in the elders but not in the young? I tell you, young man, your mother and father are bigger people than you. They have larger hearts and more generous thoughts."

Galahad was crushed, but not convinced.

"King Arthur," he said, "do you think it was right, what my parents did?"

"Do you mean, would it be right for you?"

"No, was it right for them?"

"You don't grasp an idea easily, do you?" said the king. "I can see how you are responsible for your own conduct, and how you must answer for what you hand on to your children, but how your ancestors, immediate or remote, can weigh upon your conscience—well, I give it up."

"I thought they were perfect," said Galahad.

"Shame on you if you didn't think so—and if you don't! But a grown man would have to be a bit of a fool not to know we all have faults. Your parents, like other people—I won't presume to say, like you—are a mixture of goodness and error. They'd be happy if you'd complete their lives on the good side—be what they failed to be. Would you rather punish their mistakes?"

When Galahad looked up at the king, Elaine's own frankness was in his face.

"After what you've said, I feel small and selfish—yet I can't persuade myself to be sorry I hate what they did."

"Well," said Arthur, "if you try not to be small and selfish, the rest will follow. It's not altogether your fault."

"When I came to your Court," said Galahad, "it was to be with my father, of course, but I hoped to be near you. I had no idea then of Queen Guinevere. I had heard her name, but I never expected really to know her, or to have her friendship. But I wish I could do more things in your service, King Arthur—I'm glad of this new errand. My visit to my mother wasn't the kind of service I mean. I hoped to practise arms, take part in tournaments, that sort of thing, as my father and you once did."

The king was interested.

"And there aren't any tournaments—that's the complaint, eh?"

"There's no complaint," said Galahad. "But there are no tournaments. Not since that one just after I came."

Arthur looked him over, from head to foot.

"When your father and I began, we weren't much older than you. . . . Would you have liked that wild life of ours, before we all became civilized?"

"King Arthur, that's what I thought I should find here."

"And instead, you've been spending your time indoors, learning to talk. See here, Galahad—if I bring back our old discipline, and ask my knights to be the riders and fighters they used to be, will you back me up as your father did, before there were too many women?"

"I'd like it!" said Galahad.

Arthur grasped his hand, and as they stood there in the thrill of their enthusiasm, it would have been hard to say which face looked younger.

"I'd like it, too," said the king. "You and I can do it. From now on we'll have a man's world. I knew these inward theories were unwholesome. Now you may show me what you can do with a rather difficult errand, and when you return we'll start in at once. We'll hold a tournament at Winchester, and if the women don't like it they can stay at home."

Galahad hoped he might be allowed to fight on the right side, but it seemed best not to raise the scruple too soon.

"I won't say you haven't learned something from the Court just as it is," said Arthur. "These recent worries and embarrassments have taught you more than you can tell now. But we've drifted into a life too easy and too idle, and the happiness we used to have has left us. You and I will go after it and bring it back. When you spoke as you did, I saw you were my kind, Galahad. If I weren't stupid, I should have seen it before."

"Queen Guinevere has been such a friend, and she's so wise," said Galahad, "I don't want to appear ungrateful to her Court—it hasn't seemed to me a bad life here."

"But you'd prefer this other life?"

"Yes."

"Well, be grateful to Guinevere for anything she has done for you, and be grateful to your mother and father. Think well of the good things in your past, and turn over a new leaf—that's my way of looking at it. Now this errand—you're not afraid of a hard one?"

"Try me!" said Galahad.

"You may have to kill a man this time. No great harm if you do, but perhaps it won't be necessary. Use your tact. They're as impudent a couple of rascals as I've heard of for some years. I thought the country was rid of their sort. You're to ride to the castle of a good friend of mine, Duke Lianour. We've had no word from him in several months. I sent a messenger—who hasn't returned. Lianour has a good-looking daughter. A rumor has just reached me—we might as well walk back to the castle. I'll tell you as we go."

III

GALAHAD was on his way to Guinevere's tower. In a little balcony, off the terrace, Ettard was standing, watching the afternoon sun across the country. He pretended not to see her, but she called to him.

"Was there ever anything so beautiful?"

He stopped for a moment, just to let her know he wasn't afraid of her.

"Plowed fields are always a surprise to me," he said. "From year to year I forget how neat and brown plowed earth is. One never has a chance to forget the forest."

"But then, you are always riding in it," she said. "How could you forget it?"

It occurred to him she must know he had ridden only once. Or twice, if she counted the distance to Corbin each way.

"I'm sorry you're beginning to ride out like the other men, Sir Galahad. It's lonely at the Court, when you leave us. I was hoping you wouldn't be that kind."

"What kind should I be?"

"You might stay with us," she said. "There ought to be a man or two who could live without getting into a fight every so often. If there were, women would have a place in the world."

"I begin to think they have quite a place now," he said.

"You're not very courteous this afternoon," said Ettard.

"Why not? Don't women inspire men to do their best? Aren't they honored by our achievements?"

"Where did you hear that?" she said.

He disliked her tone. She was flippant. Besides, she seemed to be making fun of him. He wished he had gone on.

"I've never been able to inspire any one, myself," she said. "Perhaps the fault's in me. But if I did inspire a man, the first thing he would do, by the way of showing the inspiration, would be to get on his horse and leave me."

"If we stayed here, you wouldn't be proud of us," said Galahad.

"If I loved a man, he couldn't stay too much," said Ettard.

"Oh, yes—if you loved him. I thought you were speaking of any man."

They both watched the plowed fields for a moment, and Galahad thought he had better escape.

"You aren't going, are you?"

"I have to see the queen," he said.

"Have to!" she said. "Then my bold plea was in vain."

"What plea?"

Ettard laughed, and he turned back to see what it was about.

"You're a strange boy," she said. "Perhaps a very deep one. I can't make you out. I was waiting here to see you."

"Why?"

"To see you."

"Yes, but why?"

Ettard laughed again. They looked at each other.

"I dare say I'm stupid, Ettard, but I don't know what you mean."

"You're not stupid—you're wonderful," she said. "I like you for not understanding. I meant simply that it's a pleasure to see you and talk with you. You'll be occupied with great doings far away from us from now on, I suppose, and we shall meet but rarely, so I hoped for these few minutes. I'm glad I had them—even though you were afraid to speak to me."

"I wasn't," said Galahad.

"To think of a great man, on his way to fight—dragons, isn't it, this time?—and afraid to speak to one dangerous woman!"

"I wasn't afraid—I was in a hurry," said Galahad. "I have an important engagement."

He was quite angry when she laughed.

"I called you," she said. "At the sound of my ominous voice, you didn't dare to keep your engagement, important or not. You must have been too scared to run."

"Just what are you talking about?" he said.

"You certainly aren't courteous to-day, Sir Galahad. I was merely teasing you because since the queen saw you kissing my hand, you've avoided me as though I were the plague."

"That wasn't the reason," he said. "I mean—"

"Yes?"

"I can't explain. You'll have to think of me what you will. But I ought to have been courteous. . . . You know, Ettard, what you say almost always sounds very kind, but you say it with a tone that makes me feel—"

She looked at the plowed fields, and waited for him to go on.

"You really aren't in love yet, in spite of what I found in your hand. Some day you will be, but now you don't even know the language when you hear it. You see, Sir Galahad, I've grown up in a world where men and women talk as though they were lovers—and sometimes they are."

"That's it, I suppose," said Galahad. "There isn't much of that sort of thing in me. I don't inherit it—at least, I think I take after my father."

Ettard could not believe she had heard correctly.

"After your father?"

"Yes. He's no more sentimental than I am."

"Just how simple do you think I am, Sir Galahad? Of course you were joking. Your father is a famous lover."

Galahad drew back as though she had struck him. His face turned scarlet.

"He must have been her lover once—I am her son. But he has had little to do with her since. I intend to imitate him—leaving out the episode which taught him so much, at such a price."

The allusion escaped her at first.

"But I'm surprised that you chose to mention my mother."

"Sir Galahad, she never came into my head! What must you think of me! I meant his great love!"

"He hasn't any," said Galahad.

"Your father not in love? Am I to believe you don't know?"

"Ettard, I've no idea what you're hinting at."

She looked frightened, and very penitent.

"I've done you a great wrong, Sir Galahad. I—I've been teasing you."

"Ettard, is my father in love with some woman now?"

"Of course not, Galahad—unless it's with your mother. I was making up nonsense, in very bad taste. I'm terribly sorry!"

"Who is the woman, Ettard?"

"It's no use, Galahad—you couldn't drag the name out of me."

His face was pale now, but he seemed turned to iron. His voice was as steady as his eye and his hand.

"If it's so, it's so. . . . I shall find out. . . . I'll ask Guinevere."

"My God! Anything but that!"

"Why not?"

"Because it's not true! I lied to you, Galahad! If you pass on this idle, wicked talk of mine, you'll smirch his name with her, as I've done with you! Oh, how sorry I am, Galahad—so sorry!"

He walked away.

"I wonder if you are as sorry as I am," he said.

"May I say one last word, Sir Galahad?"

He turned back.

"When I said he was a lover, I was praising him. You seem to take it another way. Most people think there could be no worship on earth like the love of such a man. Plenty of women would risk their souls for it."

He waited to see if she had more to say. Then he walked slowly on. Ettard stood looking across the fields, toward the distant forest, but she saw nothing.

Through her window Guinevere was looking at the

same landscape. She did not see it, either. For the past
few days she had not been happy. Galahad's trouble
blinded him, or he might have seen the worry on her
face.

"I expected you earlier," she said.

"There's no excuse for my rudeness, madam. I was
interrupted on the way, but I shouldn't have permitted
myself to be. . . . I'm riding again to-morrow—I suppose you know."

"The king said something about a new errand soon—
your father told me it was to-morrow. He's very proud
of you, Galahad."

Galahad bowed slightly, as though his father were
present. His tongue stuck to his throat.

"Will this journey bring you anywhere near your
mother?" said Guinevere.

"It will not, madam."

She smiled slightly.

"Galahad, in spite of what we said the other day, I
think you ought to visit her. You promised, you know."

He bowed slightly again.

"Very well," said Guinevere, "we'll drop the subject,
for the time being."

"You are very kind, madam."

There was a noticeable silence.

"Galahad, why did you come here this afternoon?"

"To pay my respects to you—as you've always allowed
me to do when I go away."

"Pay them, then," said the queen. "I've never seen
you so tongue-tied."

"I beg your pardon," said Galahad. "When I started
out, I wanted to tell you about this new errand—"

"It's a quest, I insist," she said.

"The quest, madam—but as I came over here I lost interest in it. There's a man named Lianour, quite a distance off—he's a duke in his country, and the king thinks he has met with foul play. He hasn't been heard of for some time, and two strange knights have been seen about his castle. Some reports make it seven knights, but the king says it will come down to not more than two, according to his experience with official reports. Duke Lianour has a beautiful daughter, and it may be that the two strangers have made her and her father prisoners. I'm to find out what is wrong, if anything is, and do what I can to mend it."

"If there are too many, Galahad, don't be rash—come back and report."

"So the king says, but I shan't have to come back. If there's anything wrong, I'll try to straighten it out."

"I foresee the end," said Guinevere. "You will rescue the beautiful maiden, and then she will capture you. Or if there is no trouble, really, you will be entertained by her father, and they will express their gratitude to the handsome young knight, and you will lose your heart just the same. Sooner or later it happens. You will be a great lover some day, Galahad, in spite of your prejudice against women."

"Do I understand you, madam? My prejudice against women? You no longer wish—"

"Galahad, I'm afraid I spoke too severely of your mother, just because she's a woman. I wanted to warn you against my sex, but perhaps I overdid it at her expense. It won't be a good thing for you to lose your respect for her. I was unjust. Lancelot was really most to blame. Your mother was only a girl, and unless he intended to marry her, he knew better than to make love."

"I thought you were too easy on my father, the other day," said Galahad. "Now I know you were."

"It seemed right to speak of it before you went away," she said. "By the time you return you will have got over the worst of the shock, and I hope you will keep your ideals without being censorious."

"Madam, I have a wretched impression, whenever we talk about this, that you are trying to draw me back from what you pushed me on to. If I'm censorious, you made me so. You taught me what feelings to have about these matters. When I first met you, I had heard the usual stories of men misbehaving with women, and I wasn't shocked by them—they seemed not worth getting excited about. If I had learned then of my mother, I could have taken it lightly, no doubt. If I had fallen myself into the snare of an enchantress, perhaps I should have boasted of it, as men do. But you are so beautiful inwardly, as well as in your face and body! You've taught me not so much to condemn foulness as to feel hurt at it. That's why argument leaves me cold. If I listened to such pleas as you now make for them, I begin to fear I might slip back rather below what I started from. I could easily be tolerant, but at the cost of what you awakened in me, for which I shall thank you as long as I live. Haven't I reason now to guess what I might become if I lost my way? It's a nightmare, thinking what impulses I must have inherited from both my parents, their history being what it is!"

Guinevere smiled at him, sadly, he thought.

"Impulses!" she said. "Lancelot may have been em-

barrassed when he learned he had a son, but I'm not sure
he was. He always wanted one. We're strangely con-
stituted, Galahad—this might help us to be charitable—
people usually are thankful for their children, no matter
how they are born. Since your mind has to be on the
subject, you ought to imagine the feelings of those men
and women who are childless. Whether they are good
people or bad makes little difference. No matter what
they accomplish, they often have to support a sense of
futility. In them something has come to an end. A
while ago you were despising the body, and I've urged
you to be creative in your mind, but it isn't altogether
satisfying to live only in the spiritual world. There must
be a joy in seeing yourself young again in your child. It
must be a kind of second chance."

"This would all be true, wouldn't it, even if the parents
were married? My mother should have been my father's
wife. Why she isn't, no one will tell me, but I shall find
out. That's where the sin of it lies, madam. There's a
secret dishonor, I'm afraid."

Guinevere astonished him by holding out her hand,
suddenly.

"Good-by," she said. "Take no risks—and come back
to us."

IV

GALAHAD was just mounted, ready for the journey, when Lancelot walked slowly across the courtyard toward him. Those who happened to be passing stopped a moment to watch the famous knight and his great son.

"You're riding now, I suppose," said Lancelot. "Be careful you don't fall into a trap as you come near Lianour's castle. That's the only danger. And remember not to tire out your horse before you get there. It's always a temptation to ride too fast."

"I'll remember," said Galahad.

"It's not a long ride—two days ought to do it. We'll expect you by the end of the week."

Galahad did not answer.

"If we don't hear by that time," said Lancelot, "one of us will come to make sure nothing has gone wrong."

"You needn't—don't come," said Galahad. "I may be later, but I'll manage to send word."

"But you must come back to report! The king expects that."

Galahad was silent again. Lancelot laid his hand on the bridle and looked up at his son.

"What's wrong, Galahad?"

"I can't tell you here. It's no use to tell you at all. That's why I was leaving without—I couldn't talk naturally with you now."

Lancelot's hand dropped from the bridle. The two looked at each other a moment.

"I'll get my horse and ride with you a way," said Lancelot.

Through the town they rode without a word. When they were well into the country Lancelot pulled his horse to a walk.

"Whatever is on your mind," he said, "tell me now, before we part."

"I don't want to tell you," said Galahad, "but if you are bound to have it—I've heard something about your life."

"I know," said Lancelot. "It was inevitable you should. I'm both sorry and glad. It makes you unhappy, naturally, and I'm not proud of it, but what's done is done. Now you know the worst."

"Do I?" said Galahad. "I heard only a whisper. I don't know who she is."

"Your mother?"

Galahad stared—then his face brightened.

"I'm glad you made me speak," he said. "Perhaps I've been misled."

"Your mother and I are not married—you haven't been misled. Our love was a sin, as you probably think. But you are my son, and I'm glad you are."

"But why didn't you marry my mother?"

Lancelot rode on, trying to frame an answer.

"What I heard, explained it," said Galahad. "I heard that you are another woman's lover. But that isn't so, is it?"

"Yes," said Lancelot, "that's the truth."

"Now I know the worst!" said Galahad. "Father, the

very idea made me sick. You deserted my mother, and
then you disgrace yourself with some degraded person,
now when you're not young, and you have no excuse. It's
dastardly!"

"This is strong talk," said Lancelot. "You know how
many men in the world I'd take it from. But I'm sorry
for all the pain I've caused you, and I'll explain more
patiently than your manners deserve. I didn't desert your
mother for this other woman—I was her lover before I
met your mother, and your mother knew I was. Your
mother tried to break up our happiness."

"Because of my mother, and because of me," said
Galahad, "the other woman wouldn't marry you, I suppose."

Lancelot let the question pass.

"It couldn't be Ettard?" said Galahad.

"It could not!"

"No, she's too young. I'm glad I don't know who
it is."

"Since you have found out," said Lancelot, "let me
tell you how I look on it. My affair with your mother,
I'm ashamed of. My love for this other woman is the one
blessing of my life."

"I've no wish to accuse you or her," said Galahad,
"and I don't want to talk of it. Nor think of it."

They rode on slowly.

"If I had my choice of fortune," said Lancelot, "I
could imagine happier and simpler experiences than I've
gone through. I wish I'd had all the good this woman
has brought me without the agony of mind along with it.
But so far as I can see, no one has a simple fate. I'm
thankful for what I've enjoyed."

"I don't understand," said Galahad, "how any real good can spring from ignoble conduct. A certain unmentionable pleasure, yes—but I suppose that's what gives you the agony of mind when you think of it now."

"You're much mistaken," said Lancelot. "The agony of mind comes when I remember how disloyal I've been. The pleasure you refer to, one doesn't mention—but that's because it's too sacred."

Galahad dug his spur into his horse, and then brought him down to a walk again.

"The relations men have with every kind of woman," said Lancelot, "are pretty much the same, everywhere and always. When you're older, you'll accept them as a fact of nature. But in addition, there are more beautiful relations with exceptional women. You've got to see it as a whole, Galahad. You can't confine yourself to the spiritual ecstasies, and discard or ignore the bodily impulses out of which they grow. Love is a common thing, and it still rests on common facts even when it becomes noble."

"You seem to be speaking of common women," said Galahad. "You forget I have known Guinevere."

"I'm speaking of what is common in women and in men," said Lancelot. "That pleasure you referred to— it's either the beginning or the end of friendship between a man and a woman. Sometimes they love in their souls, as you would say, but at last they find each other's arms,— souls are so lonely. And sometimes the body comes first, but it makes them hungry for what only soul can satisfy."

"You took my mother in your arms," said Galahad, "but your soul didn't grow much. And Guinevere has given me a soul, I think, but our love is—well, it's pure."

"Those are the two extremes," said Lancelot. "In such cases, the friendship doesn't last. I left your mother, you know."

"I haven't left Guinevere," said Galahad.

"There's some difference in age between you and the queen. And you're in the habit of consulting her as you would an oracle. The test will come in some girl who might be a companion. The woman I love has given me a soul. When you know more, you'll admit it's much the same soul as you have acquired. But she gave me herself, too. For both gifts I'm thankful."

"We shall never understand each other," said Galahad. "If you weren't my father, I wouldn't listen to such talk. I have never heard anything so base."

Lancelot stopped his horse.

"Good luck!" he said. "I'll turn back here. If I weren't your father, I shouldn't have wasted so much breath on an impudent young fool. My reason for arguing with you is simple enough, from my point of view. In a sense—I wonder if you can grasp this idea—I think of you as my son. I shall never have another. I want you to be a better man than any of us. Your distaste for meanness can't be too strong to please me. But if you're to be great, it must be in conduct—it's not enough to be a critic. Any one can recognize a fault or a failure. Don't spend your energy condemning—do better yourself. It's difficult. That's why great men are rare."

"It would be easier," said Galahad, "if I were not your son."

Lancelot wheeled his horse and spurred toward Camelot. Galahad watched him go, then pulled down his visor and turned toward his quest.

V

Lancelot avoided the Court for the rest of the day. In the evening he asked Guinevere if he might speak with her a moment. Arthur was busy with Gawaine and Bors. The queen led the way to her room in the tower. It was she who spoke first.

"I am losing my courage, Lancelot. He will find out, any day now."

"What has happened?"

"Nothing yet, but yesterday he was here, and from what he said, I'm surer than ever he will leave us. I had no idea I should feel it so keenly. Oh, Lancelot, he's the son we should have had!"

Lancelot stood looking at her, as she put her hand to her eyes. Her tears disturbed him, but he was not in the mood to offer comfort.

"Did you speak to him again about his mother?"

"Yes, I told him he ought to visit her."

"I dare say you made that revision you contemplated, to exonerate her and lay all the blame on me."

"She is very lonely, I think, and I realize a little how I should suffer in her place. Lancelot, he's absolutely through with her, as though she were a lost soul. He will judge me more terribly."

"If no one tells him your story," said Lancelot, "and while I'm alive no one will, you have nothing to worry about. I suppose he ought to see his mother, theoretically,

but I'm not sure. I don't know whether she has any influence over him, or what it would be if she had. She
wanted a life of passion—the Tristram and Iseult sort
of thing. Having missed that, she has no other re-
sources."

"Yet it seems a bit cruel. She won't improve if you
leave her alone in that stagnant existence."

"I wish I knew what you really have in your mind,"
said Lancelot. "Do you advise me to return to her, and
go on from where I left off? Even now, I presume to
think, she would have me."

"Don't be sarcastic," said Guinevere. "Galahad ought
to see her from time to time, and show the affection a
man owes his mother. That's all I meant."

"It would be more than that before we got through.
Once let Galahad begin to visit her, and—well, you don't
know Elaine so intimately as I do."

"I've every prejudice to believe what you say," said
Guinevere, "but in my heart I suspect you are unjust."

"It's too late now," said Lancelot. "We've lived it
out, and we all know where we stand. You can't make
her happy unless you destroy our love. That's the whole
case. I don't love her, and I never did. If I loved no
one else, it would be decent of me, I suppose, to give her
what attention would be necessary to content her. But
since I do love you, I'll not sacrifice my better self to
please her whim. Besides, Guinevere—"

"You were about to say—?"

"If I did Elaine even an impersonal and innocent kindness, you'd be jealous as the devil."

"I was jealous once," said the queen. "That's **all**
past."

"I'd be facing a choice between you and her," said Lancelot. "Don't let's talk of it. But if I can't return to Elaine, I certainly can't urge Galahad to do so. It's a bad business—you'd better leave it alone, Guinevere."

"Lancelot, I want Galahad to go back to her. I want him to acquire some charity before he knows of our lives."

"He knows all about my life now," said Lancelot. "I rode with him a mile or so on his quest, and he told me he had heard I was some woman's lover."

"I shall never see him again!" said Guinevere.

"Why not? He doesn't know who the woman is."

"You didn't tell him?"

"You know I wouldn't. I told him the story was true, so far as I was concerned."

"How did he take it, Lancelot?"

"He listened to me as long as he could, then he lost his temper and gave his opinion of me—or it was the other way, I lost my temper and left him on the road. Guinevere, you've made a prig of him."

"He's not so wise as you and I are—and I don't want him to be. What did you say to him, Lancelot?"

"I told him my love for his mother was a sin, but my love for this other woman—that's you—was my chief virtue."

"He probably couldn't see the difference," said Guinevere.

"At the end," said Lancelot, "I tried to tell him that any great affection between man and woman will have something in it which he, in his ignorant cocksureness, would call base."

"I don't see how that information could help him."

"It might teach him something about life, a subject in

which he's at present a child. When you first talked to me about our dreams, Guinevere, our dreams of a wonderful career, I thought you meant a vision of what might possibly be done. It's common sense, to have such dreams. But what you were after is clear now—you've succeeded with Galahad—you wanted to fill my head with ideas which couldn't be carried out."

"Couldn't they?"

"No, they couldn't. They don't start with this world as it is. You've sent that boy looking for a kind of goodness which belongs in heaven."

"Not a bad kind, then," said Guinevere.

"But it doesn't exist here. The kind of goodness he might see, you've made him blind to, and of course, to the badness as well."

"That point escapes me," she said.

"Well, when he asked me whether I was some woman's lover, I said I was. There was a little virtue in that, wasn't there? And I declined to involve you. That was decent, don't you think? He gave me no credit for frankness nor for generosity. But the mean person who told him about his mother, and the one who set him on this second story—I believe he admires them, rather, for telling what was strictly true. That's pretty bad."

"Lancelot, if you will marry Elaine, I shan't be jealous. The more I think of it, the more that seems the way out. Then you can go to him and say he was right—his criticism convinced you, and therefore you have corrected the mistake you made."

"And abandoned the other woman?"

"That would have to follow."

"The purpose of this remarkable plan is what?"

"He could go on with his own life, without further distress over his elders," said Guinevere.

"I know what you mean—he would stay at the Court. But after I'm a married man, what if he discovers who it was I loved before I reformed? Off he'd go, and I'd be left to console Elaine. No, thanks!"

"Then we ought to consider whether it's best to wait till he hears our secret from some unkind tongue, or whether we ought to tell him ourselves."

"Quite an idea! Ask him up here to your room, for an informal but intimate conference, and—just to smooth matters over—you tell him that you, being the queen, and wife to my best friend, have been my love for twenty years or so. I could watch the windows, to see he didn't jump out and break his neck. Or perhaps you've got him trained so that he'd send for Arthur, and perhaps for Elaine, and we'd have a perfectly frank family party!"

"Don't joke about it, Lancelot—I'm serious. You'd have to tell him. You could say we wished him to know all now, while we were here to explain our reasons. You could make clear in what sense we consider our love virtuous, and what good to the world has come from our embraces."

"Do you expect me to admire this sarcasm?" said Lancelot. "Or is this, after all, the vision you think you've been preparing him to receive?"

The tears in her eyes, and a certain drooping of her majestic form, made him sorry for his words. She was more deeply troubled than he had thought.

"Seriously, Guinevere, it won't do—I'm afraid it won't."

"At least we should know what he thought of us—we shouldn't have to wait. It would be our chance to put it in the best light."

"For him there would be no such light. He'd leave us, as you've said."

"Yes, he would," said Guinevere. "No doubt of it."

"Well, we needn't guess what he would do in case I told him, for I won't. No man could reveal the name of the woman who had given herself to him, and I won't be the exception for the sake of facing Galahad's scorn. But if the lady wishes to boast of her lover, that's her recognized privilege. Why don't you tell him yourself?"

"I'll die first! Lancelot, he thinks me—"

"Off and on," said Lancelot, "I've foreseen all sorts of endings to our splendid love, but I never thought of this. Our love! You're so proud of it, you'll die if the boy knows!"

"How about your own pride? Tell him yourself!" Her face lighted with a happy inspiration.

"What a wonderful idea!"

"Which one?" said Lancelot.

"I was thinking how brilliant it would be to do what you suggested—to tell everybody—go to Arthur and say we are lovers—tell Galahad—decline to recognize any shame in what we know to be pure."

"I always hoped to die with my armor on," said Lancelot. "Your idea would probably give me my wish. No, Guinevere, it's all too late. I'm for seeing it through as we began, and taking what comes."

VI

Ettard was watching the gardener planting roses. Guinevere and Anglides were walking through the paths, and they came up just as the bush was set.

"More roses!" said Anglides.

"Something for poets, ma'm, to talk about," said the gardener, moving off with his trowel and watering pot.

"Do you ever wonder, madam, what such people think of us?" said Anglides.

"I suppose they tell in their poems."

"I meant the gardener, madam."

"Oh! What should he think of us—except what every one does."

"I suppose you mean women," said Ettard. "Perhaps he thinks what the poets do—that we are the costliest form of rose-bush."

Arthur and Gawaine came down from the terrace.

"Now this is something like!" said Gawaine. "Madam, you have the art of taking advice."

"Gawaine," said Ettard, "what do gardeners think of women?"

"Why gardeners? Are they wiser than other men?"

"They had the first opportunity," said Ettard.

"This particular gardener, I happen to know," said Arthur, "is orthodox. He believes women are so many prolongations of Adam's rib."

"Gawaine," said the queen, "I thought you pretended to know everything about women."

"Please God, no, madam. I try not to. I prefer to admire."

Ettard laughed, but the queen did not smile.

"If any one had asked me what I knew about women," said Arthur, "I should have replied that I don't even understand gardens. The two things go together. While Lancelot and I were making our way in the world, we did without women and without roses. As soon as I had the kingdom in hand, I got me a garden. I learned that no castle was royal without one."

Gawaine smiled.

"I believe you married, about the same time?"

"I lost my heart, Gawaine. This garden was one of my gifts to Guinevere."

She knew they were watching her face.

"I've walked in it many a season," she said. "Gardens don't grow old, like some other beautiful things."

"You refer to women, madam," said Ettard.

"Yes, I do."

"Then I refuse to be referred to. I never felt younger."

"I expect Galahad back to-morrow," said Arthur.

Ettard started at the name, and saw that the king had his eye on her.

"I've thought of him much, these days," said Guinevere. "What an ordeal for an inexperienced boy!"

"Do you think it was really dangerous?" said Gawaine.

"He wasn't in danger—I'm confident of that," said Arthur, "but he probably had to fight. My information was rather specific. Two rascals have seized Lianour's property, and his pretty daughter, for good measure, and

they're holding the family prisoners till they get formal
consent for the matrimonial relations they may have estab-
lished already."

"Arthur! How shocking!" said Guinevere.

"It's the worst thing that's happened in a long while,"
said the king. "It came just at the moment to try out
Galahad. He can handle the two, but they won't think
so. If I had sent Lancelot, they would have run away.
Now, against a mere boy, they'll come out and fight. He'll
have to kill them both. That's just about what I want."

"Arthur, you're reverting to the savagery of your
youth!"

"I am. For a while there I fell away and became
polite, but the kingdom, in my humble opinion, has gone
to the dogs. Now I'm on my feet again, and I'll begin
once more with youngsters like Galahad. He'll do well, if
I can get some sense into his head. So far as fighting
goes he's his father all over."

Guinevere walked toward a garden bench, and the
others followed. Gawaine had no intention of letting the
conversation die.

"You feel there's a need of starting once more from
the beginning? Isn't the kingdom going to suit you?"

"Going?" said Arthur. "Nothing goes on here but talk.
That means we have surrendered to the women. Galahad came to us with an ambition to do a man's work.
Now he is trying to prop up the universe and abolish
human error, chiefly by meditation and dialogue."

"He did well till he met Ettard, here," said Gawaine.
"She paralyzed the active side of his nature. Love works
that way with some men. A different type, like you and
me, will become quite busy."

"Well, we'll see what Galahad can do when his lady

is watching him," said Arthur. "As soon as he returns I shall hold a tournament at Winchester."

"I haven't heard that word for years," said Guinevere. "A tournament!"

"You'll hear it frequently now," said the king. "We've grown too soft. And I've had another idea, too. You women ought to find something to do."

"What, for instance?" said Guinevere.

"What you please, so long as it's useful. When I was young, even the ladies worked. Now the servants cook and clean, and fine women consent to exist. I thought it out the other night, when I couldn't sleep. I've never liked the theory that women should inspire men to great deeds, but I couldn't see what was wrong with it. Now I do. If the women want to inspire anybody to work, they should inspire each other."

"What sort of work would you prescribe for me?" said Ettard.

"Go home and get married. Guinevere has Anglides to look after her. You've seen enough of the Court to know how to care for a house of your own, and you could brighten up a small place."

"Hadn't I better wait till a lover appears, King Arthur? I hate to confess publicly, but no one has asked for me."

"I'll find you a husband," said Arthur. "Some good, honest man who'll love you all you need, and if you want a larger sphere for your affections, you can find it in your children."

"You needn't be indelicate," said Guinevere. "I thought we had got beyond the doctrine that women are here just to increase the population."

"Well," said Arthur, "it's still their one distinctive contribution."

"I think I'll go back to the castle, if you don't mind," said Guinevere.

"We'll all go," said Arthur. "But I'll ask Ettard to stay a moment—there's something I want to ask her."

When the others had walked ahead, Ettard felt uncomfortable. There was nothing friendly in the king's face.

"I shan't keep you long. . . . Are you making love to Galahad?"

She hesitated.

"I've flirted with him."

He waited without change of expression.

"You haven't answered my question."

"I suppose I've made love to him—but I didn't think of it that way."

"Do you love him? Do you want to marry him?"

"I love him."

"It will be best for you to leave the Court voluntarily," said Arthur. "It would embarrass your family as well as yourself, if I sent you. I'm assuming that Galahad has not made love to you."

"What have I done that's wrong, King Arthur?"

"Nothing, I dare say—but you're a disturbing element. You're doing no good here. You might upset Galahad, and I'm taking no chances. I'm going to clean up this place, and I count on him to help me."

"Let me stay, King Arthur! I'll do nothing you don't approve!"

"My dear child, it makes no difference what you promise, nor what I approve. There will remain you and

this boy you're in love with. If it were the other way
around, if he were wooing you, I shouldn't interfere. But
when the woman is the one, it's a bad business, whether
she gets him or not. Galahad's mother was a fine girl,
but I don't wish that episode to repeat itself in the second
generation."

"You insult me!" said Ettard. "You've no right to
speak so. I said I loved him, but you know how much
older I am than he—it's more like a mother's love."

"Not having a father, the boy seems to have too many
mothers. He has an unbalanced life. I'm less unkind
than you think. When do you intend to leave?"

Ettard sprang to her feet, white with rage.

"We'll return to the castle together," said the king.
"The walk will cool you off."

He was so impatient, he could hardly wait till Anglides had announced him.

"I saw the king first, madam, and then I hurried to tell you."

"You are home again, safe," said Guinevere. "You need tell me nothing more—that's enough good news for one day."

"I killed a man," said Galahad. "The other one's horse was too fast, or I should have killed him, too."

"Galahad! How dreadful!"

"It wasn't. I was angry all the way, and when I got there and they rode at me, I understood how the king feels—some methods are better than talking."

"And having rescued the beautiful maiden, you fell in love with her?"

"No."

There was a strain in his voice that made her look at him.

"She was dead. I got there too late."

He dropped into a chair, bowed his head suddenly, and sobbed as though his heart were broken. She went to him, and tried to lift his face to her.

"Don't, Galahad. You've had to go through too much—that's what's the matter. You were in no condition to ride on that terrible business. You poor boy!"

He got up and walked to a window. Guinevere let

him recover himself. He cleared his throat, and turned toward her, but said nothing.

"I shan't forgive myself for letting Arthur send you. This is the sort of thing we used to have all the time, when I was young. I stood it better then—my youth and ignorance, I suppose. He simply made an executioner of you!"

"No, madam, I'm glad I went. Now I've seen what needs to be done—we should go at such fellows before it's too late. As soon as I'm rested I want to ride off again. After the tournament."

"Oh, the king told you!"

"Before I started out. I meant to speak of it that last day I saw you. We're going to revive tournaments, all the old chivalry, madam—the king says I may help him—of course with your ideals added. If I got on well with my errand, he said we might begin at once."

"Yes, he said so the other evening, but I didn't know you and he had thought it out together. I suppose you will become rough and hard, as the men who did that sort of thing used to be. Well, I'm glad I knew you in your unspoiled days."

"I shan't change so—I promise, madam."

Guinevere smiled.

"Madam, if you knew my thoughts as I rode out to Lianour's, you would understand what your ideals count for with me. Except for you, I would not have returned. Not even for King Arthur, and our plan together."

"What have you against the king?" said Guinevere.

"Madam, when I'm near him, I have to be near my father."

Guinevere felt the moment was at hand. In a flash she saw how she must meet it.

"You ought to have forgiven your father by this time, Galahad."

"You don't know," he said. "You don't know!"

"If I don't, you'll have to tell me. What were you thinking of, on your ride to Lianour's?"

"Just before I came to say farewell, I heard that my father is the lover of some woman. I couldn't keep my mind on what I was saying to you, madam, with that last horror fresh in my ears. As I rode out, my father joined me. I asked him, and he admitted it."

They looked at each other.

"Madam—don't tell me you knew this about him, too?"

"Yes—I have known this."

He caught his breath.

"Madam—for God's sake!—because I worship you!— don't tell me I ought to forgive him and this woman!"

"No, Galahad, I won't. I don't see how you possibly can."

He sat wiping his brow.

"You've known it a long time?"

"Before your father met Elaine, this woman was his mistress. She wasn't generous enough to love him openly, and of course she was the reason he couldn't marry your mother."

"You always find excuses for him," said Galahad.

"This time, perhaps we might find an excuse," said the queen. "When you know who the woman is—"

"I don't know her, and I don't wish to learn her name. It would be only another person to hate."

"You would hate her?"

"Perhaps hate is too strong a word. I've never met her, or I should have had some suspicion of it. But if

it were a woman I had met and had respected—yes, I'd
hate her, for the harm she has done. I couldn't stay where
she was. You know why I can't meet my own mother.
What could we talk about? How could either of us
pretend we weren't thinking of our history? It would
be too horrible! To meet this second woman would be
worse."

"Galahad," she said, "you hoped I wouldn't ask you
to forgive. I shan't. But wouldn't you try to understand—to imagine how it happened? I think you ought
to have a proper curiosity to know why people—"

"I've no curiosity whatever," said Galahad.

She waited a moment.

"You must remember," she said, "I'm used to the
strange and wicked things people do—I've lived more
than twice your years—dear boy, I'm fifty times as old
as you are! Nothing surprises me now. I can suppose
this reason or that, a little extenuation here and there, for
what you and I would both deplore. Your father does not
love your mother—never did. He's a lonely man, as
all his friends know. If there's a woman who could
comfort and help him, who perhaps ought herself to have
been his wife and his son's mother, if fate had been
kinder—will you condemn them for saving as much as
they could?"

"It wasn't so—my father told me he loved this woman
before he saw my mother."

"Very well," said Guinevere, "take it that way. Suppose he loved some good woman before he met your
mother, and suppose your mother, by some temporary
fascination, managed to break down your father's loyalty,
and suppose he went back afterward to his real love, who

was generous enough to understand and forgive. Suppose, that is, it wasn't this woman who prevented his marriage with your mother, but your mother who made any happy love impossible for this woman. What then?"

"He ought to have married one of them, at least," said Galahad. "I can't follow these suppositions, madam. Perhaps, as you say, because I know so little about the world—but what a world it is I am to learn more about! My father ought to have made up his mind."

"You told me I was finding excuses for him," said the queen. "I suppose you think this affair of his has degraded him—has somehow debased him, from the man he once was. In fairness to the woman, I must say she helped him outgrow many rather crude traits. I can remember when his senses were not what we should call delicate, and his manners, beyond rough honesty, were undeveloped. Arthur and he were setting up the kingdom then—or they had just finished it—and skill with a battle-ax they thought the supreme accomplishment. She helped him to be gentle, and to have the desire for fineness. You might say, he ought to have had all that inspiration without the sin. He should have loved a better woman. I agree. But in those days the choice of women wasn't large. I dare say, if your father had known an altogether good woman, this story of his past would not now be troubling you."

"If he could have come here when he was young," said Galahad, "and found you!"

"There's one other thing. You ask why he didn't marry one of them. I'll tell you. He couldn't marry your mother, because he loved this woman, and he couldn't marry her because she already had a husband."

"He hasn't stolen a purse at any time, has he?" said Galahad. "Nothing else remains."

"There's no excuse," said Guinevere, "but of course the woman was most to blame. No doubt she would say her husband disappointed her, or he was out of harmony with her nature, or he bored her. It is thought her husband didn't consult her wishes about their marriage—he took her as a sort of payment on a debt—he had done some valuable service to her father. You ought to have these feeble lights on the problem, Galahad—they are the best I can offer you. When all is said, we are where we started from."

"Not quite," said Galahad. "At first you said you didn't know how I could forgive them. I wish, for once, madam, you'd tell me why you think they are wrong."

"I will," she said.

To his surprise she rose from the tall chair, came slowly toward him, took his face in her hands, and kissed his forehead.

"My knight!"

He thought she had lost her wits. She seated herself once more, and smiled at him. He remembered, with a pang, his mother at Corbin door.

"This woman is unforgivable," she said, "because she was false to a man who loved her, who was true to her, who spent his youth trying to give her honor and happiness. She is unforgivable because she never gave herself entirely to your father, as your mother did. I suppose that's why she disliked your mother. She wouldn't give your father the son he longed for. She hadn't your mother's daring.

"And your father is unforgivable because the woman's

husband was a friend of his. He was false to every kind
of trust. He has pretended for years to be the husband's
friend, while he has been the wife's lover."

She spoke as though she were pronouncing sentence
in court. Galahad listened fascinated. She waved her
hands, as though that were all.

"You and I are one," he said. "I can never forgive
them."

She did not answer, and the silence became awkward.
He stood up.

"Good-by," she said.

"I've tired you with my troubles—thank you for all—"

She shook her head and motioned him to go. He had
almost reached the door when she called him back.

"From the day I came to Camelot, your father and I
have been lovers. He would have married your mother,
if he had not loved me still. I shall love him till I die."

He clutched at the side of the door.

"You!" he gasped. . . . "King Arthur!"

She sat watching him.

He turned and left her.

PART FIVE

THE WHITE ELAINE

THE WHITE ELAINE

I

"I'VE an idea you ought to go to the tournament, after all," said Guinevere. "They'll connect your absence with the fact that he rode away."

"They would be right," said Lancelot. "Arthur arranged the tournament chiefly for the boy. I couldn't put any heart into it now."

"Well," said Guinevere, "I lost my interest in tournaments years ago, and I shan't make an issue of your attending this one. . . . But Lancelot, you could ride on an errand for me, if you would."

"I will," he said. "What is it?"

"I want you to see Elaine once more, and cheer her up. My jealousy is ended. She lost her man, and now she has lost her son. I'm somewhat responsible. I wish you'd ride over and be kind."

"It's quite safe for you to urge me," said Lancelot. "You know I won't do it."

"Yes, you will. I want you to."

"Guinevere, you don't want anything of the sort. You enjoy the exaltation of an unselfish idea, but you and I both know where to stop."

"I mean exactly what I say—I want you to see Elaine and cheer her up. You needn't overdo it, of course. But my jealous disposition has left me, and I hope I'm beginning to be just."

"If you begin again on this subject," said Lancelot, "I'll let you talk, but don't imagine I take it seriously. The truth is, I think you're verging on the hysterical. Galahad's disgust and his disappearance over the horizon, look to you like a masterpiece of character-training, and in the flush of your triumph you want to dispense largess. We'll leave it there. Any comfort I gave Elaine would turn out to be too much. I haven't the skill to tell her how sorry I am she has lost me, nor to explain why you are elated to have driven Galahad away. And you don't want me to overdo it. Really, Guinevere! What would you think of comfort which stopped short of affection?"

"Not even that would trouble me now," she said. "I've had what life could give. I've done what I was intended to do."

"It sounds," said Lancelot, "as though you were through with me. If you are, don't try to designate your successor in my devotion."

"You can't exasperate me to-day," she said. "Your sarcasm is vain. Yes, if you wish to know, I believe the fiery part of our love is burned out. From now on we shall have our friendship—and our memories, Lancelot. All the heart I had left, I gave to the boy."

"I'm not through myself," said Lancelot, "and I doubt if you are. The quickest way to prove it would be for me to visit Elaine."

"Prove it, then—I've asked you to."

"I won't."

"Didn't you promise?"

"I was hasty."

He sat looking at her. In spite of his grudging words, he knew how beautiful she was, and even after their quarrels and resentments, he still loved her. Since Galahad's going away she had taken on glamour. Her eyes were feverishly large, her color more delicate than when she was a girl.

"Couldn't you ride there and back in one day?"

"I suppose so."

"That would satisfy me."

"Would it satisfy Elaine? You really haven't considered her, though this is supposed to be for her pleasure. Shall I tell her you sent me? If I went of my own will, there'd be no excuse for treating her coldly, or for leaving her at once. She won't believe you are sorry for what has happened—she'll think you wanted to flaunt your success."

"I am not sending you with a message," said Guinevere, "I'm sending you. She'll appreciate the difference. Do anything you like, comfort her as you think best, and I'll understand. I know now what excuse she had."

"What was it?" said Lancelot.

"A craving for a son."

"Nonsense!" said Lancelot. "Complete nonsense!"

"I'm not sure a man can judge such things," said the queen. "To you it would seem more plausible if I said she couldn't resist your charms. But having Galahad—and losing him—has taught me much."

Lancelot continued to look at her. A slight smile came over his gaunt face.

"If you would go to-day," said Guinevere, "I'd be very grateful."

The smile left his face, but he said nothing.

"Will you, Lancelot?"

"No, I won't."

"Not even for love of me?"

"Do you think that's a fair argument," he said, "after telling me your own love is burned out?"

She came to where he was sitting, on a low bench against the wall, and took his large hand in her white fingers. He was as unresponsive as the tapestry behind them.

"I'm not going to be wheedled into it," he said.

She reached up toward him—he couldn't help kissing her lips. She let the argument remain in that state for a while.

"When the boy returns," he said, "he can visit his mother. He'll be ready to forgive her now."

"Is there any word of him?"

"No," said Lancelot. "There isn't a trace."

"He won't return," she said. "I'd be disappointed if he did. He will make his name in the world—a great name, but somewhere else."

"Well, if it's a mistake for him to return to us," said Lancelot, "you shouldn't ask me to revert to Elaine. I do very well, where she isn't."

"Haven't you a particle of affection for her—not really?"

"We've discussed it enough," said Lancelot.

"Not quite," said the queen. "The question is whether you still love me. If you do, get on your horse and ride to Elaine. Go now."

"But, Guinevere—"

"Go in any case," she said. "If you won't do this for

me, I can't pretend to be happy with you. I'd rather you
went off somewhere for a while, Lancelot."

"You don't mean what you say—"

"I do. I want you to see Elaine. If you won't, you
hurt me—it isn't pleasant to learn you've ceased to care.
There was a day you would have done harder things for
me. But since you won't, I'd rather not have you here—
not till Arthur returns from the jousts."

"You excel in sending people away," said Lancelot.
"Very well, I'll go. I've never been dismissed so mildly
before, and you ought to be encouraged."

There was no discourtesy in his tone, but he walked
from the room without looking at her. She had expected
his kiss.

Anglides found her in a slightly acid humor.

"Where have you been, Anglides?"

"In the next room, madam, in case you should call
me."

"Very thoughtful! You've kept me waiting. Where
is the new embroidery?"

"I'll fetch it, madam."

By the time she brought it, Guinevere's temper had
improved.

"Thank you," she said. "I found myself alone here,
with nothing to do."

II

GUINEVERE listened for hoof-beats in the yard. She had the disconcerting impression that Lancelot would not ride—his casual manner suggested a new independence of her wishes. More than an hour passed, and she was wondering how she could meet this rebellion in her lover, when she heard what she had waited for.

"Who is riding out, Anglides?" she said.

"I don't know, madam. It's a man in armor, as big as Sir Lancelot, but it's not his armor. Nor his horse."

Guinevere went to the window herself.

"That's Lancelot," she said. "No one else."

She went back to her embroidery, but Anglides stayed.

"Why should he go in disguise, madam?"

"I don't call that disguise," said the queen. "A man of his size is difficult to conceal, even if he does get himself a new horse and a new suit of armor."

"But the armor isn't new," said Anglides. "It's rusty."

Guinevere made no reply. She kept at her needlework till Lancelot had gone a good half-mile.

"Which road is he taking, Anglides—the one to Winchester?"

"He's just getting to the fork now," said Anglides. "He's slowing up—yes, that's the one—no, madam, he's turning back—he's taking the north road."

Guinevere's embroidery dropped in her lap. She picked

it up, and went on with unsteady fingers. Anglides faced into the room.

"I've forgotten what there is on that road, madam. I thought he was riding to the tournament."

"I thought so, too," said the queen. "The north road was a suggestion of mine—which now I regret."

"It's a very roundabout way, I should think," said Anglides.

"That's the trouble with it."

Lancelot saw nothing to do but ride, since Guinevere was in an arbitrary mood. It occurred to him that a little solitude would not be amiss, to think over the disaster of Galahad's indignation, and the danger they had passed through that all the world should find out their stolen love. Guinevere had behaved with great poise, he was ready to admit, but largely because she had made her educational theory work. He had some doubts whether she was sane. The best women, he had heard, were liable to turn queer.

When he reached the fork in the roads his instinct was to keep on toward the west. It might be well to join the tournament before it was over, and he had a half-formed plan to look on, at least. The borrowed horse and the old armor might hide him in the crowd. Perhaps not, but the disguise suited his mood.

It came to him suddenly that he was still in sight of Guinevere's window. He had stood there himself, and watched to see which road Arthur or Gawaine might be taking. Well, two could play at that game. He turned in his tracks, and took the path to Corbin. He knew well what would happen to Guinevere's serenity if he really seemed to be going back to Elaine. She deserved to suffer

for a day or so. Afterward, when she learned he had
been at the tournament, she would admit she had brought
it on herself.

It was a long time since he had ridden through the
woods with so little weight of business and obligation.
He was free to go leisurely, and enjoy the early summer.
He thought of the journey on which he had brought Guinevere and her company to Arthur, for the wedding. The
scent of the woods then had crept into his soul. Until
then he hadn't known the wide difference between the
morning perfumes, when the dew is drying, and the cool
evening smell, when the dew begins to fall. It had worried him to be so unnaturally sensitive, and he mentioned it to Guinevere. By good luck she had noticed it,
too. His fear was that he might be softening into a poet,
but she explained to him, some time later, it was love.
That was long ago, but he could still recognize the smells.

Then there was that ride at night to Case, through the
damp woods— He reined in his horse, to think. If he kept
on, he would arrive at Corbin, or near by, before the day
was over, and some one might recognize him. There used
to be a cross-road to the west—it led to Winchester, if you
had patience.

It was hardly more than a path when he found it,
so little used that the grass showed no hoof-prints. It
hadn't seemed worth while to the woodsmen to clear it
that spring—the young branches struck his face now and
then, and the horse would come to a standstill, fretted
by the rough going and by the leaves in his eyes. Lancelot urged him on. They would find a deserted hermitage,
or at worst a soft bank in a clearing, for the night's shelter. Meanwhile he was alone.

He wondered what Arthur would say to his arrival at the tournament, after all. There had been a day when he had known all of Arthur's thoughts. Would it ever come again? And Arthur had known his heart—what was the phrase?—like an open book. He wished Arthur knew it so now. It would be a great relief. Looking back, he could see what a steady friend Arthur had been—kind to Elaine, for his sake, and wise with Galahad. They three together—what couldn't they have done! Oh, well—

He thought it was a clearing he was coming to, and he started to debate with himself whether he ought to stop there, though the afternoon was not ended, or push farther, on the chance of finding another such spot. But suddenly he rode out of the trees, and stood before an old house, not strong enough to be a castle, but guarded in a fashion by ivied walls, crumbling peacefully here and there, and surrounded by a moat, still as a mirror. Not a soul was in sight. As he watched, a swan came swimming around the corner of the tower, regal and slow. The slight ripples streamed back, and hardly moved the lilies along the shore.

Lancelot rode to the gate, and called. For a moment he believed the place was deserted, but an aged porter stuck his head out of the tower window.

"I have lost my way—will you give me a bed?"

The porter considered the question.

"Or will you show me a clear road to Winchester?"

The porter put his hand behind his ear.

"The road to Winchester," said Lancelot.

"This isn't it," said the porter.

He and Lancelot looked at each other.

"Who lives here?" said Lancelot.

"Sir Bernard of Astolat," said the porter.

"Oh, this is Astolat! I've heard the name. Well, you tell Sir Bernard that Sir Lancelot is here, on his way to join King Arthur, and disposed to get inside these gates, if you'll open them."

The head disappeared, and before long the gates were lifted and Lancelot rode in. Sir Bernard was there to greet him, a tall man with a gentle face.

"We were discourteous," he said, "only because we didn't know who you were. I am the only fighting man in the house, you see. It's a good thing you and King Arthur keep us in such peace, or poor men like myself would have a hard time."

"I've no right at all to trespass on your kindness," said Lancelot. "I've put you out."

"Not a bit! There's always a dinner in the house, and more beds than we fill—and we don't see a guest often enough, Sir Lancelot. . . . My people will help you with that armor and look after the horse. We'll walk in the garden till the cook is ready."

The servants weren't expert, but they got the armor off. They seemed to know better what to do with a horse.

"This is a very beautiful garden," said Lancelot. "I've seen few so well cared for. Such roses!"

"It's my wife's garden," said Sir Bernard.

"She must give all her time to it," said Lancelot. "This shows affection as well as skill."

"My wife," said Sir Bernard, "died five years ago. She was very fond of roses."

"I beg your pardon—I didn't know," said Lancelot. They walked through the paths.

"We've heard accounts, now and then, of your very extraordinary son, Sir Lancelot."

"That pleases me," said Lancelot. "Galahad is promising, I think."

"More than that, I should say. We have had reports of his unusually noble character. It is what we should have expected of you, Sir Lancelot, to bring up the boy so well."

"No credit to me at all," said Lancelot.

"That's what the modest father always says, and I'll admit the mother has most to do with it, when a boy turns out well," said Sir Bernard, "but the man has something to do with it, too."

Lancelot thought the subject might as well be changed.

"You have a son yourself, Sir Bernard?"

"I had one. He died."

Lancelot felt mortified to stumble a second time on a family sorrow. Sir Bernard's household was evidently under a blight.

"You do some farming, Sir Bernard? Of course, not here in the woods."

"My fields lie farther west—you'll pass them on the way to Winchester."

"And what do you raise mostly?"

"Hay, Sir Lancelot. Your horse has probably eaten my hay before. I send it up to Camelot, you know."

Lancelot was startled.

"Ah, yes, I remember," he said. . . . "We have always used the hay from this region."

"It's good grass land," said Sir Bernard. "The king has always expressed himself as satisfied."

Lancelot tried for another line of thought.

"Why is it we never see you? You keep home too much, I fear, Sir Bernard. The Court would be better for your visits."

The tall man with the gentle face smiled slightly.

"I'm not very exciting company," he said. "This old house suits me and my poverty. I was born to be a simple person, Sir Lancelot—my one success in life is that I've avoided the great world."

"Do you call the Court the great world, Sir Bernard? We often think it a narrower spot than such a restful home as yours."

"I don't know—I've never been there—but it has seemed to me, Sir Lancelot, that I should come to grief if ever I ventured even to the edge of your fine life. Understand, I say nothing against it—the danger might be that I should love it too much."

"Nonsense," said Lancelot. "We have faults enough to dampen the most ardent affection. You would only have to know us."

"That's it," said Sir Bernard. "My temperament is to love people first and know them afterward. A costly way. I was wise, I'm sure, to take what life has sent me, without seeking."

"Have you thought of a monastery, or a hermitage, or something of that sort?" said Lancelot. "You seem to have the gift."

"Well, to tell the truth," said Sir Bernard, "I'm much too worldly, after all. I love this old house."

Lancelot found the conversation growing difficult, and he was glad when the porter came out to announce dinner. From now on, it appeared, the porter was the butler. The table was set in the hall, not a large room, but suggesting history. There had been wealth once. The windows looked upon the garden, but the vines were grown up over them, till only patches of light made the shadows green.

There were places for three at the end of the long table. Lancelot wondered if the butler was a relative of the family.

"My daughter presides at my table," said Sir Bernard. "With your permission, Sir Lancelot, we'll wait for her."

Lancelot was living in a dream.

"Her name isn't Elaine, is it?"

"It is," said Sir Bernard.

Lancelot waited with his gaze on the dark oak door. If it had opened, and if a girl with golden hair and clear, friendly eyes—

"Daughter," said Sir Bernard, "you and I have the honor to entertain Sir Lancelot."

"Sir Lancelot!" she said.

She had come in silently another way. When he turned, she was standing by his side. She was tall, like her father, but as yet she seemed very young. Her hair was black, and her eyes even darker, perhaps because her skin was so pure a white. She wore a red gown, scarlet, with pearls embroidered in the sleeves. She had put on her best.

Through the dinner Lancelot could hardly keep his eyes from her. And whenever he glanced up, she was looking at him, with wonder in her child-like face.

III

Before breakfast Elaine was in her mother's garden. There Lancelot and Sir Bernard found her, gathering a flower or two and trimming the dead stalks. She had on a plain black gown, long and close-fitted. Lancelot thought her face would not be so white if she went in for gardening more often.

"Good morning, Sir Lancelot. So you insist on leaving us?"

"It's too bad you have to go," said Sir Bernard. "Elaine and I agree we need to see more people. Your chance visit has brightened us up. Perhaps you'll come again, now that you've discovered the road—if you call it a road."

"I'll certainly come," said Lancelot. "You've welcomed me most kindly, Sir Bernard; your house has strange charm. I haven't had such a sense of peace for years."

"Well, why not spend another night with us on your way back? You can give us news of the tournament."

"I think I'd like to. I will, Sir Bernard—on one condition, that you promise to bring your daughter to Camelot."

Sir Bernard seemed pleased with the idea.

"We might do that, Elaine. What do you say?"

"I'd love it, father. If they are all like Sir Lancelot."

316

"They don't send me out for a sample," said Lancelot. "You'll find better people there."

"Well, we'll come up soon and learn for ourselves," said Bernard. "Meanwhile, we'll look for you after the tournament."

"You won't get hurt, will you?" said Elaine.

"I promise not to, this time."

"Your son isn't at the Court now, I believe," said Bernard.

"Not now," said Lancelot.

"I want to meet him. From what I hear, he's the sort of young man we've needed."

"He has admirable qualities," said Lancelot. "You say you need him?"

"I refer to his—may I say, his unworldliness?"

"You may. He isn't what I should call worldly."

"That's a remarkable thing," said Bernard. "I was afraid the mood of dedication was lacking in the young people to-day—and here's a boy with every advantage in life, birth, breeding, wealth, who takes a high tone from the start. I think better of the Court, I don't mind saying, Sir Lancelot, since I know he is a part of it. That sort of goodness, I used to think, could flourish only in the meditative life, but if a young man can be so active and yet keep his ideals, there's a new day coming for us, wouldn't you say?"

"I'm not the best one to answer that question," said Lancelot. "He's my son, of course, and I've watched him at close range."

"I knew you must have brought him up carefully. Elaine here has never been out of my sight, since the day she was born."

"I meant," said Lancelot, "that though Galahad is un-usual, I doubt if he will ever become typical."

"Certainly not," said Bernard. "If he's unusual he won't be typical. But if the other young men, even a few, take life as he does, it will make a difference."

"I can't understand where you heard so much about him."

"Why, Sir Gawaine passed this way, a short time ago, and talked of him for hours."

"I don't like him," said Elaine. "He talks as if he were really poking fun at people."

"Only the Court manner," said Bernard. "I tried to explain it to my daughter. But I'm glad you haven't it yourself, Sir Lancelot."

The porter showed himself at the end of the garden.

"Ah, there's breakfast," said Sir Bernard. "I was wondering what had happened to it."

"Not yet," said the porter. "It isn't quite ready. May I have a word with you?"

Sir Bernard hurried after him into the house.

"The cook gets nervous," said Elaine.

"Now I've upset your housekeeping," said Lancelot.

"No, it happens when we're alone. He sees visions."

"The cook?"

Lancelot started to laugh, but Elaine was serious.

"He has a vision of angels, every now and then. Father won't have him disturbed. He says we shouldn't interrupt an experience about which we know so little."

"Very wise," said Lancelot. "And while the vision is on, what happens to the man?"

"Just the vision," said Elaine. "But some one else has to do the cooking."

"Most extraordinary!"

"Why, doesn't your son see visions, too?"

"Not that I know of," said Lancelot.

"Sir Gawaine thought he did. Father told him about the cook, and Sir Gawaine was profoundly interested. He said he would give five years of his life to see angels himself, but it had been withheld from him. Perhaps because he lacked humility, he said. He couldn't bring himself to be a cook."

"And what did your father say to that?"

"He asked him whether Sir Galahad didn't see angels, and Sir Gawaine said practically nothing else."

Lancelot cast his eye in the direction of the house, to see if breakfast might not be ready.

"Sir Lancelot, will you do me a great honor?"

He was too surprised to answer.

"You saw that dress I wore last night? I've taken off one of the sleeves with the pearls on it. When you fight at the tournament, will you wear it on your helmet, as a token of me?"

Her eyes were brilliant and pleading, and he didn't like to see how much in earnest she was. A cold thought went through him that here was trouble.

"Elaine, I'm not at all sure I shall do any fighting at this tournament."

"Oh!" she said.

The world had collapsed, her tone was so sad.

"But I may, of course. . . . Elaine, I ought to tell you I've never worn a token of any woman. My friends expect to see my armor plain. Isn't it rather late for me to change?"

"But last night you told father you were wearing

strange armor and riding a new horse, just so your friends wouldn't recognize you. Wouldn't it help to wear this, too?"

He looked down at the white face, and knew it was guileless.

"It would make a great difference, whether I wore it or not?"

"Greater to me than to you, Sir Lancelot."

"I'll wear it. And when I come this way again, if it isn't ruined, you can put it back on the gown. That was a pretty dress. . . . Ah, there's your father."

"We'll eat now," said Sir Bernard. "I don't know whether you'd call it breakfast or lunch."

IV

Bors was the first to return from Winchester.
glides met him in the castle yard, as he came f
the stables.

"Well, was it a success?"

"More like the old days than I expected to see aga
Of course, they missed Galahad."

"And his father," said Anglides.

"No, Lancelot was there. He won the tournament.'

"Aren't you mistaken, Bors? I saw him ride anothe
way."

"He was there. We all recognized him, in spite of his
rusty armor. He fought in his usual style."

Bors was going to his room, but Anglides stopped
him.

"You must tell me. Why was he wearing the rusty
armor? And when did he get to the tournament? We
thought he was at Corbin."

"Well, perhaps he was," said Bors. "I shan't ask
him myself, but all the tongues are wagging. It looks
as though he has gone back to her."

"Elaine?"

"Yes. He wore her token—a red sleeve. He never did
so much for the queen. They say he went to her after
Galahad disappeared, and they are reconciled. In fact, he

got to the tournament only toward the end. Now the question is, will he marry her, so late in the day."

"How terrible!" said Anglides.

"Not at all. It's a good thing. I admire Elaine—my cousin should have married her years ago!"

"But the queen!"

"I've no patience with her," said Bors. "She spoiled his life. I'm not squeamish—their love affairs don't worry me—but she ought to have known her own mind, and stuck to him or else sent him away. She hasn't cared her little finger for him, these last fifteen years; she has just grown accustomed to scolding him and ordering him around."

"That's not fair," said Anglides. "Her life is wrapped up in him. When he took that road to Corbin, you should have seen how she went to pieces. When a woman gives everything, the man ought to be faithful."

"I'd say it was Elaine who gave everything," said Bors.

"What had she to lose? The queen has risked her name and her safety for his sake, and he was just like the rest of you, when another woman came along."

"A number of us begin to have a fairly settled idea of the risk the queen took. She took none at all."

"She's a very beautiful woman," said Anglides.

"What has that to do with it? Yes, she has looks, but as I grow older I'd rather have Elaine across the table from me every day in the year. There's a girl with spirit and a sound heart!"

"I've looked at the queen for a long while," said Anglides, "and I love her. She has faults—she grows harder to please, but that's because of her worries. I've

seen her pleading with one man after another in this
Court to be a truer knight. Arthur will get the credit, of
course, but I know of the talks in that tower room. She
has worked day in and day out for the happiness of others,
for their true success."

"She never worked over me," said Bors. "When you
count up, you'll find she specialized on her husband, on
Lancelot, and on Galahad. And the last two, you'll admit, had no business to pass their time in that tower room
being inspired. They were as regular as clockwork, waiting their turn to climb those stairs and be talked to. We
wondered how long it would be till Lancelot came to himself. Galahad set him a wise example, and I'm thankful
Lancelot is imitating it."

"Is he leaving the Court, too?"

"Oh, no, I meant he has left Guinevere, and gone back
to the boy's mother. He really has gone back—he's at
Corbin now. He rode that way as soon as the jousts
were finished."

"We must keep this from Guinevere," said Anglides.

"I won't, for one," said Bors, "and the others feel as
I do. We shan't deliberately tell her, but if the story
starts of itself we'll let it spread naturally. It's the surest
means to separate her from him."

"When she sent him away, long ago, he went crazy,"
said Anglides.

"That was an error—he won't do it again. You'll see."

Anglides looked crushed.

"Bors, this Court is going to pieces!"

"It's gone already," said Bors. "One good shake and
down it comes. I'm glad of it, Anglides. The king is
in the saddle again, and we'll start fresh. No offense

to you ladies, but this time it will be a man's world, absolutely uninspired, unrefined and unencumbered. Please God!"

"I'm willing," said Anglides. "I assume you'll permit us to live, and I'd like to see an unencumbered man. When I was young I thought I would marry one, but as you say, they don't exist as yet. They've always fallen in love, long before, with some other woman of whom they've become tired. She, poor thing, encumbers them. And the famous ones, the Lancelots, have outlived their affection for so many women."

"He loved Guinevere," said Bors. "If she had been capable of a true passion, he would love her still. But you can understand that Elaine has the real claim on him."

"Why do you think she let him wear her sleeve?" said Anglides. "To notify Guinevere?"

"That's an idea—she may have been glad to publish her victory. But I took it that Lancelot was tired of his position, and served warning on us that he belonged from now on to Elaine."

"If he marries her," said Anglides, "I suppose Galahad may return."

"Of course—they've thought it out, you may be sure. Lancelot isn't the man to stand by and let his son's career be ruined."

"I hate to think about Guinevere," said Anglides.

"The subject has become distasteful to me, too," said Bors. "I think of her as seldom as possible."

V

WHEN Lancelot returned to Sir Bernard's house, he drew rein at the edge of the clearing, to enjoy once more the charm of its quiet, against the forest, with the mirror-like water under the walls. He waited to see if the swan would come swimming to greet him. The place was friendly, and he was glad of another night beneath the ancient roof.

Sir Bernard welcomed him in the hall, and asked for news of the jousts.

"I'm out of touch with such sports myself," he said, "never was good at them, but my daughter has been in a fever about your safety—she was certain you'd come to harm."

"Nothing to worry about," said Lancelot. "We were all friends, and I've had practise in taking care of myself. I'm sorry for Elaine. Where is she?"

"She'll be here presently. She's too sensitive, poor child—life will be hard."

"You and she must keep your part of the bargain, and visit the Court," said Lancelot. "Then I'll make it up to her for having caused any concern. She's a fine girl, Sir Bernard. You are fortunate."

"She is like her mother—that makes her dear to me. . . . Ah, she is coming now."

Lancelot saw how strangely she was changed. She

appeared to be recovering from a long illness. Her skin
could not be whiter nor her eyes darker than before, but
her body drooped, as though she lacked strength to stand.

"You are safe, Sir Lancelot!"

"Quite so. And the sleeve is torn in only one place.
With a stitch or two you can wear it again."

She smiled.

"I'll keep it as it is, to remember you by. I wanted
it to be torn a little. Did you fight hard to protect it,
Sir Lancelot?"

"Some of the men think so, I believe."

"Then perhaps it helped you a little?"

"No question of it."

Her evident delight disturbed him. It hadn't been
much of a tournament, or perhaps he was growing old.
The child exaggerated.

"I wish I had been there," she said. "But I could almost see what you were doing. You were wonderful, Sir
Lancelot."

"Dear me, no! Very average, Elaine, I assure you."

Sir Bernard seemed to like the conversation. He sat
by, gently interested. Elaine kept her large admiring eyes
on Lancelot. He felt rather foolish.

"There were ladies there?"

"A few—I didn't notice which ones."

"Was the queen there?"

"No," said Lancelot, "I happen to know she stayed at
home."

"I've heard she's very beautiful," said Elaine. "Father
saw her once, and he thought she was, didn't you, father?"

"Very beautiful indeed," said Sir Bernard.

"She's my ideal woman," said Elaine. "So splendid

to look at, and so good. When father says the life at
Court isn't helpful to the soul, like our calm existence
here, I ask him who could be better than Queen Guinevere, even if she lived in a nunnery. I've always loved
King Arthur and his knights because of her. You know
her, don't you?"

"Well," said Lancelot, "I've been in Arthur's service
since we were of your age, about."

"I'm nineteen," said Elaine.

"Just about that," said Lancelot.

"You think she's rather an exception among the ladies
of the Court?"

"I'm sure of it," said Lancelot.

"I've understood so," said Elaine, "yet it makes me
sad to think so. Why can't more women live in the great
world, and be an example to us?"

"It's an important question," said Lancelot. "Have
you thought of an answer?"

"I suppose some of them, even among the rich, haven't
had good homes," said Elaine.

"Particularly among the rich," said Sir Bernard. "My
theory is, the influence of early years determines everything, and wealth in the cradle is a sort of contradiction
of childhood. When you can have everything you want,
you have no imagination."

"The queen in her youth," said Lancelot, "was rather
poor, as you know."

"Exactly," said Bernard. "There you are!"

"But you think it's safe to have the wealth later on?"

"No, I don't," said Bernard. "A simple fortune is
best."

The old porter began to bring in the dinner service.

"You might show Sir Lancelot the new blooms in your mother's garden," said Bernard. "After the meal it may be dark."

Elaine led him to the row of hollyhocks, where a delicate trumpet or two appeared on each stalk.

"They're just beginning, since you were away," she said. . . . "Sir Lancelot, may I talk to you alone before you go away?"

"Talk to me now—we're alone," he said.

"I thought perhaps in the morning, here in the garden—I'm always here then, and father usually has his breakfast late."

"Now's a good time," said Lancelot. "Begin now."

"Father will call us for dinner in a minute."

"Well, what's left can go over till to-morrow."

"I ought not to ask such a thing—but I must know, I really must, Sir Lancelot!"

Her face was as child-like as when he had seen it first.

"Sir Lancelot, are you leaving us to-morrow?"

"Yes."

"Will you take me with you?"

"I hope your father will soon bring you to Camelot, Elaine. I wish it with all my heart."

"That's not what I mean, Sir Lancelot. I had to ask. . . . I had to know if you understood!"

He stared at her, unable to believe she was saying what he thought.

"If I understood?"

"I love you, Sir Lancelot," she said.

Sir Lancelot rode away before daybreak.

VI

"I've no wish to see you again," said Guinevere. "I have nothing to say to you, and I should think you had nothing to say to me."

"It isn't what I want to say—it's your strange behavior," said Lancelot. "You have treated me, in the presence of your household, as though I were a beggar, a rather unwelcome one. The meals in the great hall have been dreadful experiences. For five days I've asked to see you, to know what is wrong, and to-day when Anglides said you were not at liberty, I told her—well, you know what I told her."

"You are in this room for the last time, I hope," said Guinevere, "and since you are here against my will, it's useless to ask you to leave. For the moment I am at your mercy. Say what is on your mind, but don't expect me to discuss your infidelities as we used to do."

"There are no infidelities to discuss, madam. I came only to ask why you are discourteous to me."

Guinevere looked hard, but he showed no disposition to wilt.

"Why, madam?"

"We won't discuss it, Lancelot."

"Why won't we discuss? If there's a reason why you should insult me daily at the king's table, tell me. It's either true or it isn't. I'm accustomed to your wrath, Guinevere, but usually I have known what it was about."

"And you know now."

"I don't."

She took her sewing from the table, and walked to the other side of the room.

"Will you excuse my back?" she said. "The light is better here, and I must go on with my work."

He waited for her, but she ignored his existence. He thought an hour must have gone by, and he wondered what would be said if some one came in and found them at this unusual vigil. To be ridiculous—

He got up ostentatiously, and strode toward the door.

"Good-by," she said. "Under the circumstances, you ought to live there, you know. If your meals at my table are uncomfortable for you, perhaps your conscience is troubled, to be so much away from your wife."

"Is this a form of humor?" he said.

She sprang to her feet and turned on him.

"It's a tribute to your impudence, Lancelot, cheap liar that you are! You cared nothing for her, oh, no! You had to be urged to see her, of course! You feared I might be jealous if you waved your hand to her, from a safe distance! And you were her husband, all the time!"

"Whose, for God's sake?"

"Have you several? Don't you know which one?"

He was too bewildered to think it through.

"Will it please you, Guinevere, to have me repeat what you know is true, that I have no wife?"

"Is it pleasant for you to hear again, what you know is true, that you are a cheap liar?"

For the first time he realized he was disgusted with

her. Whether or not she had gone mad, he didn't care. He only wanted now to get away from her with some grace and self-control.

"Guinevere, I have loved you for many years, and I've disappointed you too often, but never have I told you what wasn't true. I have no wife, I never had. When I asked you who it was, I wanted to know what name you connect with mine. I know, myself, that you are mistaken, no matter what the name is."

"I saw you ride to her—Anglides saw you."

"Oh . . . Then you were looking."

"We saw you, Lancelot. What's the use of—"

"But I didn't go to Corbin," he said. "I knew you'd be jealous if I did, and anyway I had no wish to visit Elaine. I was at the tournament, and you know I was. The men have been talking about it with me at your table, before your face."

"You certainly were at the tournament, Lancelot, but you were at Corbin, too. Doesn't it occur to you that the men talk also behind your back?"

"Guinevere, I was not at Corbin, and no one can say I was. I did take that road at the fork—because you might be watching, and you had asked me to go that way, but when I was well in the forest, I turned west again."

"You wore a woman's sleeve on your helmet."

"That is true, I did."

"Whose sleeve, then?"

"Elaine's, Sir—"

"Yet you haven't seen her!"

"I see what the trouble is, Guinevere—"

"So do I!"

"It's not the same one, Guinevere—this is Sir Ber-

nard's daughter, of Astolat. She's a mere child, and I
wore the token to please her fancy."

"Who is Sir Bernard? I've never heard of him?"

"He's an obscure knight who lives in the forest with
a few servants and his motherless daughter. They took
me in that night, after I left the Corbin road. I stopped
there on my way back. Send and ask him, if you don't
believe me. I've neither seen nor heard of Galahad's
mother."

"You ask me to believe there are two Elaines, both in
love with you?"

"I didn't say they were in love with me."

"No, but of course they would be. And no doubt this
second one, of whom you never told me before—"

"I didn't know of her existence till I arrived at her
father's house that night."

"So? Yet you wore her token next day. A rapid in-
timacy!"

Lancelot did not answer.

"She probably told you she loved you?"

He was silent.

"Did she?"

"As a matter of fact, she did."

"Even though you couldn't marry her, she wanted
you?"

"That is true."

"And you wish me to believe this is not the same
one?"

"Guinevere," said Lancelot, "we have reached a point
where I don't wish you to believe anything you'd rather
not. But since you have asked for the truth, I've told you.
They are two distinct women. There's a difference of

twenty years or more in their ages, and the difference of
a whole world in their temperaments, and they don't look
alike. But they have the same name, and to my great
misfortune, both have chosen to admire me."

"You'll have to provide for your next son yourself,"
said Guinevere. "I'm too old."

As he watched the hard lines come and go with
her anger and wounded pride, he wondered how he could
have thought that face beautiful.

"There will be no more sons," he said. "I don't love
this girl—I didn't love the other, of course, but this
time I have nothing to regret."

"I still think it's shabby of you not to live with her at
Corbin," said Guinevere. "I was sorry for her when I
thought she was deserted. I feel much more sympathy
now I know the sort of husband she has."

Lancelot began to laugh.

"Have it your own way. I haven't married her, nor
any one else. But suppose I had married Galahad's
mother; wasn't that what you urged me to do? And
didn't you swear you wouldn't be jealous?"

"Then you admit you married her!" said Guinevere.

He threw up his hands.

"I'm not deceived by your silly story," she said, "nor
moved by your argument. I did say I wouldn't be jealous, but you knew better—you knew I was trying to be
fair to her—you knew I loved you! You knew I forgave you before—how many times? And tried to lift
you up again when you—acted as you did! But perhaps
you didn't know how a woman feels, even toward a man
unworthy of her, if once she has given herself to him.
She belongs to him, and he to her—that's all there is to it!

A woman can't drift from one affair to another, as a man can, and leave memories behind—she gave so much, he ought to think of her when he has the next victim in his arms—"

"Now this is too much," said Lancelot. "You've got beyond decency!"

She dropped into the chair, and breathed hard, as though she had run up-stairs. But she seemed to regain her old poise—the lines went out of her face, and he was annoyed to observe that she was beautiful after all.

"Well, Lancelot, my lover," she said—

"Yes, Guinevere, your lover. For a moment you forgot that."

"I wish you'd do something for me, Lancelot."

"What?"

"Go home to your wife."

When he was well down the stairs, Anglides hurried in. "I couldn't tell you while he was here," she said. "I doubt if he knows yet, but Galahad's mother is dead."

Guinevere froze into marble.

"Madam! Madam! . . . Are you faint?"

Guinevere brushed her away. "How do you know?"

"She is here—they are going to bury her at Camelot?"

"Why here, of all places?"

"They have a letter she wrote when she knew she was dying—when King Arthur read it out, a few moments ago, I was at the back of the crowd and couldn't hear it all, but I gathered that Lancelot had invited her to come to Court—"

"Ah!" said Guinevere.

"And she said she thought he could forgive her most easily if she came this way."

Guinevere thought a moment.

"Where did all this happen?"

"In the chapel. They brought her there, and the king came, and they uncovered her face for the last time. The king said he would tell you himself, but first Lancelot must know."

"She was a rather handsome woman," said Guinevere.

"I remember her years ago," said Anglides, "and I wouldn't say she was handsome."

"Is she changed?" said Guinevere.

"I don't know. I was behind the others, and I came to tell you."

"I'm sorry for Galahad," said the queen. "They should have been reconciled . . . Let me have my black shawl, Anglides . . . I suppose I ought to go."

She put the shawl over her head, and drew it down around her face with her exquisite hands. When she came to the door of the chapel, the castle folk drew back, and left an aisle for her. She walked like a queen, and her face, framed in black, was an unforgettable beauty.

At the foot of the dead she knelt a moment in prayer Even Gawaine was struck by the splendid irony of the drama before them—the slighted woman praying—or was it giving thanks?—over her departed rival. Then without haste, Guinevere walked to the head of the casket, and looked down.

She gave a little shriek, or an hysterical laugh, and then checked herself. They were astonished to see her turn to them, with wide eyes, and clasp her hands, and clear her throat as though she were going to make a speech. It might be a funeral oration.

"There were two of them," she said.

VII

LATER on, Lancelot lost his self-respect, and shortly afterward he entered the religious life.

Brother Martin, wise in the cure of souls, used to pace the abbey cloisters with him, in the intervals of their devotions, trying to clarify Lancelot's state of mind. Brother Martin reported that Lancelot's states of mind were really in a class by themselves.

"The trouble with me is that I've no practise in confessing my sins," said Lancelot. "I sincerely believe I'm penitent, and I thought when you were sorry for your sins, it was all quite simple. But of course it's like other things—you have to learn how."

"When did you go to confession last, before you came here?"

"Let me see. . . . Why, it was just after Arthur and Guinevere were married."

"Twenty years!" said Brother Martin.

"All of that, and more," said Lancelot. "You see, I went to confession regularly till I was Guinevere's lover, and once after that. When I confessed the sin, the priest asked me if I repented, and wishing to be honest, I asked him what he meant. He said the question was whether I was sorry Guinevere was mine, and I said I wasn't. He said there was no absolution for me, so I never went back."

"How is it with you now?" said Brother Martin.

"Why, in a sense I do repent now. Of course I can't say I regret the good part of our love."

"What would that be?" said Brother Martin.

"Her beauty—and the desire I had to be worthy of her—and the recollection of her lips, when we were young."

"That's what you call the good part, is it?" said Brother Martin. "I'd like to have your idea of the evil side of it, that you're sorry for!"

"Why, it was wrong—I couldn't marry her—our nerves were under a strain and we weren't entirely happy—it turned to ashes toward the end. I'm not clever at saying it, but you'll understand. Whatever wasn't wrong, I'm glad of, and for all that was sin I repent. Won't that do?"

"I'm not sure you know which is which," said Brother Martin. "But you may go on for the present."

"Well, just after our love began, a year or so, I met a girl who offered herself to me—not in a brazen way, I must admit, but with frankness. She asked for my love for one moment of her life, knowing all the time that I loved Guinevere. I've been in the habit of saying that she tricked me into it, but now I'll confess I wanted her. She was very compelling. I've repented it, for one reason or another, ever since. Will that do?"

"That seems to be a clear case," said Brother Martin. "But I've been wondering why you told of Guinevere without mentioning the element in the affair which would trouble me most. You don't seem to ask yourself what Arthur would think of it all, her husband and your friend."

"I know what Arthur thinks of it," said Lancelot.

"How can you?"

"I asked him. That's why I'm here. I couldn't stand the thought of treachery to him, and I reached a point where I'd rather die on his sword than hide the secret longer. So I went frankly to him, and explained that I loved his wife too well. I thought that was the honest way out."

"When was this?" said Brother Martin.

"Recently."

"You loved her too well," said Brother Martin, "but you didn't love her much. I should call it the honest way if you had gone to Arthur twenty years ago. What did the king say?"

"He said he had known it for some time. Soon after their wedding, he said, he found out she had married him to reform him. He wouldn't have minded, he said, if he had had more leisure, but with the kingdom on his hands he was too busy to be reformed. Then he saw she had turned her attention to me, and though it hurt him, yet there was something to be said for the arrangement. Well . . . that's why I'm here. When Arthur talked that way to me, I couldn't look the world in the face."

"Are you confessing your sins, Brother Lancelot, or reciting your misfortunes?"

"I've admitted my confusion," said Lancelot. "I told you about that girl who offered herself. Well, she had many charms, but innocence wasn't one of them. She knew everything there was to know, and a chapter more. But I happened to come to another house, only a month ago, and my host said we'd wait for his daughter to preside at dinner, and her name turned out to be the same as that first one's. I had a queer feeling that perhaps the first one would come in the door pursuing me after all those years. But when the daughter came at last, she was a mere child—innocence and nothing else. Yet they had the same name."

"Why not?" said Brother Martin. "The name means little till it's on you."

"I don't know," said Lancelot. "Before I left that house, this innocent girl made exactly the same proposals to me as the wise one did—exactly. Wanted my love, or wanted to be my mistress, or—in short, wanted me."

"We don't always have a second chance," said Brother Martin. "I hope you did better this time?"

"I did," said Lancelot. "I told her it was a temporary aberration, and when it was over she'd marry the right man some day and we'd all be friends. That was better, wasn't it?"

"Nothing the matter with that at all."

"Yet when you come to consider it," said Lancelot, "your best conduct can do so much harm, and your mistakes do turn out amazingly. When I sinned with that woman who threw herself at me, we had a child. The result of that wrong was Galahad."

"You don't mean the great Galahad?" said Brother Martin.

"I don't know how great he is," said Lancelot, "but there's only one."

"He is devoting his life, we hear," said Brother Martin, "to the search for the holiest treasure in the world."

"That's how stories grow," said Lancelot. "And then, Galahad wouldn't have been on the way to this greatness, if I hadn't loved Guinevere."

"That's far from self-evident," said Brother Martin.

"She was jealous of his mother, and jealous of him, and angry at me," said Lancelot, "and it occurred to her to get the best of us all by making a masterpiece out of him. Before she got through, she loved him, I think."

"I see," said Brother Martin.

"And then," said Lancelot, "the one time I did right, when I spoke so gently and wisely to that little girl, it killed her."

"She probably died from natural causes," said Brother Martin.

"Perhaps," said Lancelot, "but my impression is that if I had said yes, she wouldn't have died."

"You know," said Brother Martin, "I don't think you are in a way of grace!"

"You can judge that better than I," said Lancelot. "But can't a man be in a way of grace and still ask questions?"

THE END